LADY OF DRAGONS (PART ONE)

SHELBY ELIZABETH

*For all the young readers who dream of worlds filled with dragons
. . . and for the grown readers who still dream of the same thing.*

CONTENTS

Magic flew through the air in the form of the serpentine dragon spiraling overhead.

Finlay leaned forward to watch the dragon and rider, one hand gripping the worn bark of the tree, both feet at the very edge of the moderate cliff. Just another inch and she could see them fully, practicing above the distant treeline. Her palm edged past the smoothed section of bark she'd made gripping it like this so often. She extended her torso, fingertips clinging to the rougher bark to keep her steady, toes of her boots pressing onto open air—

A firm hand grabbed the hood of Finlay's cloak and tugged her back. "You've been leaning out over the edge more every day lately. Don't you remember falling in last time?" Facing Finlay was a strongly-built young woman with intense black eyes and sharply cut, short black hair level with her chin—her best friend, Elsie.

Finlay held her head high. "Yes. I got wet. But I had an amazing view of Isla and Muir on the way down."

Elsie rolled her eyes. "I don't want to fish you out of the water again."

"Isla fished me out. You just laughed."

"It was pretty funny. You looked ridiculous as you fell."

Finlay sat down at the base of the tree, wrapping her pale, slender arms around her knees to fend off the morning chill, and looked out over the lake. She supposed she had been leaning over the edge more, desperate to catch every glimpse of her adoptive sister training with her dragon that she could. Muir's need for water meant Isla trained outside the walled compound much of the time, near the lake. This was the only spot Finlay could see a Knight in training.

"I want to be out there with her," Finlay said. She watched as the blue-green dragon dove, skimmed a foreleg on the surface of the water in a wide loop that left a trail of ripples in his wake, and coiled and uncoiled his sinuous body to climb back into the sky. Finlay's heartbeats lined up with each ascending motion of Muir's, the sight simultaneously filling her with a sense of peace and a desire growing more urgent by the day. She needed to work with dragons. She had to be able to train with them, as Isla did each day.

Elsie dropped down beside her and knocked against her shoulder. The affectionate bump still had enough force to make Finlay reach out a hand to steady herself. Elsie had quite a strong build. There was a reason she'd been asked to work in the forge.

"Isla won't be the only Knight in the family for long," Elsie said. "We'll be out there with our own dragon partners before we know it."

If we pass the trial, Finlay thought. Elsie never let her talk about 'if' they passed the trial that would allow them to train as Dragon Knights. With Elsie, it was only 'when.' Elsie's unshakeable confidence was one of the things Finlay loved about her. Finlay couldn't help worrying about it, though. She reached for a strand of her coppery hair and started twining it around her fingers.

"Can't believe we're finally eligible to compete," Elsie continued, her dark eyes on the cloud-covered skyline. "Seems like forever that we've been waiting, doesn't it?"

Actively waiting? Since the last trial, two years ago. Dreaming of it? "Since I came here."

"Before Isla was a Knight," Elsie said with an upturn to her lips.

"You're taking way too much pleasure from that."

"She's my big sister. And she brags about being a Knight all the time."

"Maybe she does," Finlay admitted. Muir entered her line of sight again, diving steeply and leveling off at the last moment, maintaining his speed. He flew just above the surface of the lake, serpentine body coiling as he flew in a tight loop. The water responded to his motion while he continued circling, rising in a ring. Muir increased his speed at a command from Isla and climbed higher into the air with each loop, bringing the ring of water with him. Finlay inhaled sharply. "We never got to see things like that until she became a Knight, though. I'll take a little bragging to see this."

Muir was a cyclical blue-green blur until he lunged away from them, body straightening in a whiplike fashion. The ring of water shot forward and burst, and Isla's laugh echoed with the crashing water. Two kelpies across the lake peeked their horse-like heads above the water, apparently as captivated by the girl and dragon as Finlay. Part of Finlay wanted to admire the elusive creatures. She couldn't look away from Isla and Muir.

"Three weeks," Elsie said. "Three weeks and we'll pass the trial and be able to do things like that." Finlay felt Elsie's gaze shift to her. "Have you thought about which dragon you'd like as your partner? Which type, at least?"

Muir and Isla ascended out of view again. "I've thought about every aspect of becoming a Knight. I don't really have a preference, I guess."

Elsie scoffed. "Typical. *I* have a preference. No water dragons for me. I want one that's sturdier."

"Not even in the running and already choosing a dragon partner? My, my, we really are getting ahead of ourselves."

Finlay jolted at the familiar masculine voice and turned to find Meric a few paces away, looking at them sternly. Tall and broad-shouldered, with rich black skin and calculating eyes, many assumed him unapproachable without a very good reason, fearing his ire. The severe expression he naturally wore didn't help matters.

"What do you mean, not in the running?" Elsie asked.

The half of Meric's mouth not permanently tugged down by a scar ticked upward. "If others caught you slacking in your duties, you might not be seen as eligible to compete. Don't worry. Secret's safe with me, as long as you both get to work now."

Finlay tried to hide her smile. They technically weren't supposed to be here at all, on the border of the property private to the Knights, watching any of the Knights train, but it was just like Meric to ignore that. He'd ignored it all the times he'd caught them here. Finlay rather suspected he approved of their devotion. Of all the Knights, the seasoned warrior Meric knew best how fiercely Finlay and Elsie sought to join them.

He was the only one to teach them fighting techniques and sparring skills; something he certainly could have gotten in trouble for, but volunteered to do whenever he could. Something that made it impossible for Finlay to see him as unapproachable, regardless of the grumpiness in his expression or his massive, intimidating stature.

"Any time for a lesson between now and the trial?" Elsie asked.

"I suspect we'll be plenty busy until then. Now scoot, before someone else sees you and we all get in trouble."

Finlay and Elsie walked past him, heading to the path that would take them back to the village.

"You don't need more lessons," Meric called over his shoulder, as soon as they were past. "You're ready."

"That's a vote of confidence I didn't expect," Elsie said. "Meric doesn't fluff about with his words."

Finlay choked on a laugh. "Fluff about?"

"Oh, you know what I mean, Fin!"

She always knew what Elsie meant. Everyone did.

"It is encouraging to hear that from Meric," Finlay admitted.

They reached the path to the communal section of the village, where Finlay had to tend left to reach the healing den and Elsie had to continue straight to the forge. Elsie stopped Finlay before she could turn. "Promise me we'll both become Knights."

Finlay studied her friend for several heartbeats, weighing the statement in her core. She may not have had the absolute confidence Elsie did, but combined with Meric's reassurance and the determination and desire burning in her gut, enough of Elsie's confidence sank through to allow Finlay to grasp her hand firmly, look her dead in the eye, and say in earnest, "I promise."

Elsie shook her hand. "No going back on it, now."

"Wouldn't dream of it."

Finlay turned to walk to the healing den. The structure stood larger than the cottage Finlay called home, stocked full of medical supplies, raw ingredients, and finished salves and tinctures. The lead healer Finlay had been apprenticed to for the last four years, Moira, had her own space, as all leaders of trades did. She had access to her own dwelling. Still, she kept a room in the back of the healing den, behind a thick curtain, as she claimed she sometimes couldn't sleep until a new idea for an elixir had been attempted—even if it was the middle of the night. Finlay had only seen her bit of a room once, but in that glimpse, she'd seen papers and ingredients filling all available space aside from the bed and fireplace. Moira was a bit eccentric, but tremendously talented.

"Morning Moira," Finlay said upon entering.

The healer peered up at Finlay through her thick glasses, hunched over powders she was measuring and adding to a flask on her desk. "Oh, morning," she said absently, looking back to the spoon. "Did I add one dose of ground scales, or two?"

"I only saw you add one."

The healer studied the metallic powder and dumped the heaping spoon into the flask. "Even if I did already add two, a third will only make the elixir stronger!"

Finlay stayed by the doorway. "Moira, is there something specific you want help with?"

"What? Oh, no. You can see we're not in high demand today." She put the top on the flask and shook it. "You can go to the sanctuary if you'd like. I'll send word if I need you."

"I can gather more supplies there."

"And see a certain young man."

Heat crept into Finlay's cheeks. "Evander is in charge of the sanctuary. Of course I'll see him."

Moira opened the flask, sniffed, and coughed. "That'll put the hair back on their chests!" She resealed the flask and limped over to the cabinet, placing it with some of the other healing salves and solutions. "Let's see, where did I put that quill?"

Finlay plucked one from the desk and strode to Moira's side.

Moira blinked owlishly. "Ah. Perfect." She scrawled a hasty label in front of the flask and shut the cabinet door, glancing at Finlay when she turned to limp back to her desk. "What are you keeping that boy waiting for?"

Chapter Two

Finlay

Finlay adjusted her cloak and walked out of the healing den, her step quickening to that of a jog as soon as she passed the busiest part of the village. The dragon sanctuary began in the collection of trees just behind it, closer to the base of the mountain. Crystals shimmering with an inner light that never seemed to fade marked the borders of the sanctuary—small blooms resembling flower buds suspended in time, emitting a soft blend of lilac and periwinkle light that created a magical sphere of energy. The dragon-paw tattoo on the back of Finlay's hand glowed with the same light when she passed between two of the crystals, permitting her into the protected area.

A slim young man with artfully disheveled blond hair knelt not far inside the magical dome, his back to her. He held the paw of a small green dragon, and turned his head when Finlay approached. Liquid brown eyes the color of nurtured soil brightened when they fixed on her, and Evander stood in a fluid motion.

Excitement sang through her veins and sped her heart's pace to an uneven gallop. Purely because the dragon sanctuary was easily her favorite place, of course. This reaction had nothing to do with the attractive young man before her. Nothing to do with the lean muscle apparent beneath his sand-toned skin, or how his dark blond hair curled loosely against the nape of his neck, or the way he seemed to light up when he first saw her—every time he saw her.

Evander smiled, that dimple on his right cheek appearing. "Finlay!"

"Hi, Evander."

"What brings you here? Not that you're not welcome or anything. I'm actually really glad you're here. Just surprised. Happily surprised." He cleared his throat. "What's up?"

Finlay's lips wobbled with the smile she worked to repress. He would take it the wrong way, and there was no need to embarrass him, though she found his rushed speech more endearing than anything. "Moira doesn't need my help today, so I thought I could lend you a hand."

"That'd be great! Let me finish changing the bandage on this guy's paw, and we can make the rounds."

The little green dragon, Forrest, held one paw up obediently when Evander crouched beside him again. Forrest was five years old, and should have been almost ten times his current size by now. For some reason he hadn't grown any larger than a youngling, still able to be cradled in human arms with relative ease. Evander had a theory relating to Forrest's time in his egg, but it didn't seem like anything could be done to encourage his growth. To keep his spirits up when other dragons his age grew larger, Evander had asked Forrest to act as his dragon assistant about three years ago, when he'd still been in training himself. It was a role he took to heart. Most of the time.

"What did you do this time, Forrest?" Finlay asked.

I was the only responsible one, Forrest grumbled, turning yellow eyes like sunshine on leaves to Finlay. *Do other dragons my age clean up their messes? No! They leave it to me and Evander! I stepped on a sharp rock that used to be a boulder, before Jasper broke it with his skull. He's got a boulder for brains, but everyone fawns over him for breaking things.*

"The bandage is mostly for show," Evander said in a low voice. "He's spreading a rumor that he hurt his paw hitting Jasper against the boulder."

Forrest whipped his head back to Evander. *I didn't start that rumor!*

"You didn't discourage it, either."

Never you mind, Forrest said. He flexed his bandaged paw and spread his wings. *I'll start rounds in the opposite direction, meet you in the middle.*

Evander chuckled, watching the tiny dragon fly away. "He's so mature sometimes I forget he's basically a teenager, and then he does things like this."

"Let him have his fun," Finlay said.

"Why do you think I put on the bandage?" Evander walked with an easy pace, looking all around in casual observation. Finlay matched her step to his. "I spoke with Chief Stewart yesterday about extending the range of the sanctuary. I know the dragons can come and go as they please, but we have a good population, now. And I'd like to find more." His eyes went to her. "Would you like to come with me, if he lets me scout for more dragons soon?"

"Do you think he would let me?"

"If I told him how incredible you are with dragons. You have this way with them. They know they can trust you."

"Says the dragon whisperer."

"Dragons have excellent hearing. Whispering works quite well."

Finlay brushed against him. "Especially when you're in tune with the hearts of dragons, which is what I meant. You get them, Evander."

"Almost as well as you get me."

Pink dusted his cheeks, and Finlay longed for a moment to place her palm on one and feel the warmth there. She shoved the crazy impulse aside.

"So would you?" Evander asked. "Accompany me to find more dragons, that is? I'm sure I can get permission for you to come."

Was it even a question? Maybe just a formality. He had to know that answer was a resounding, "Yes!" From the flicker of emotion behind his eagerness, Finlay was sure he'd expected that answer, and her heart did a little somersault.

Within the dragon sanctuary, there was always something to capture your eye. This time of year, a month or so past the vernal equinox, several pairs of mates were expecting their eggs to hatch. Evander pointed out a male dragon Finlay almost overlooked, he blended into the ground so well. He had a larger nest, with three eggs. Most had only one, maybe two. Finlay spotted five nests, large eggs gleaming in a rainbow of hues. There would be plenty of baby dragons soon.

As they neared the mountain she noticed more aerial dragons. Adolescents, mainly, from the daring of their acrobatics and dives. One of the fully grown dragons that had been there as long as Finlay could remember stood on a ledge on the mountain, watching the adolescents carefully. Gaea. One of the most formidable dragons within the sanctuary, Gaea towered over all but one of the others, and his massive build left no one in dispute of his claim as dragon leader.

Fortunately, he was a gentle giant the majority of the time. He dipped his head in greeting when Evander and Finlay walked nearby, and then returned his scrupulous attention to the gold dragon showing off in front of him.

"Are they training harder than usual?" Finlay asked.

"They're in the running to be chosen to work with future Knights. Chief Stewart gave me a list of things dragons who have met the minimum age requirement have to be able to do. I shared that list with Gaea, and he's getting them as prepared as he can."

Gaea's deep bass sounded in Finlay's mind. *Wait, Evander.*

Evander stopped and looked over his shoulder. Finlay mirrored him just in time to see the gold dragon crash into a blue one. The gold dragon rolled past the blue one and into a tree.

"Are you all right?" Evander called.

Told you not to add the spin at the end, Gaea grumbled. *I could see you would crash. I warned you. You think I'll let you train with a Knight with that kind of foolishness? You need another two years to mature.*

His words were harsh, but not cruel. A trial occurred every two years, and the handful of people that passed and trained as Knights selected their dragon partners. Finlay didn't think many of the dragons chosen were as young as this group. Of course, many of the humans chosen weren't as young as she and Elsie, both eighteen within the last several weeks. They would be competing against men and women ranging from nineteen to early thirties (the cutoff for the trials), with much more experience . . . she pushed the thought away.

The gold dragon hissed when Evander touched his tail. *Kaiser bit me!*

Because you crashed into me! the blue dragon spat.

"Easy!" Evander said. "It's not deep, Gem. Let me clean it out and it'll heal quickly."

Can you talk to him? Gem whispered when his peers went back to practicing and Evander started cleaning the bite mark on his tail. *Let me try again? I let the others get in my head, but I swear I'm ready!*

Evander didn't pause, dropping some of a healing potion Moira had made over the wound. "I'll see what I can do, but I trust Gaea's judgment."

The gold dragon sighed, let Evander finish, and mumbled a gratitude before flying back over to his friends and Gaea. Evander put his supplies back in his satchel and returned to Finlay's side.

"You really never wanted to do the trial?" Finlay blurted out. She swallowed. "I just think you would be a really good Knight."

He started walking again. "I'm sure being a Knight has its merits, but it's never the life I imagined for myself. I've always wanted to care for the dragons. Not that Knights don't care for them, but—"

"But it's different," Finlay said.

Evander nodded. "It's too much excitement, for me. I get plenty of excitement making sure this lot is taken care of, and there's very little fear. I think that would be different if I'd somehow become a Knight."

A different future played before Finlay's eyes. One where she didn't compete in the trial and become a Dragon Knight, but instead came to work by Evander's side at the dragon sanctuary. Still working with the creatures she loved. Working closely with Evander.

Something inside her stirred, suddenly picturing this future with tangible clarity. Something that wanted it fiercely, but knew if she altered her course now she would always wonder if she'd had what it takes to become a warrior to protect dragon-kind, beyond the dome of this sanctuary.

"There is some danger in what they do," Finlay allowed. To say otherwise would be naïve. They'd known Knights who left on patrols and never returned. Fights with Mages on the border often had devastating consequences.

"That little bit of fear that comes with the position, and that chance of danger, doesn't discourage you like it does me," Evander said, pulling Finlay from dark thoughts. "You like the promise of that adventure. And honestly, I've never met anyone more suited to it. There is one thing I used to want, that I thought only the Knights could ever have." Serious brown eyes met hers. "Can I tell you a secret?"

"Absolutely."

He reached out to take her hand, his palm warm and rough against hers. "Stars above, your hands are always freezing," he murmured. He covered her hand with both of his, sandwiching it, and Finlay sighed as his warmth seeped into her.

He led her to a boulder large enough to sit upon, and both seated themselves. Evander angled his body toward her and started to let go of her hand, but paused with a look at the tattoo on its back. "You'll receive a permanent mark to let you into the sanctuary when you become a Knight. I probably won't have to reapply the temporary one you have now. You'll also receive a second mark, recognizing you've been bound to your dragon partner. When you'll have access to some of your partner's magic."

He released her hand. "It isn't only Knights that can use dragon magic. You don't need to go through the binding ritual to share a dragon's magic. They decide which humans to share with." He leaned in closer and lowered his voice. "They've shared some with me, and I'm learning how to use it to help them the most."

Finlay gaped at him before recovering herself. "They choose who to share magic with?"

He nodded slowly. "The ritual is more for show than anything, though it is a fast way to form a magic bond. Anyone could bond with a dragon, if the dragon wanted them to."

"Which dragon bonded with you?"

He held out his palm, and a brown light flickered above it. "Care to take a guess?"

She took in a small breath. "Gaea?"

"He doesn't rely on his magic very much, but he's a healer by nature." Evander closed his fist, dousing the glowing light. "I haven't used it on anyone but myself yet, in case I do something wrong and cause more damage, but yesterday I accidentally sliced my palm. I used my shared magic to encourage its healing. Within minutes there was no mark. I'll be ready to use this to help the dragons in the next few days, I think."

There was such a selfless eagerness in his voice that Finlay could only stare at him in awe for an extended heartbeat. He'd been given a gift no one thought possible for anyone but a

Knight to receive, and while she knew it excited him, his excitement wasn't for himself, but for how he could use it to benefit the dragons he loved.

"You're amazing," she breathed.

He rubbed the back of his neck.

"I've been meaning to ask you something," Finlay said, forcing herself to look away. "If I don't pass the trial, I have to choose which career path to follow, at least until the next trial." The words rushed out. "Do you think I could come tend the sanctuary with you?"

Evander froze. "You'd really want to?"

Finlay nodded, fisting her hand in her skirt.

Evander placed his hand over hers. "You'll always have a place with me, Finlay." He sighed. "But you won't need the sanctuary. You'll pass the trial."

There was pride in his voice, and confidence in his words, but it was the sigh that Finlay puzzled over. Had he been a bit disappointed? Regretful? Was she reading too much into a simple exhale?

She wasn't sure, but she decided that if he had sighed because part of him wished she would join him working in the sanctuary, she could relate. That path, which she'd never let herself fully picture before this morning, was incredibly enticing.

It was a good thing the part of that path she most wanted, even if she wouldn't admit it to herself, would stay in her life regardless.

CHAPTER THREE

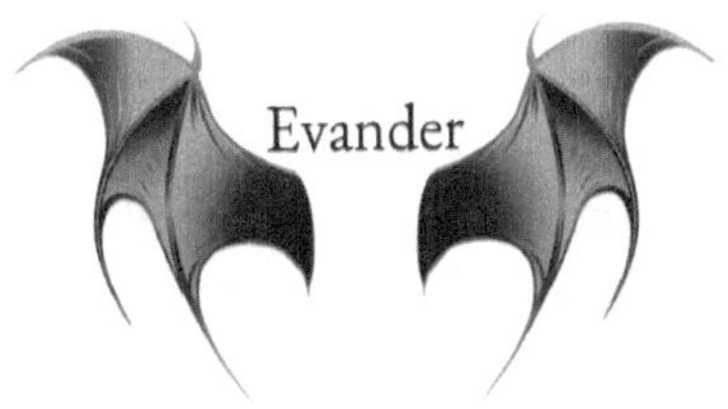

Evander watched Finlay leave the sanctuary several hours later, his heart sinking down to his stomach as it did every time she left, lately. He supposed it balanced, since it soared into his throat every time she came. It tended to flutter somewhere between those regions when they were together, based on the conversation—and how he vacillated between being completely smitten and being the friend he'd always been to her.

You're drooling like a lovesick puppy.

Evander spun at Forrest's mocking, to find the tiny green dragon hovering just behind him. Forrest came to land on Evander's shoulder, front paws resting over it, hind scrabbling against Evander's back until they caught in his shirt and he stabilized. "I don't know what you're talking about," Evander told him.

You are a bit of an idiot sometimes.

"Hey!"

Only sometimes. Happens to the best of us. But you seriously don't see how you feel about Finlay?

Heat rushed to Evander's cheeks, and of course, Forrest noticed.

You do know! I knew it!

"You guessed," Evander corrected, walking toward his cottage. "If you'd known, you would have said something a long time ago."

I don't like to interfere.

Evander snorted. Interfering was one of the things Forrest did best, and had since he hatched. It was almost always good-natured, though. "I guess you don't want to go see Chief Stewart with me then, to ask if Finlay can come along to find more dragons?"

Forrest's tail curled around Evander's neck. *That depends. Can I come with you too?*

"You know it isn't safe past the border, Forrest. I'd really like you to stay here."

Forrest sighed and pushed off of Evander's shoulder. *You can ask the chief on your own.*

"Forrest, wait!" Evander groaned. "I need you safe. Okay? That's all. My heart's already going to be close to exploding having Finlay in potential danger, and if you come too it'll push it right over the edge."

Forrest hesitated, hovering in the air immediately in front of Evander. *I am pretty important in your life. Okay, I get it. I'll still let you ask the chief on your own. I'm gonna check in with Gaea.*

Evander almost laughed, watching Forrest fly away. For all his talk, he could be extremely sensitive. He was also incredibly young . . .

Evander made his way to his cottage, grabbed his parchment with the current numbers of the dragon population, pocketed it, and headed out immediately to the Knights' compound. Should he wait and let the chief reach out to him again, since they'd spoken only yesterday? Probably. But Finlay wanted to go with him, and with the trial approaching, he thought it would do her some good to have another thing to focus on.

She tended to worry things over, and she tended to do it silently and, often, hid it very well. He'd learned to see it, over the years. The way she bit the inside of her lower lip, so lightly he doubted she noticed. How she toyed with her long hair. How her warm brown eyes seemed to see right through her surroundings, the power of her thoughts claiming her vision. She wasn't always worrying when she did these things, but when he noticed them more frequently, he was sure she had something heavy on her mind.

His thoughts strayed back to when they'd first become friends. When it had taken months for him to see her truly smile, and the first time he had, he'd determined to make her do it as often as possible. That soft smile lit up the world–and he had seen it when she first stepped into the sanctuary, and saw a dragon up close. Something that told him she loved the creatures as he did. Though he knew he'd been too young for it to really have happened then, Evander swore he started to fall for her that day.

He'd been falling every day since, without even knowing it until recently. Immeasurably deep as it was, all he knew was that, at this point, he would never surface from his affection for her. How could he, when loving her had become a part of his very being?

He really did wonder why Forrest hadn't said something sooner. Evander had only fully realized it in the last year, but it must have been written across his face every time he saw her. Then again, he didn't think she'd ever caught on, so maybe it wasn't as obvious as he thought. Forrest did know him better than just about anyone other than Finlay, after all. He certainly spent enough time with him.

Many of the Knights had finished training for the day, and already left the courtyard. Several were still hard at work, Isla and Meric among them. Evander waved at them as he passed. The pair seemed to be sparring, as their dragons clashed overhead. Meric raised a hand for an instant. Isla merely nodded in his direction before rushing toward Meric.

Finlay talked all the time about how different Isla and Elsie were, despite being sisters and looking so similar. Evander didn't think they were as different from each other as Finlay did. He saw the same stubbornness in both girls, and the same dedication. Honestly, he saw those same traits in Finlay, too. Maybe it was something to do with them all being raised together. But the youngest, the boys, did seem very different to him, and they'd had the same upbringing . . .

Chief Stewart sat on a bench on the far side of the compound, watching those left training with a calculating eye. He smiled when he saw Evander approach. "Ah, I was wondering when you'd come to ask again."

"I brought my notes, as you requested I do next time we talk." He handed the parchment over. "It has the current population count, and the breakdown of males and females, adults, adolescents, younglings, and eggs. We might need to expand soon, but still, we can do so much more. Have you decided if I can scout for more dragons or not?"

The chief's eyes scoured the page he held in his stubby fingers. "You've certainly kept detailed notes, my boy. You're a fine keeper of the sanctuary."

This was nothing compared to the notes Evander had in his cottage. He'd compiled pages detailing all the types of dragons he'd seen, with sketches and common characteristics, into a book. A master tome, as he liked to think of it. One copy rested in his cottage. The other he'd given to Finlay. "Thank you, sir," he said, blinking away the thought.

Chief Stewart handed the paper back after several long moments. "I agree there's more we can do. So much in our world needs to be changed. We need to do what we can now to make that happen, so yes. I'll grant permission for you to go on a scouting trip near the border. With Knights to accompany you, of course."

Evander folded the parchment and slipped it back into his pocket. "Chief Stewart, I was also hoping to have someone else accompany me. Finlay McDonough." He watched the man's reaction and rushed to add on, "She helps me in the sanctuary whenever Moira doesn't need her, and she has a way with the dragons. I know she could help convince any we see to live here."

The chief took the better part of a minute to respond. "If you speak so highly of her, you must really believe it. All right, then." He smiled. "We'll get it arranged so you can go in the coming days."

Evander held out his hand. "Thank you, sir."

Chief Stewart shook it with a nod. "Anything to help make our world better."

Chapter Four

Finlay

Not the best soup I've made, but not the worst, Finlay thought, dropping a handful of leafy kale and chopped carrots into the pot of water. She wished she had some chicken to add, as it really enhanced the flavor—and kept her full longer. She'd used the last of her weekly allowance of meat last night, and wouldn't be able to take more until tomorrow.

She added two small, peeled potatoes to the pot, a generous measure of the barley she used to make everything, and a pinch of seasoning herbs, before leaving it to cook over the fire. It would suffice for her supper. While it cooked, she did a quick sweep of her little cottage. It didn't take nearly as long as the soup needed to tidy the small space.

Finlay remembered how excited she'd been when Elsie and Evander had helped her build her own space, almost three years ago. Finlay had been living with Elsie and her family before that point, and with Elsie's mother having more children, space under their roof was in short supply. Elsie and Evander had helped her secure a patch of land and the materials they would need to make a cozy stone cottage for Finlay to call home.

Within the one-room structure, Finlay had minimal furniture, so it didn't take more than a few minutes to straighten everything into relative tidiness, at which point Finlay sighed and sat herself in her armchair. Restless energy demanded she do something while she waited for her meal to cook, so though she was horrible at it, she picked up the weaving she'd been slowly working on. For two years. Someday Elsie would get this pouch.

There was a reason beyond her dislike of the practice and total lack of skill that Finlay was taking so long with it. She only picked it up by the fire, in her soft chair, and found it mind-numbingly boring. Her restlessness faded by the time her supper was done, and after eating it, she returned to the chair to finish her current section of weaving with a sense of duty.

Before long, her head bobbed up and down, blinks lengthening, hands slowing over the loom, and against every intention, she drifted off.

"Take that!"

Finlay thrust her imaginary sword forward, and Michael doubled over with a theatrical gasp. He pressed his hands to his stomach and staggered before falling to the ground.

"Another stab to the stomach?" he said a moment later, leaning up on one hand to raise an eyebrow at her. "You need to get more original with your swordplay."

Finlay extended a hand to help her brother up. "You're just jealous I broke through your shield."

"I let you break through because I'm a good older brother who lets you win sometimes." He smiled. "Now it's my turn."

"Michael, Finlay, time for your chores!" Mam called from the house. The day was practically over, Finlay realized. The light had already started fading from the sky.

Michael groaned, raking a hand through his brown hair. "Next time, it's still my turn to be the warrior."

Mam told Michael to go chop some wood for the fire, and Finlay to wash the dishes from lunch, while she mended some clothes. Da came in from the paddock where their cow and horse stayed after a few minutes.

"It's getting dark," he said. "Where's Michael?"

"He should be along any minute with firewood." Mam set down one of Da's work shirts and pulled on her boots. "I'll see if he needs a hand."

She walked out. Da came over and took the last wooden bowl from Finlay. "I can finish that, sweet." He scooped up a cupful of clean water and poured it over the bowl, then picked up the soapy rag to wash it. "Did I hear you and Michael playing warriors again?"

Finlay nodded and bounced on her toes. "I beat him."

Da laughed. "Both of my children are fierce warriors. Soon enough you'll have the chance to show"—he cut off when a loud noise cut through the stillness. He set down the half-washed bowl and strode to the door, and stopped just outside, looking all around.

A bit of fear crept over Finlay as she went to stand behind Da. "What was that?"

The same sound, something incredibly loud and deep, made Da tense. "Power," he said. "Dragon's power." When he turned sharply to look at her, Finlay's heart almost stopped. Da had a look in his eyes she'd never seen him have before. Terror. His hands gripped her upper arms. "Finlay, I need you to stay here!"

"Where are you going?"

"To get Mam and Mi"—he took in a sharp breath. Bright orange lit a patch of the night, angry flames growing bigger by the second. Da turned and pulled Finlay inside with a jerk.

"Why is there a fire? What's going on?"

"Everything's going to be fine, but you need to hide here until I come to get you. Do you understand?" He pulled up the trap door leading to the cellar space where they kept their supplies and urged her down the wooden ladder. He thought for a second, and then ran out of sight, returning with a dagger. "Don't let go of this, either. If anyone but me, Mam, or Michael comes for you, you use that and you run."

Tears formed in Finlay's eyes, and her breath became shallower. "Da, I'm scared!"

She could see that he tried to smile at her, but that terror was too bright in his eyes for it to be reassuring. "Stay here and safe, sweet. I'll be back in a few minutes."

He shut the door, blocking out the light from the lantern completely. Finlay cowered next to the base of the ladder, hugging her knees. She tried singing the lullaby Da always sang, softly to herself. Her voice wouldn't work.

A few minutes passed without change, alone in the dark. A shattering tear sounded above her. The cellar door shook, sending dust sprinkling down on her. Crashes accosted her ears, and bright orange light entered her darkened surroundings; the light of a fire, visible in the cracks between the cellar door and the floor. A wave of heat followed the orange light, washing over her. Uncomfortably warm.

It swamped her in the next moment, blistering and dry, the flames generating the heat and light drawing closer: the cellar door caught fire. Finlay crept out of the way when the door burned to splintering pieces and fell next to her, feeling her way along the dirt floor. She had to stay put. Da had told her to stay put. Smoke coiled in the air around her. Finlay buried her head in her lap.

When the heat and light from the fire had faded, and Finlay hadn't heard any sounds in a very long time, she unlocked her hands from around her legs and inched toward the cellar opening. The wooden steps of the ladder had burned with the door.

"Da?" she called. Her voice scratched. "Da?" she called again, louder.

She couldn't wait any longer. She jumped, latched onto the edge of the floor, and scrabbled up to the house. To what used to be the house, really. Ash coated everything in sight. The roof and walls were gone.

"Mam!" Finlay yelled. "Michael! Da!"

She looked back at the cellar opening. She had to go find them, but she couldn't leave without the dagger Da had given her. She jumped back down and retrieved it, and tied it around her waist with twine she took from around one of the sacks of potatoes she'd been hiding near. That done, she once more climbed from the cellar and set out to look for her family.

Finlay startled awake to a knock on her door with a gasping breath, eyes flying open. Wetness stained down her cheeks, and her heart pounded.

She scrubbed her hands over her face and stood as another insistent knock hit her door. "Fin? You in there?" Elsie called.

"Coming!"

Finlay took in a steadying breath, plastered on a smile, and opened the door. It was a mark of their friendship that Elsie looked at her for an instant and understood exactly what had happened. She dropped her lantern and stepped into Finlay's cottage and wrapped her tightly. Finlay imagined the powerful grip must be similar to a bear's, but it wasn't crushing. Her throat closed.

"I'd hoped the nightmares had slowed down," Elsie said over her shoulder.

"They're not quite every night now, but close enough," Finlay said.

Elsie let her go and inspected her. "It's time for the moonlight flight. Do you want to skip it tonight?"

Finlay shook her head and went to light her lantern. "We can't miss it. Isn't it Isla's night to go on patrol?"

Elsie hummed a response, and once Finlay had her lantern lit and had wrapped her cloak over her shoulders, they walked to the site the Knights gathered. Each night, shortly after full darkness claimed the skyline, several of the dragon riders and their partners flew to the border and back on a scouting mission.

Seeing the handful of Knights preparing to take off calmed Finlay. No surprise attacks in the night could happen with the patrol so dutifully surveilling the border. It was the better part of an hour flying on a dragon, over terrain that couldn't be crossed easily on foot; since the Mages killed dragons in order to claim their power, their travels required more mundane transportation. They would be spotted, if they tried to launch a raid in the night.

Chief Stewart—elected leader of Aerouant Glèidh long before Finlay joined—stood with his dragon partner, watching as he always did, arms loosely crossed and resting on his paunchy belly. Finlay couldn't remember the last time she'd seen him take part in the moonlit surveillance flights, despite that he watched them leave every night. It was common knowledge that his dragon partner, Ghillie, had something wrong with his muscles. He fatigued more rapidly than he should. The braces he had around his paws straightened legs that would be bowed otherwise. Finlay guessed Chief Stewart didn't want to tax Ghillie with the flight. She also suspected that it might be good for Ghillie to go, once in a while. Every dragon loved to soar.

But it wasn't her place to say anything.

Ghillie rested calmly next to the chief, purple eyes serene as they swept over those nearby. He certainly did his part for the Knights, even without going out on surveillance flights. Ghillie's camouflaging magic hid them from view of the Mages and the wider kingdom, Alocasia. Only those whose hearts hadn't been darkened by killing dragons, or conspiring with those who had, could see past the camouflage, so long as Ghillie's magic surrounded it. One Mage had stood within the range of a bow and not once shown any sign of seeing the Knight and dragon staring at them from this spot. Finlay had seen it, and marveled at Ghillie's ability.

"Finlay, Elsie, you two are here as reliably as I am," Chief Stewart greeted.

"Can't resist the chance to see the Knights," Finlay said.

Chief Stewart huffed a mild laugh. "Most people wouldn't think watching them take to the sky is worth so much enthusiasm."

"But you watch every night," Elsie said.

Finlay almost elbowed her. Thankfully, the chief seemed amused. "Are either of you planning to participate in the upcoming trial? You're eligible now, aren't you?"

"Both of us," Elsie stated, standing taller.

Chief Stewart looked at them appraisingly. It seemed to Finlay his gaze rested on her a second longer than necessary. "I look forward to seeing your attempts."

"Ready?" Meric asked the other four Knights.

Finlay turned to watch them climb onto the saddles on their dragon partners. Within a minute they were all climbing into the sky, Isla's serpentine water dragon appearing to swim through the air while the others flapped large wings to ascend. Longing stirred deep inside Finlay.

The only other spectator, a young boy called Jayne, left as soon as the Knights were out of sight. Elsie left after a few minutes, yawning hugely and complaining about a hard day at the forge. Even Chief Stewart didn't stay the entire time, leaving soon after Elsie, Ghillie walking behind him. Finlay pulled her cloak closer against the chilly night, fisting her hands tightly in the soft material, but stayed in the same spot until the Knights appeared on the horizon what had to be two hours after they'd left, massive shapes in the darkness until they drew near.

"You didn't need to stay," Isla told Finlay after sliding off Muir's back.

"I wanted to see everyone home safely."

Isla softened. "No threat tonight, Finlay. No activity anywhere near the border of the kingdom."

Finlay allowed herself to smile and started back to her cottage, much more at ease than she'd been before the patrol.

Her nightmare could remain merely a memory, for another night at least.

CHAPTER FIVE

You sure you don't need me?

Finlay pursed her lips and looked at Evander, who regarded Forrest with a long-suffering amusement. "Forrest, I do need you," Evander said carefully. "I need you to keep watch over the sanctuary while Finlay and I are looking for more dragons."

Forrest exhaled sharply. *I could sneak away with you.*

"But then you wouldn't be doing your job."

Forrest grumbled, then stood on his hind legs and dipped his head to Evander. *The sanctuary will be safe under my supervision!*

Evander's shoulders shook when Forrest flew away. "I don't know what to do with him sometimes."

"He's getting much better with guilt-tripping."

Evander looked back to Finlay. "I feel like he may be getting lessons from someone."

"I'm sure I don't know what you're talking about."

She felt Evander's smile on her back, but didn't give him the satisfaction of looking over her shoulder. Instead, she strode to Gaea and climbed onto his back. Evander joined her, seating himself behind her, and asked Gaea to take off.

Evander's arms circled Finlay's waist once Gaea spread his wings and launched from the ground. His hands rested loosely over her hips, perfectly still, barely pressing against her. There was nothing improper about his touch—he merely had to hold on, and this was the most secure way to do so with two riders—yet Finlay's pulse quickened, all the same. His breath warmed the back of her neck, and she was tempted to lean against him.

But they were only flying to the launch site, to meet the two Knights who would be escorting them to the border. Finlay brightened when she saw that Isla was one of them. She didn't know the other personally, though she knew he was called Bryson. What made her pause after Gaea landed was the sight of Elsie, running toward them.

"What are you doing here?" Isla asked before Finlay could.

Elsie panted for a moment. "Thought you could leave without me?"

"You're not coming," Isla said.

"Yes I am. I'm not missing the chance to save some dragons before I'm a Knight."

"You don't have permission to join us," Bryson said.

Elsie waved a hand dismissively. "I can ask forgiveness after. Now, are we going?" She stared between Isla and Bryson. "I'll take any blame if Chief Stewart does disapprove. But I don't think he'll mind very much."

Isla groaned and climbed onto Muir. "Come on, then. You can ride with me."

Evander frowned. "I guess we're not discussing our flight route."

Finlay climbed back onto Gaea with a sigh. She was certain Isla would have taken several minutes to go over the flight route if Elsie hadn't come. Finlay had seen it enough times to know nothing frazzled Isla more than her little sister. Even their four younger brothers couldn't exasperate the Knight as quickly as Elsie; something in which Elsie took great pride, and Finlay didn't understand.

This time, Finlay sat behind Evander. Since he had the bond with Gaea, she thought it only right he should be in the lead position to ride him. Isla and Elsie flew in front of them, Bryson behind.

Trepidation and eagerness warred in her blood as they left Aerouant Glèidh behind. Finlay focused on the eagerness, extending her arms once they leveled off above the flat gray clouds. The spring afternoon was chilly, especially up so high, but she made no move to tighten her cloak. No bit of cold could taint this experience. Both the edges of her cloak and her hair flew out behind her, strewn by the breeze that brushed past her cheeks, and a bubbling laugh escaped her.

You act like you were born for the sky, Gaea told her, turning his head enough for her to see one giant brown eye.

"How can you resist flying all the time?" Finlay asked.

Sometimes I can't, Gaea admitted. *The air calls to all dragons. My pull to the land is almost as strong, as is Muir's pull to the sea. But air is integral to all dragons. Few humans are comfortable in the sky.*

"Further proof you're secretly a dragon," Evander said over his shoulder.

Finlay lowered her arms, wrapping them around Evander's waist again. "I wish!"

You don't need to be a dragon to understand them. The two of you are as kin to dragons as humans can be.

The weight of Gaea's praise took a few moments to settle over Finlay. Moisture pricked at her eyes. Once she got past the block in her throat, she placed one hand palm down on Gaea's scales. "Thank you."

He rumbled in response and turned his full attention back to their flight.

They'd been given until the end of day to search for dragons. Only a handful of hours, but it was better than nothing. Finlay knew most of the dragons that used to live in this section of the mountains had long since fled, moved to their sanctuary, or been killed by Mages seeking their power, but felt no area was completely devoid of them.

They traveled carefully, alert to any signs of Mages or dragons, for much of their allotted time, without sight of anything but the fresh growth of the wild in the mountains.

"We have company approaching," Bryson called.

Finlay whirled to see two dragons, adolescents by their size, climbing into the sky from a cavern entrance below them.

"Let's land and have a little chat," Isla called back.

Finlay turned around in her seat to watch the two dragons adjust their course to meet them on the ground. One of them kept catching her eye more than the other. Its scales shone the color of sunset, orange and red and gold mottled together. It wasn't merely the color that captivated Finlay. It was the dragon's wings. Bright, feathered wings.

"They're beautiful," Evander breathed.

Elsie's cry shattered the silence. "Look out!"

Finlay realized she wasn't the only one to have been focused on the adolescent dragons. A bolt flew over their heads. Directly over their heads.

"Head back!" Isla demanded, diving towards the origin of the bolt. Two figures stood below, one holding a crossbow. Mages.

Bryson and his dragon charged down to help Isla fight them off. Bryson raised his sword high. His dragon snarled, low and menacing.

"Please, come with us!" Evander called to the adolescent dragons as Gaea turned them around. "We can keep you safe!"

The dragons hesitated only a few seconds.

Long enough for a second bolt to fly through the air, and burrow into the chest of the sunset-colored dragon. Finlay watched its orange eyes widen and its wings jerk before it fell slack, freefalling to the ground. A scream tore from her throat. It was still alive. It had to still be alive.

"Evander!" Finlay cried.

Evander was already in motion, leaning forward urgently. "Gaea, take us to it!"

Gaea spun and dove so quickly Finlay had to cling to Evander to stay astride him. He collided with the ground with a dull thud, making a crater, and lowered himself as close to the ground as he could.

Finlay slid off his back and ran to where the injured dragon had fallen, and froze. The dragon was on fire.

A heavy scent emanated from the fierce blaze. Her throat constricted. She imagined smoke choking her, though none filled the air yet. Why was she freezing? She didn't have time to let this fear paralyze her, when a dragon was dying in front of her!

She barreled past the fear, ignoring the lurch in her stomach the sight of the flames caused. "It must have been a fire Mage, enchanting the bolt," she said to herself. Rage made it easier to ignore the fear. A string of curses left her mouth, and she raced back to Gaea and grabbed a jug from the supply pack he wore. "Don't worry, we'll save you," Finlay said, returning to the ailing dragon's side.

"Finlay, don't!"

She threw the top off and upended the jug over the dragon, spilling the water over the worst of the rapidly spreading flames. An angry hiss marked the fire being quenched, but a chill went down Finlay's spine, and she turned to Evander.

He stood as though transfixed, a look of horror on his face. "She's a phoenix dragon."

Finlay brought her gaze back to the beautiful dragon by her feet, taking in a rattling breath. Most of the flames that had been spreading across its scales were gone. Finlay pressed a fist to her mouth and fought the urge to be sick. Its coloring, its feathery wings . . . the stories were true. Phoenix dragons existed. How could she not have put it together? Her voice came out in a strangled whisper. "She was healing."

The dragon wheezed, blood spilling out from the quarrel in its chest. It raised its head from the ground and looked at Finlay with dulling orange eyes.

You didn't know.

The voice was quiet, feminine and soothing. Guilt snapped Finlay's spine, forcing her to her knees before the dragon. Her voice refused to work.

You didn't know, the dragon said again. *But your intentions were pure. It's all right.*

Finlay forced herself to meet the dragon's gaze, shoving the apology that could never be enough for her mistake past the bile and grief in her throat. She met the kind orange eyes, determined to be strong for her.

The dragon blinked, eyes glowing brighter. Finlay gasped, a painful jolt searing across her chest.

Everything faded.

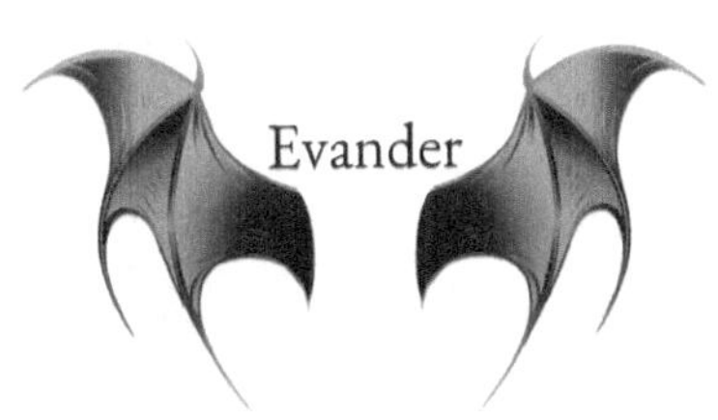

CHAPTER SIX

Wings the color of a burning sunset, with delicate feathers instead of the tough hide he'd seen most . . . Evander stopped in his tracks on the way to the dragon the Mages shot down. It couldn't be, could it?

Flames spread from her wound, climbing over her scaly body and reaching towards her soft wings, and he knew for certain. She was a phoenix dragon.

That was when he saw Finlay grab the jug of water. His cry reached her too late, the water already sloshing through the air. It hissed over the phoenix dragon's body, extinguishing the flames. "She's a phoenix dragon," he said, in a stunned sort of voice.

Finlay turned to him, incredibly pale, and then looked back at the dying dragon. Evander's gaze cycled between the two as he stepped slightly closer, helplessness tearing at his stomach. "She was healing," Finlay whispered, behind her hand.

Evander bit the inside of his cheek, using the sting to force the shock and sadness away. There had to be something he could do. If he could stop the bleeding somehow, she could try to generate another flame and finish the healing—he just needed to help her start healing.

That was when Finlay's knees hit the ground, and Evander's frantic attempt at planning fled from his mind. He wasn't sure if he said her name aloud or not, but he rushed to kneel beside her, to brace her at the least. The phoenix dragon's eyes seemed to glow in his periphery, and just as he reached his arms out, Finlay tensed and slumped over.

Evander lunged to catch her, then pushed himself upright, studying her. She was so pale, hair fanned around her startlingly bright in comparison. Had she passed out?

He glanced at the dragon and did a double take. There seemed to be something coming from the dragon, which was still breathing weakly, and moving toward Finlay. A spark. He watched the bit of fiery energy touch Finlay's hand, where it lay on the ground, close to the dragon, and sink inside her skin. The glow of that spark, orange and bright, seemed to continue inside her, traveling along her arm, spreading across her body.

"Finlay?" Evander asked.

The spark stretched and grew beneath her skin like a spidery thread, thin lines, smaller tendrils connecting and fracturing in opposite directions. It peeked over her cloak and climbed her neck, curving along her face and curling in front of her ears, where it stopped on either side.

She showed no sign of hearing him, of being anywhere near waking. She showed no sign of anything, until the spark reached her temples, and then her mouth opened in a pained cry. Her eyes remained closed, but she whimpered and tensed, clearly in pain.

"Finlay? Finlay, can you hear me?" Evander gathered her close, pulling her head onto his lap. He held the back of his hand to her forehead and her cheeks and found them unusually warm. What was the dragon doing to her?

Another pained cry cleaved his heart, and he brushed her hair back, looking helplessly from her to the dragon.

The dragon shuddered and went still, and the absence of its shallow, pained breathing was deafening. "I'm sorry," Evander breathed, looking at the beautiful creature. It would be gone in moments. The first phoenix dragon he'd ever seen, and he'd watched it die.

The loss took a back seat to his fear for Finlay now, though. Fear that he might lose her, as the dragon had just been lost, shook him to his core. He searched her face and found it smoothed over, the pain gone from her expression. Just blankness. The glowing lines of the spark faded and disappeared. Whatever the dragon had been doing, it stopped with the dragon's death. What harm had she done before that, though?

"Finlay, please wake up!"

Evander adjusted her in his grip, pulling her up more so her head was cradled against his chest. *Don't die,* he pleaded. *Don't die, don't die.*

It seemed an age in itself that he held her close to him, feeling the beating of her heart, listening to her steady breathing, praying to anyone or thing that would listen for her to recover.

The other adolescent dragon landed nearby. *She's gone?* he asked in a slight tenor voice.

Evander nodded. "I'm sorry . . ."

Arget.

"Arget," Evander said. "Please follow us. We have a safe place for dragons."

The dragon dipped his head and took off. Evander knew he should speak to him more. He couldn't. Finlay demanded every thought. His attention shifted to the phoenix dragon when a golden yellow glow covered her body. In a glittering display, the phoenix dragon's body lost its form, magic essence dissolving and dispersing in the air.

Part of Evander had hoped that whatever damage had been done when the phoenix dragon tried to reach Finlay, with whatever that spark had been, would be undone when the last of her magic faded, and her body dissolved. Finlay remained in the same state, dashing that twisted hope.

"Finlay, please!" he whispered.

A small hitch in her breathing made him pause, and then his heart leapt when he heard her murmur, "Evander?"

Chapter Seven

There was fire everywhere.

Crimson claimed the sky, everything washed in red light. Ashes swirled in the hazy, boiling air, churning restlessly above the inferno. Earth scorched black burned the bare soles of her feet.

The fire called to her.

Choking on the blistering heat and breathing in cinders, she trudged toward the clearing where they chopped their wood for the fire.

The flames beckoned.

She clutched the dagger and made her way, stumbling and swaying the nearer she got. The heat seemed more concentrated here, each step hotter than the last. Breathing hurt. Walking hurt. Balance tipped, the world coming in and out of focus.

She inched forward, pulling herself toward the blaze.

She took another step and staggered. Something with heavy charring rested on the far side of the clearing. Three somethings, broken husks of shapes, two closer together . . . her knees gave out.

Wings reached the outermost tendrils of flames, which leapt to them with a destructive joy, eagerly claiming fresh material to burn.

Agony scorched along her arms, fire racing toward her torso, overwhelming her body. Embers crackled over her flesh and sank inside, scorching through blood and bone and muscle.

She bathed in the flames, became the flames, energies mending and merging as they destroyed and, at the same time, restored.

She screamed without being able to produce a sound.

I'm so sorry, she thought to the other. The girl was being pulled into her consciousness, torn between burning and her own nightmare . . . she retreated, unwilling to risk the life of the girl.

The fire quenched and swirled away, and Finlay fell backward into cool nothingness . . .

"Finlay? Finlay, can you hear me?"

A voice floated around her. She knew that voice. Warm, deep, silky tones laced with emotion. It quickened something inside her, clearing away char and soot that had encased her. Light played behind closed eyes, which she shuttered open a crack.

Even the minimal rays filtering through her mostly-lowered lashes were blinding.

"Finlay, please wake up!"

Evander, Finlay thought.

Her eyes shut of their own accord, and his voice receded.

Finlay found herself back in the clearing, on the ashen ground. Her eyes were locked on the three shapes ahead of her.

Her world had burned to the ground. Though she didn't want to, and fought it bitterly, the realization crept inside her all the same. She clutched Da's dagger in trembling hands, throat hoarse from exertion and ash, eyes streaming from grief and smoke. Mam. Da. Michael.

Despite the ache, she heard an inhuman wail come straight from her soul, and fell forward, holding the last remnant of her family close. The dagger's tip pierced the skin near her collar. Finlay didn't feel the pain, hugging herself tightly with her hands fastened to the hilt. She only noticed the wound when she stood, some unknown measure of time later, hollower than she'd ever been, and saw the blood running down her shirt.

She touched the wound absently, still unfeeling. It wasn't too deep.

She tied the dagger around her waist again and cast a final look at the broken shapes that used to be her family before walking away.

Time was meaningless, but she had a vague direction in which to travel. Mam and Da had taken Michael to a nearby settlement the day before, hoping to look into moving there. Finlay had stayed home with a cold, with the neighbor checking on her, but knew the general direction they'd traveled. She headed that way in the deep of night, stiffly moving forward.

The sky wasn't as black when she saw signs of a settlement, hints of color playing along the horizon. Dawn had to be near. Part of Finlay glowered at those hints of light. Most of her didn't care either way, and trudged on through the craggy terrain and around small bodies of water until she came upon a row of cottages and other modest homes. Could this be the place? She guessed it was about the right distance, though they'd traveled with a horse and cart.

She winced against the images that flashed across her memory. Everything was gone.

A feminine voice startled her and made her whirl. "Are you all right?"

A girl stood in the opening of one of the larger homes in the row, probably close to Michael's age. She seemed around three years older than Finlay. Her dark hair hung down to her waist.

"You're bleeding!" she cried, eyes going to Finlay's chest. "Mam, come help!"

Mam. The word pierced, and suddenly Finlay was running. Staggering, really, but hastening away from the girl, away from the memories and the pain . . .

Tears obscured her vision again, and she knocked into someone and fell back to the ground. The boy looked at her with confusion that swiftly changed to concern. "Hey, it's all right," he said quietly.

Finlay swallowed hard. He wasn't asking if she was okay. He must have seen she clearly wasn't, would never be again. He had a kind face, with dark blond hair reaching almost to his chin. He kneeled next to her.

"My name is Evander. Who are you?"

A tiny passageway opened, allowing her to answer this one question, at least. "Finlay."

He smiled, and a little dimple appeared on one of his cheeks. "I like that."

The girl from before hurried over, another, younger girl just behind. From their shared features, probably sisters. A woman walked behind them, also noticeably similar to the girls. "Isla, Elsie, give her room," the woman said. "You too, Evander."

The boy backed up several paces but remained on the ground, anxious brown eyes never leaving Finlay. The woman crouched beside her.

One look at her face was too much. She may not have been Finlay's mother, but there was a distinctive mothering look in her almond-shaped eyes, and Finlay hadn't had nearly enough time to process. The numb state she'd entered fractured and broke apart.

So did Finlay, surprised as she was to find she had more tears to shed.

"Finlay, please!"

Consciousness returned swiftly and completely, Evander's whispered plea tearing her from the nightmare and back to reality. They were both on the ground. Evander had his arms wrapped protectively about her, her head resting against his chest. "Evander?"

He sucked in a breath and leaned back to look at her. "Thank the gods you're all right!"

Finlay moved to sit up, but found her strength all but gone. "The dragon."

He pulled her close, one hand cupping the back of her head. "It's gone, Finlay. Dissolved, like all dragons when they d"—he broke off. "At the end," he said instead.

Motion nearby made both flinch, and panic stabbed through Finlay. "I killed a dragon. Evander, what will they do to me?" Her voice rang hollowly in her ears. Remorse tore at her stomach and lashed her throat.

"Nothing. They won't find out."

"What do *I* do? What have I *done?*"

Something didn't feel right, beyond the physical weakness currently lapping at her. Had she been burning? Was she still on fire? There seemed to be a lingering memory of pain, and emotions so strong she wasn't sure where they came from. Her thoughts spun at a sickening pace, and she closed her eyes in an attempt to sort through them, fully leaning against Evander. Everything was too much and too little. What was going on?

She wondered if Evander thought she'd passed out again, because his hold on her softened. He pressed his lips to the top of her head and whispered, "I'll take care of you."

You always take care of me, Finlay thought. For one wonderful moment, she felt herself again. Loud footfalls entered her range of hearing, and Elsie's distressed cry, and Finlay's mind resumed its chaotic frenzy to process.

"She's all right," Evander said, louder than before. "Just fainted. We tried to save the dragon, but were too late."

A rough hand touched Finlay's forehead. Elsie.

Finlay couldn't face them yet, and pretended to still be unconscious.

"We drove the Mages back," Isla said. "One might not make it."

"If we're lucky," Bryson said. "The world needs fewer dragon murderers."

It took all of Finlay's efforts not to tense. "We should get back," Evander said. "The other dragon has agreed to follow us. Arget is his name." He adjusted his hold on Finlay and stood, one arm beneath her knees and the other supporting her torso, her head against his chest so she could hear the rapid beat of his heart.

"You got her?" Bryson asked.

"Let's go," was all Evander said in response. Finlay felt him walking, and he carefully climbed onto Gaea's back. He tucked her against himself before asking Gaea to bring them home, and

Finlay both heard and felt the great dragon's wings move to bring them into the air.

"I know you're awake," Evander said once they leveled out in the sky. "I also know you weren't ready to answer any questions. I'll get you home without having to talk to anyone else."

As before, Finlay latched onto his reassuring voice and reclaimed her sense of balance. This time she clung to it, forcing the swirl of emotions and thoughts to slow and stop. She opened her eyes to glance up at him, certain it would give her the courage to start to face what she'd done. As if he knew she would and wanted to be ready—or, more thrilling and nerve-wracking, perhaps he had been watching her already—his gaze was set on her when she opened her eyes. Warm, steady earth. "Thank you," she murmured.

He flashed the dimpled smile of his that made her heart flutter in her chest, and didn't say another word until they approached home. Even then, he merely asked Gaea to drop them both off at Finlay's cottage and go back to the sanctuary himself.

"I'll take her inside," he called to the others when they started descending. "She's fine, just needs a good night's sleep. She's coming around now."

"I can bring something from Moira," Elsie offered.

"That won't be necessary," Evander replied. "I know just what you need," he whispered close to Finlay's ear.

"I can walk inside," Finlay said.

"It'll convince the others to leave us alone longer if you let me carry you."

Finlay acquiesced and let him carry her into her cottage. Once the door closed she opened her eyes, expecting him to set her on her feet. He kept his grip on her and walked to her cozy armchair, placing her in it.

"I can walk now," Finlay said.

"Your strength may be back, but you've just been through something traumatic. Hold on while I get what you need."

She could at least start the fire, and moved to do so. She turned when he walked to her cabinet in the kitchen area of her cottage as she grabbed a match, and watched him reach onto one of the narrow shelves and pull down a bottle. "Wine?"

He looked at it and replaced it on the shelf, picking up the bottle next to it. "No. Something stronger."

Finlay lit the kindling she'd preemptively placed in the fireplace that morning and returned to her chair. Evander took two cups from another shelf and poured a generous measure of the amber liquid into each, then went to her side and handed her one. He grabbed one of the chairs from her table and brought it over, seating himself by her side, then held up his own cup.

"Drink."

Finlay obeyed, swallowing back the alcohol and showing him her empty cup to prove it was gone. He drank his, refilled both, then leaned back in his seat.

"Now, what exactly happened back there?"

CHAPTER EIGHT

F inlay took another sip from her cup, holding it between both hands in her lap.

"It was so strange, Evander. One second I was looking at the phoenix dragon, and the next I was trapped in a familiar nightmare and something I've never experienced before. I was burning, but I wanted to be part of the fire . . ." she trailed off. "I heard the dragon."

Evander leaned closer. "She spoke to you?"

"Before I passed out, or whatever it was that happened, she said it was all right, that she knew I had pure intentions. But in the dream, I heard her again." Thoughts that had still refused to coalesce into semblance latched into a shape that made sense, and Finlay understood what had happened. "It was the phoenix dragon's consciousness. She tried to do something, and didn't realize it was hurting me. That was the conflicting dream: my mind and hers, overlapping somehow. Right before the dream ended I heard the phoenix dragon apologize and say she couldn't risk my life . . ."

"Take it slowly," he encouraged. "And take another drink."

She downed the rest of the cup and then told him the specifics of the dream. It was a little hazy, with the switches between what she now knew were her memories and the memories/dreams of the dying phoenix dragon.

Evander refilled their cups once more before she finished, and Finlay drank that one with greater gusto. She didn't usually relish the feeling of alcohol. It was why she'd had that same bottle for months, when she could have gotten some each week from the market. The blurred, indistinct air it induced was usually unappealing. It was numbing the grief, now, letting her talk about it without breaking down, and her appreciation for it grew.

"What I saw makes more sense now," Evander said, after both stared into the fire for several long moments. "It looked like a spark went from the dragon to you, the instant you collapsed. Kind of an orange glow, spreading from the dragon toward you. It faded quickly. Must have been when the dragon stopped whatever she was trying to do."

Finlay stared at the floor. She may not have been feeling the grief anymore, but alcohol only numbed it. It was still there. The fact remained that, due to her actions, a dragon had perished.

Evander's hand reached out and rubbed between her shoulder blades, and without a word they drank again.

"I didn't think phoenix dragons existed," Finlay murmured. "They seemed like stories those who didn't want to believe phoenixes had gone extinct clung to."

His hand paused in its circular movement on her back. "The war between the dragons and the phoenixes was so long ago, no one really knows what happened. They're both creatures of fire, so it makes sense that they would be compatible."

"But you've never heard of anyone seeing a phoenix, have you?"

He pulled his hand back. "No."

"So either they're gone, or there are so few left that they're as good as. How many phoenix dragons could there potentially be, then? Was the one I . . . was she the only one?"

"Don't do that to yourself. I'm sure she wasn't."

Evander seemed intent on distracting her, telling her about Forrest's latest story.

It worked. The numb grief fled from her mind, at least temporarily, and she lost herself in his reassuring voice. Tension melted from her shoulders. The knot of stress and emotion that had settled in the pit of her stomach unraveled and dissipated, and warmth spread from her core. She was getting uncomfortably warm, and realized she'd never taken off her cloak.

Fumbling with the clasp, Finlay inched closer to Evander, a request for him to help on the edge of her lips. She misjudged the space and slipped from the chair. Evander made a swooping motion to steady her, hands flying to her sides, and both sank to their knees on the floor. Finlay's breath hitched to find him so close—so wonderfully, wonderfully close—and for an extended heartbeat they stared at each other, his hands still near her hips from helping her. Wordlessly, Evander removed her cloak, eyes intent upon the clasp, shadowed by his hair, and as he set it to the side, Finlay reached her hand out to frame one rosy cheek. She couldn't help herself.

"Evander," she breathed. Just his name. It was all she could think to say, all she wanted to say, the taste of his name on her lips an alcohol in itself.

He paused, his face still inches from hers. His gaze was on her collar, and his fingers whispered over the pale scar visible above the neck of her tunic. "You're breathtaking."

Her hand traced along his jawline and cupped the back of his neck, urging him closer. He swept an errant curl behind her ear, his touch feather-light again. Everything about Evander was light, and warm, and home.

"I was so worried the day we met," he whispered, tracing her scar again. "I didn't even know you, but the blood . . . I couldn't bear the thought of you dying. And today, I was so worried again . . ."

"I'm right here, Evander," she said, her other hand finding his cheek. *Right here, with you . . .*

Something crumbled in his eyes when they met hers, revealing a thing she'd never seen in them before. Something sharper, darker, than usual. When he leaned forward and brought his lips tantalizingly close to hers, she realized it was desire.

"Finlay."

Longing and affection resonated in that murmured exhale of her name, his breath warm and sweet on her lips. It stirred her very soul, leaving her no choice but to pull him closer and meet his lips with hers. He reached out to draw her fully against him, their bodies crashing together. Her hands traced his perfect chest, feeling the lean muscle beneath soft skin even through his shirt; they traced his jaw and twined in his air, roaming over his top half. He held her at the small of her back with one hand, steady and warm, and trailed over her shoulders and behind her neck with the other, his palm cupping the back of her neck. All the while their lips remained locked together.

The frenzied need to touch each other ebbed gradually, hands moving slower, kisses softening. They were on the floor by the fire, wrapped up in each other's arms. They cuddled there, Evander toying with a lock of Finlay's hair, Finlay tracing the shape of his lips in a captivated kind of wonder at what had just occurred. Exhaustion pulled at her, her hand stilling and dropping to Evander's chest. She nestled against him.

"You're beautiful," she murmured.

He breathed deeply. Asleep. Finlay knew she was seconds away from sleep herself, and her lips tugged up.

My Evander.

Another reason Finlay didn't usually drink very much: the after-effects were the absolute worst.

A dull pressure fixed behind her eyes right when she awoke. The feeble pre-dawn light filtering through her window stabbed at her if she looked at it directly.

She groaned and sat up, only realizing when her hand pressed against Evander's slim but muscular chest that she wasn't alone. A jumbled mess of the events of the night before entered her mind, firelight and kisses and heat . . .

Her cheeks burned. Evander roused, wincing as he pushed himself upright. He blinked sleepily at Finlay, and then his eyes widened. "I, uh . . . hi," he stammered. "How, uh . . . are you all right?"

"Regretting drinking so much."

He stared hard at the floor, his cheeks reddening. "I wasn't trying to . . . I hope you don't think I was trying to take advantage. I'm sorry I let anything happen."

Finlay sucked in a short breath, something crumpling in her chest. "What?"

"Last night, we kissed . . . I don't want anything to ruin our friendship, Finlay."

"Neither do I." More details of the night before became clear. She'd pulled him that final distance. She'd started the embrace. Would she have done that without the alcohol's influence?

Would he have reciprocated, if not for the drinks lowering both of their inhibitions?

She recalled the feeling of his lips against hers and knew the answer to the first question. Pushed past her limits after the incident with the dragon, with the boy she trusted most in the world helping her heal . . . she absolutely would have barreled past the barriers she'd been skirting for months, even without the alcohol. No more denying how badly she wanted something more with Evander Robertson.

But if he didn't want something more himself . . . He was hard to read sometimes, impenetrable as frozen soil whenever she wondered if his smiles were conveying anything beyond friendship.

"You seemed warmer than usual after the phoenix dragon, like you had a fever. You're all right now?"

So the burning feeling had been real. "I don't feel it anymore."

Evander stood, grabbing the cups from last night and putting them on the table. "Can I get anything for you?"

Finlay shook her head before she realized he wasn't looking at her and wouldn't see the gesture. "No, thank you."

He looked over his shoulder, murmured that he would check on her again soon, and left, without truly meeting her eyes.

Finlay stared at the closed door, all traces of warmth disappearing, and mechanically rose and got ready for the day.

Chapter Nine

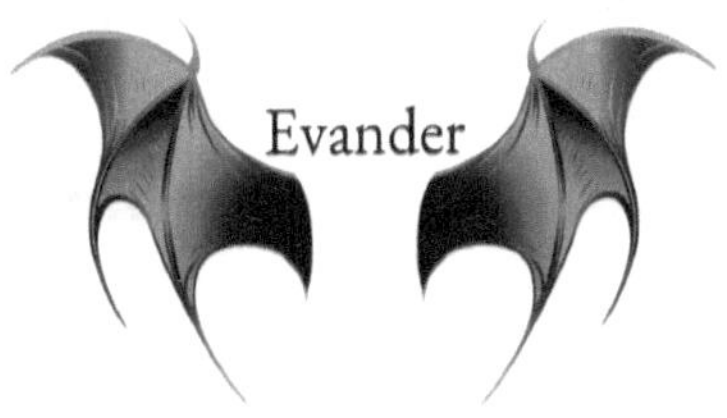

How could a span of hours be filled with profound pleasure, mind-numbing fear, and crushing grief, with each experience bleeding into the other?

What had started as a wonderful outing with Finlay (and the others, but really . . .), flying on Gaea's back, Finlay's arms wrapped around him as they scouted for dragons, had shifted into one of the most terrifying experiences of Evander's life, holding her limp form in his arms while a legendary dragon died next to them.

He'd seen the grief he felt, mirrored and magnified in her pale face when she'd finally woken. He'd seen the shock setting in, and known he had to do something to help her. So he let her pretend to still be unconscious when the others found them, and held her close as Gaea flew them back to the sanctuary. He brought her into her cottage and made sure she sat down, and got her the only thing he knew to help with people experiencing shock: alcohol. Something to dull the pain trying to break her.

It had dulled other things as well, in both of them. He'd done what he'd wanted to for ages, and kissed her, and she'd kissed him back, and it had been the most amazing thing in the world.

If only he could feel he hadn't taken advantage of her.

Evander walked from her cottage the following morning with a hurried step, shame burning his cheeks. How could he accept his first kiss with Finlay being a result of too much to drink? Of course he hoped she would have kissed him, but she was in such a state, devastated and overwhelmed, and with alcohol thrown in, who was to say she had really wanted to kiss him?

And that he kept replaying it in his head, as he walked back to the sanctuary? That he kept remembering the feeling of running his fingers through her loose curls, and her hand tracing over his chest. That he remembered the feeling of her mouth on his, the sound of his name on her lips, in a warm breath that tickled his skin, and that the memory made him happier than he thought he'd ever felt.

He felt even guiltier about that, because he knew no matter how he felt about it now, nothing would take the pleasure from the experience. So that selfish joy sat in stark contrast with the fear that he'd overstepped her boundaries and ruined their friendship. He hadn't even been able to meet her eyes before he'd left.

Gaea waited for him near his cottage, dwarfing the structure with his massive size. *How is she?* he asked in his deep rumble of a voice.

You didn't come home last night! Forrest cried, leaping from Gaea's back and flying in front of Evander.

"She's all right. I fell asleep at Finlay's," he said, addressing both dragons at once.

Ooooohhhhh, Forrest said, wiggling in anticipation.

What happened? Gaea asked.

Evander sank to the ground and told them everything. He had his head in his hands when he reached how he'd left her that morning, and dug his nails into his scalp. He'd made things worse, no doubt, by leaving that way. Why couldn't he get things right with Finlay?

A warm feeling spread over Evander, with a puff of moist air, and he looked up to see Gaea leaning over him, using a light form of his healing breath. The heaviness of Evander's thoughts—the weight caused by the alcohol, at any rate—faded. Some of his irritation did as well. A wonderful lightness replaced it, a sweet contentment.

You always say how Finlay overthinks things, Evander, but I think you've matched her here, Forrest said. *Just talk to her!*

He shouldn't talk to anyone right now. Go about your day as usual, and then go see her, Gaea recommended. *You both need a bit of time to put things into perspective.*

And realize they're crazy for each other, Forrest added.

Gaea rumbled in what Evander thought was agreement.

"You really don't think I ruined anything?"

It's not for us to say, Gaea said gently, *but you've never been anything less than kind with Finlay. She knows that. Trust your instincts. You aren't the type to take advantage.*

Evander took a deep breath and stood. "Thank you, Gaea. And you, Forrest," he added when Forrest's chest puffed out. "I needed that."

He took his time to go inside, make himself some porridge, rinse his face, neck, and torso with water, and change into fresh clothes. That done, and feeling significantly less like the world had lost all its splendor, he emerged from his cottage and found both dragons still in the same position, waiting for him.

The new dragon, Arget, could use reassuring, Gaea said.

Without a word Evander climbed onto Gaea's back, and the great brown dragon flew him deeper into the sanctuary. Forrest flew alongside them, barely the size of Gaea's snout. Evander had been around dragons all his life. He'd studied them more intensely than just about anyone he knew. Still, he had no idea why Forrest was so small. He wasn't a pygmy dragon. His snout shape and wingspan didn't match the characteristics of the smaller races of dragons. He looked just like other forest dragons—on a miniature scale. It had to have been something that happened during his incubation period . . .

Evander took note of the dragon nests he could see as they flew. The eggs would be hatching any day now. One egg had been very close yesterday. He would have to make his rounds after this, and see if the hatchling had emerged yet. He didn't see all of the nests as Gaea flew; they didn't fly for very long before the adolescent dragon from the day before came into view, tucked up close to a large tree, tail over his snout as though asleep, yet perfectly awake.

Evander slid off Gaea's back and walked up with slow, measured steps, raising his hands placatingly. "I don't know if you remember me, but I was with the group of people yesterday. My name is Evander. I'm the keeper of this sanctuary. And I'd like to offer you a home here. Please, tell me anything I can do to help you feel comfortable." He swallowed a lump in his throat. "And I'm sorry about your friend. We tried to save her."

Tears welled in the Arget's eyes. *No one will hunt me here? It feels like Aithne and I have been running since we were old enough to fly.*

Evander crouched near the dragon's head and placed a hand on the ridge between his eyes. "I promise you, no harm will come to you here."

Arget's tail slipped from his snout, and he blinked back his tears. *Aithne would have liked that.*

"I really am sorry."

I know. Me too. Arget sniffled. *So what do I have to do to stay here? What are the rules?*

Evander offered him a small smile. "You just have to live."

And not pick too many fights, Forrest put in.

"That would be best, but I don't think Arget plans to pick any fights right now, Forrest. Gaea is the leader of the dragons," Evander said, gesturing to him. "He'll help you get settled. As far as I'm concerned, my job is to keep every dragon here safe, happy, and healthy. You come to me with anything you need, and I do my best to help. All right?"

Arget nodded. *All right.*

"Oh, you're fine," Evander crooned as the baby dragon made a pitiful squeak. He reached out with two fingers to take the piece of egg shell stuck to the baby's head off. "Come on, climb the rest of the way out. We've been waiting for you, little one."

The baby crag dragon blinked its silver eyes at Evander and cocked its head to the side, as if wondering why it hadn't already been freed from the egg.

"It's a rite of passage," Evander said through a chuckle. "You need to stand on your own for the first time."

The dragon made another squeaking sound. The egg shuddered and then cracked apart, and the dragon hopped as the egg broke and freed it, spreading steel gray wings and landing with a wobble. A male, Evander noted. The telltale ridge pattern along his back, with some of the features of the jaw and the angle of his wings, confirmed it.

He's beautiful, the dragon's mother, Soren, said, as she leaned down and ran her tongue over the baby for his first wash. *Help me name him, Evander?*

You sure about that, Soren? Forrest asked.

"I'd love to," Evander said. He frowned at Forrest. "Why shouldn't I help name him if she wants me to?"

You're not exactly the most creative person.

"I'm pretty good with names, I think. I've named a lot of the dragons here."

You named me Forrest. I'm a forest dragon.

Evander opened his mouth to say he'd thought it amusing, saw the expression on Forrest's face—and worse, the surprised expression on Soren's—and raked a hand over his face. "Fair point."

Finlay would really help you name him, Forrest said innocently. *She's great at getting you to be more creative.*

Evander's chest tightened. "I'm sure she would help. She'll come when she's ready to see me. I won't force my company on her."

Forrest let out a long-suffering sigh. *I've been going between the two of you for the last few days. How much plainer can I be when I say you're both pining over each other, but too stubborn to admit you know it's true?*

The thought warmed Evander slightly. He really did miss her. Would it be so wrong to be the one to breach this horrible separation that, if Forrest was being truthful, neither of them really wanted? "Maybe I will go see her later. For now, how about the name Aerie?"

Soren considered. *I like it.*

And we can ask if Finlay has any better suggestions before we set it in stone, Forrest agreed.

"Evander!"

Chief Stewart stood nearby, panting slightly.

"There you are. I need you to come to the compound as soon as you can, to check on Isla's partner, Muir. He wasn't feeling his best. Could you check on the other partners of the Knights, as well? With the trial coming up, we need everyone in top condition."

Evander stood in a fluid motion. "Of course. I'll be right there."

"Finish what you're doing first," the chief said. He smiled at Soren and her hatchling. "It's just as important to tend to the newest additions to our home as to the old. I'll leave you to it."

Evander watched him go, then turned his attention back to the newly-named Aerie. He took out his parchment, quill, and ink, and started a new page for the baby crag dragon. "Just need to take a few notes," he murmured as he began a loose sketch. Worry for Muir made his hand faster across the page, and he left Soren and Aerie with a quick smile and a promise to check on them again later.

I'll go see Finlay, Forrest said, after riding on Evander's shoulder on the walk to the sanctuary's border. *I expect you to come see us later.*

Evander's lips tugged up. "As long as Muir and the others are healthy, I'll be there before you know it."

Chapter Ten

Finlay ended up hiding in the healing den all day the morning she woke up nestled against Evander.

Moira took one look at her, tutted, and made a drink she promised would have Finlay feeling better in no time. "I was young once, too, and this tonic saved me a few times!" She handed the frothy vial to Finlay. "Not like you to get yourself in this state. Something happen?"

Too much. "We ran into some Mages yesterday. I couldn't save a dragon."

Moira sighed. "Poor thing."

Either she assumed Finlay had a residual headache (which she did), or she knew she didn't want to talk, because Moira didn't say anything else. For hours they worked in a companionable silence that was broken only to issue directions or ask for a certain ingredient. Moira's tonic worked wonders, so by midday when they broke to find lunch, Finlay was confident the effects of the alcohol were completely gone.

It was a good thing, because Elsie just about broke down the door to come get her for lunch.

"Finlay, have you been in here all morning?" Elsie demanded.

"I had work to do."

Elsie grabbed her by the wrist and pulled her out of the healing den. "I went to check on you this morning, to get you to go watch Isla train, and you weren't there. Then Patrick saw me and gave me a ton of work, so I didn't get to watch Isla train at all!" Elsie led Finlay to their spying spot and let her go. "So, really late, but are you okay, after yesterday?"

"I'm all right, I think." Finlay accepted some of the bread and cheese Elsie unwrapped from a cloth bundle in her satchel. The sight of the food reminded her how long it had been since she'd eaten, as she'd completely forgotten about it that morning. She took a large bite and chewed slowly, trying to figure out how to tell Elsie the decision she had almost made.

"It's a shame we couldn't save both of the dragons, but we got one back here," Elsie said around a mouthful. "Isla really gave one of the Mages a thrashing, too."

"Elsie—"

Elsie raised one hand in a stop motion. "You're going to tell me you don't know about being a Knight anymore, right?"

Finlay frowned. Elsie was her best friend, and it was clear she cared about her, but . . . "How did you—?"

"Isla guessed you'd be pretty shaken. I get that. I do. But don't say anything definitive now. Don't break your promise to me."

But I killed a dragon. The words burned the edge of her tongue, almost coming out, but Finlay imagined the judgment she would find in Elsie's eyes if she knew the truth. She already felt like she was losing Evander. She couldn't lose Elsie too.

"I tried to save the dragon," she finally said, deciding to share most of the truth. "I just made things worse."

Elsie stared at her directly. "You tried. That seems like something a true Knight would do. You owe it to that dragon now, and to yourself, to pass the trial and really become one, so you can save others."

Finlay's doubts started disappearing under Elsie's stern gaze and absolute faith in her. "Okay."

You can't avoid the sanctuary forever.

Finlay tightened her grip on Forrest, cradling him closer. He didn't let her hold him like this often, but the last few days he'd been with her for hours on end, letting her carry him or curling up on her lap in the evenings.

He misses you, Forrest said. *But he thinks you'll come to him if you want to see him.*

"It's not Evander I'm avoiding, Forrest." Not entirely, anyway.

You know you miss him too. But you're distancing yourself from everything and everyone, trying to figure out the right course of action, for some reason. Am I right? Don't answer that. Of course I am.

"The right thing to do would be to drop out of the trial, but I'm not. I still want to be a Knight."

It had taken her over a day to realize it, but the death of the phoenix dragon added to her motivation. She had to do everything in her power to keep more innocent dragons from being killed. Still, telling Elsie and Chief Stewart when she watched the moonlit guard two nights ago that she planned on taking part in the trial had been one thing. Telling the dragons, looking them in the eyes and knowing she had, however unintentionally, killed one of their kind? Even swearing to devote herself to saving them for the rest of her life, it was hard to face seeing them again for the first time since that horrible day.

"How can I face the dragons?"

You're facing a dragon right now!

"You're different."

His shoulders shook in a swaggering little dance. *I <u>am</u> a prime example of dragon-kind. No one thinks you did anything wrong. I know some of the humans have been teasing you, saying you're weak because you're still sad. You can bet Evander and I would have squashed any talk like that among the dragons.*

Finlay breathed in sharply and nodded. "Okay. Let's go."

Forrest turned his head to look at her. *Seriously? Sweet! But Evander isn't there right now. He's in the compound, checking on one of the Knight's dragon partner. Can't remember which.*

"Did something happen?"

Don't think so. He got word from the chief just before I came to see you that he should check on them. The guy probably wants everyone in top form with the trial starting tomorrow night.

He couldn't hide the jealous undercurrent in his voice. Forrest wasn't in consideration to be a Knight's partner. He was too small. Finlay didn't think he would want to do it anyway, but she knew he would have liked the option.

"Do you want to fly ahead?"

You'll need me to get through. I can say I have urgent business with Evander as assistant keeper of the sanctuary, and you're assisting me.

"So I'm the assistant to the assistant to the keeper?"

Forrest tilted his head. *I like the sound of that.*

"Somehow I can't see it catching on."

As they approached the border of the Knights' compound, Forrest leapt from Finlay's arms and coasted in the air next to her. The high walls of the compound had always elicited an urgent desire in Finlay, to know exactly what lay beyond. Entry beyond the walls was prohibited without express permission from a Knight or Chief Stewart. Finlay remembered trying to sneak through with Elsie about a year after coming to live here, and being forced to do menial labor for a week as punishment.

Evander was the only non-Knight aside from Moira allowed to enter freely, since he cared for all the dragons.

The compound had two entrances: one facing the village, the other the mountains. The entrances were metal gates between the slabs of stone that formed the walls. Graham, a pale man with sun-bleached hair, was permanently stationed at the entrance facing the village. He had a little stand, and a comfortable chair, and always seemed to be reading. Finlay suspected he'd made a special arrangement to be given this position, simply so he could have freedom to read all day. He frowned when he saw Finlay and Forrest draw near, putting one hand in his book to keep his place.

"What's your business?" he asked.

Forrest flapped his wings in an even pace, staying airborne immediately in front of Graham. *Evander asked me to retrieve Finlay and report back to him. He wants our help.*

Graham squinted at Forrest, then at Finlay, and sighed. "Go ahead."

He had his book opened again before Finlay and Forrest passed the gate.

Not as magnificent as you thought, right? Forrest said.

Finlay looked all around in wonder. It wasn't a utopia, but she certainly found it magnificent. Wide open spaces for training and sparring, both human vs. human matches and dragon vs. dragon. An armory, and a dormitory. Everything tended carefully, and kept in pristine condition.

Three people clustered near a massive boulder, two on the ground on either side of someone lying on the grass, the third standing in front of them. Isla, Meric, Cormac . . . their dragon partners paced nearby, Muir coiling in the air behind Isla. Finlay's heart crept toward her throat. Stress radiated from all three of the Knights, and the figure on the ground wasn't moving. Several steps closer revealed a very familiar head of dark blond hair. And a very dark red stain coloring it.

"Evander!"

Finlay

Finlay sprinted the remaining distance, falling to her knees by Evander's side and banging into Cormac in the process.

"What happened?" Finlay demanded.

Oh gods, Evander, Forrest worried, trembling against Finlay on the ground.

"He got in the middle of our sparring match," Isla said, from Evander's other side. "Muir and I were fighting with Cormac and Paisley, high up. We didn't see him. He must not have seen us. The force that radiated out when the dragons collided sent Evander flying, and his head struck the boulder hard."

Finlay watched the rise and fall of Evander's chest while Isla spoke, and when Isla finished, forced herself to look at his head-wound. She suspected it was the collision that had knocked him out, but to be bleeding so much, he had to have a cut of some sort. The blood dripped down one side of his face, and he seemed much paler than usual . . .

"We were just going to fetch Moira," Meric said.

Blood roared in Finlay's ears, almost drowning out Meric's voice. Evander couldn't die.

She was vaguely aware of Meric jumping onto his dragon's back and taking off. Isla and Cormac had some sort of conversation that drifted around her without sinking into comprehension. The only sound that meant anything was the soft inhalations and exhales coming from Evander's slightly parted lips.

He's gonna be okay, right Finlay? Forrest asked. He shook his wings out and puffed out steam. *I mean, he's gonna be fine. He will be.*

"Of course he will be," she whispered. "He'll be back running the sanctuary in no time."

Forrest edged closer to Evander, nudging his arm. *I'd really like it if you woke up now,* he said.

Finlay's last comment kept going through her mind. The sanctuary. The dragons. "Gaea," she murmured. She breathed in sharply and leaned closer, brushing hair back from his face. "Gaea," she said, with greater force. "I'll get you to Gaea, he can help!"

"What was that, Finlay?" Isla asked.

Forrest jumped up, flying low behind Finlay. *Gaea can help!* he crowed.

"We need to take him back to the sanctuary!" Finlay said, snapping her gaze to Isla.

Isla hesitated.

"We're here!" Meric called.

Isla and Cormac stepped back when Meric helped Moira slide off his dragon's back and come over. Finlay sat rooted in her spot, unable to move.

"No one's moved him?" Moira asked.

"He's in the same position as when he fell," Meric confirmed.

Moira went to Evander's other side and skimmed her fingers over his scalp. "It looks like a lot of blood, but the wound isn't deep. His head striking the rock likely caused more damage." Her fingertips came away red, and moved to the back of Evander's neck. "Lift him, just a bit," she directed.

Finlay grabbed his shoulders and coaxed him into a more elevated position. Moira continued her analysis, tracing her fingers along his spine.

"I won't be able to tell the full extent of the damage until he wakes up, but I can't feel anything broken. I can't even feel any muscles in spasm, which is good. We can move him, carefully."

"We need to bring him to the sanctuary," Finlay said, as everyone moved to grab Evander. Finlay and Moira supported his head and shoulders. Meric and Cormac each held one leg.

"Why the sanctuary instead of his house?" Meric asked.

"He'll want to be near the dragons," Finlay said. The words flew from her quickly. They weren't a lie, either. He was most comfortable near the creatures he adored, and that cottage in the sanctuary was more home to him than the house reserved for him outside it. She kept the part about Gaea potentially healing any damage between herself and Forrest, though.

They moved him to the dragon's back, keeping him as level as they could in the process. Forrest continued his pacing flight nearby, until Finlay gave him a meaningful look and he took off.

"Isla," Finlay started.

Isla grabbed Finlay's wrist and led her to Muir wordlessly, and a rush of gratitude went through Finlay. Muir ascended elegantly behind Meric, Moira, and Evander, as if Isla and Finlay weighed nothing atop his back. He kept them steady, following Hugh's flight from the compound to the dragon sanctuary. Even Hugh seemed completely unburdened in his flight, despite carrying three adults.

"We didn't know he was coming," Isla said over her shoulder.

Finlay touched one hand to Isla's arm. "I don't blame you. And Evander won't either. It was just a lack of communication."

Finlay couldn't worry about that now. All her focus was on Evander as they pulled out a cot and placed him upon it, just inside the cottage within the magical dome protecting the sanctuary.

Moira set her parcel on the table and started pulling things out. "Finlay, you may stay. Everyone else needs to leave. The stress is enough to keep the poor boy unconscious." The second Isla and Meric had taken off on their dragons, Moira chuckled. "That should give you more alone time with the boy."

Finlay blinked. "You're laughing. Is he not that seriously wounded?"

Moira waved a hand. "The outer wound will be healed in under an hour, with my salve. Inside, we'll have to see, but his coloring is good and his breathing is steady."

The pressure that had been mounting in Finlay's chest eased at Moira's words. "Thank you."

Moira slathered some of her salve onto Evander's scalp. "This is my job, child. I know you would have gone for this salve yourself, if it hadn't been the other half of your heart in danger, mucking with your reasoning."

Finlay ignored the heat rising in her cheeks. "You're incorrigible, Moira."

Moira cackled. "Your cheeks say I'm spot on. But don't worry, I'll leave him in your care now. If there's any sign of something amiss when he wakes, send for me."

Finlay thanked her again and watched her leave, then turned at the short beats of tiny wings against the air that sounded behind her. "Forrest? Did you tell Gaea what happened?"

Forrest flew through the open doorway and landed by her feet. *He's right behind me.*

The massive brown dragon landed several paces outside the cottage. *Can you bring him out here?* he asked.

The cot slid across the ground easily enough, though it was a tight fit through the door. "Evander said you have healing abilities. Is there anything you can do?"

Gaea leaned his head over Evander, closed his eyes, and hummed in concentration. He stayed in that position for an extended moment before backing up, lowering his head as close to ground level as he could. Mouth opened, he blew out a silver breath, eyes still closed. Finlay watched the silver hover over Evander's body and sink inside, then brought her widened eyes to Gaea.

He'll be all right, Gaea promised in his deep voice, *though my healing breath will keep him unconscious for several hours. It's a side effect.*

"As long as he wakes up, that's fine!" Finlay cried, throwing her arms around Gaea's neck. His warm scales trembled with his amused vibration.

Finlay turned and just managed to catch Forrest as he flew against her chest. She staggered against Gaea and held Forrest tightly, and laughed. Should she be laughing? All the dread that had been pulling her into a sinkhole had faded, leaving her curiously buoyant. Forrest diving into her for a hug had really prompted the sound, she decided. That, and absolute relief.

Gaea stayed with them for some of the time, but eventually it was just Finlay and Forrest left keeping watch over Evander. Finlay moved the cot back into the cottage and kept place beside him. She filled a shallow bowl with water and used a cloth to wash away the blood clinging to Evander's hair and staining his skin. When that was done she simply waited, holding one of his hands between hers. Forrest curled into a ball against Evander's side, resting his head on Evander's stomach.

A groan startled Finlay from roaming thoughts some indistinguishable amount of time later. Forrest picked up his head and looked at Finlay questioningly. Finlay studied Evander, and leaned closer when she saw him stir further.

"Finlay? Your hands are warm . . . ah, what . . . what happened?" Evander asked. He blinked a few times and took in Finlay and Forrest, and groaned again. "Right. That was really not fun."

I leave you alone for half an hour, and you do this? Forrest demanded, stepping onto Evander's chest.

"Sorry."

"How are you feeling?" Finlay asked.

Evander reached up to stroke Forrest's scales. "Embarrassed, mostly. Physically I'm fine."

Forrest huffed and jumped to the floor. *Well don't do it again. I'm going to patrol.*

Evander sat up and looked after Forrest. "He was really worried about you," Finlay told him. "We both were."

"I think worry has been going around lately. Though I'm feeling pretty good right now. Relaxed." He looked at her. "Gaea helped me heal."

It wasn't really a question, yet Finlay nodded.

"I'm sorry I made you worry about me."

"I don't think I could ever stop worrying about the people I care about."

A hesitant smile tugged at his lips. "That's just caring about someone, I suppose. Always thinking about them." He reached out and brushed the back of his hand against her cheek. "I believe you're not overly worried anymore. I hope not, anyway. Still, there's always such sadness in your eyes, Finlay."

He sounded, and looked, like that bothered him. Like he wanted to change it, to be the one to relieve the grief Finlay feared would never leave her side. But perhaps that was wishful thinking, and Evander was just pointing out something anyone who truly looked could see. Her chest tightened in disappointment at the thought.

She put on a slightly teasing smile. "There's always such kindness in yours. Maybe we balance each other out."

He shifted, that dark glint of desire appearing in his eyes. "Maybe we should spend more time together, then. So we can both have balance."

Finlay had unconsciously moved toward him and now he was much too close, voice husky, hand warm on her cheek . . . it was entirely too easy to close the minimal space between them, to surrender to the want burning inside her. She thought she could see that want in him, too. Their lips met fleetingly, brushing, warm, before a noise startled them apart.

Elsie ran into the cottage and stopped, staring between Finlay and Evander. Evander had half jumped out of his cot. Finlay stood several paces away, pulse drumming. Elsie looked from one to the other and blinked. "So everyone is all right now?"

Evander cleared his throat and looked to Finlay. "More than all right, I think."

Finlay feared she would catch on fire, her cheeks were burning so. "Right."

Elsie grinned. "Great. We really don't have time to not be. Time for the trial!"

Finlay frowned. "The trial is tomorrow night."

"There's a major storm coming tomorrow. Tempest can sense it. Chief Stewart met with the Knights and decided to hold the trial tonight instead."

Tempest was one of the older Knight's, Aileen's, dragon partner. Another rare dragon from the east like Muir, Tempest was more serpentine than the others, and lacked wings. While Muir was a dragon of the sea, though, Tempest belonged to the sky. She always warned them of severe weather, detecting changes in the air. As far as Finlay could recall, Tempest had never been wrong.

Finlay had difficulty swallowing for a second. She'd expected another day to prepare herself. Another opportunity wouldn't present itself for two years after this trial.

She took in a sharp breath and touched the dagger strapped to her waist. Confidence seeped into her. She didn't need another day.

"Let's go become Knights."

Chapter Twelve

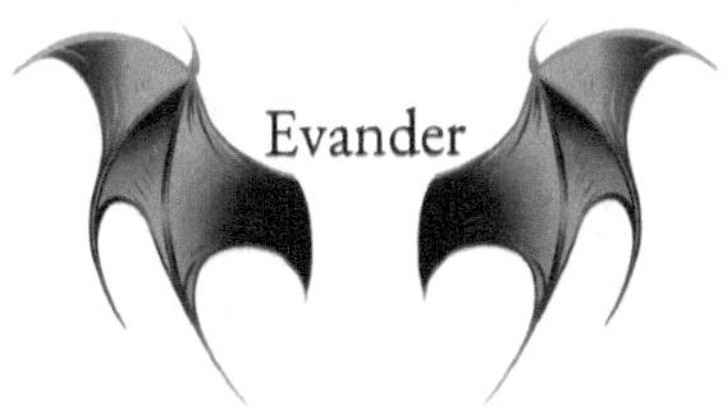

He really should have been more careful, approaching the training pavilion. That was one of the things the former keeper of the sanctuary had drilled into Evander's head all through his apprenticeship. Always be careful approaching training dragons.

And he'd managed to forget that rule completely, thinking they were expecting him and worrying about Muir so much he rushed in his approach. Isla and Muir had been flying above, circling Cormac and his dragon partner, Paisley. A dragon-riding mock battle. He'd slowed his step in spite of his concern, momentarily captivated by the whirling dragons above. Despite having been allowed in the compound where the Knights trained for years, he rarely saw them actively training like this.

He'd waved as he approached, and thought he caught Isla's eye. For that instant, it seemed like she was surprised to see him. Then Cormac and Paisley moved, clearly not seeing Evander, and . . . well, in the next few seconds Evander moved the only way he could to avoid a human-dragon collision. The last thing he remembered was slamming headfirst into a boulder.

Waking up with Forrest's weight on his chest was familiar. Waking up with Finlay's hands holding his was not. It took him a minute to realize it was her. She was warm. Finlay was never warm. He'd brave the usual chill to hold her hand whenever he could. Now, without that cold, it wasn't just pleasant, but incredible, to feel her hand on his skin. The callouses on her palm and fingertips from where she held her dagger contrasted with the smoothness of her touch.

He couldn't keep himself from reaching out to brush her cheek, after commenting that caring about someone meant worrying about them. It had been days since he'd seen her. Any fears he'd had that she was upset with him faded.

There was a teasing tilt to her smile when she said maybe they balanced each other out. He had to do it now. To tell her how he felt, before it ate him alive.

"Maybe we should spend more time together, then. So we can both have balance."

He cursed himself for saying it in such a roundabout way, and then his heart jumped when she leaned just a hair closer—she'd understood him after all. He was sure of it. And his pulse raced as they drew closer, his lips just brushing against hers . . .

Enter Elsie, with the worst timing in the world. Evander stifled his groan after jumping from his cot. He couldn't stifle the frustration mounting inside him.

"So is everyone all right now?" Elsie asked.

"More than all right, I think," Evander managed, making his voice as steady as he could and looking to Finlay. She met his eyes briefly, an adorable blush entering her cheeks. Evander thought there was a smile burgeoning behind that blush, but was distracted from this line of thought—and his frustration at the almost-kiss—when Elsie said the trial was tonight, and Finlay's lips turned down.

He watched all the levity fade from her expression, that distance of worried thought clouding her vision as Elsie told them the trial date had been moved up due to a storm. He wanted to reassure her, but before he could do more than open his mouth he saw her move, her hand going to the dagger at her waist. He pressed his lips together and exhaled a puff of a laugh through his nose. He knew that gesture as well as any other. She didn't need words of reassurance, as long as she had that dagger by her side to remind her to be strong.

"Let's go become Knights," she said to Elsie, standing at her full height.

"A promise is a promise," Elsie said, with an even wider grin than before. "Come on, Fin. Evander, you coming too?"

"I wouldn't miss it," he told them. "I just have one thing I need to do first. I'll meet you outside the compound."

He could feel the trace of curiosity coming from Finlay, but she didn't ask what he had to do. She let Elsie start to lead her away, and after a few steps, the girls were practically pulling each other, their steps lengthening from steps to strides as they broke into an excited run. Evander chuckled.

He wondered about the storm. Tempest usually gave them much more warning than this for significant weather events. It must be a fast-moving storm to prompt the chief to conduct the trial early. Evander supposed it didn't really matter. Everything was ready. Still, it was surprising.

He found the box with the ribbons the chief had given him the day before. Part of the trial would take place here in the sanctuary, as it always did. The ribbons had to be distributed to certain dragons before that point. Evander had to make sure he reached the outside of the compound in time for the opening words . . .

"Gaea?" Evander said, sending his thoughts out along with his voice.

It took several seconds, but Gaea's comforting rumble answered in Evander's mind. *Yes?*

"Can you help me distribute these ribbons? The trial's been moved up, and I can't miss any of it."

I'm on my way to you.

Evander opened the box and inspected the ribbons. Technically, he supposed he was meant to distribute them himself, to tie them to the dragons and ensure they stayed. Since he was pressed for time, he didn't mind forgoing that aspect. The dragons that needed these ribbons would have them.

Gaea's sturdy footfall outside the cottage prompted Evander to close the box back up and walk outside. Gaea lowered his massive head and looked at Evander with amusement in his eyes. *I was surprised you reached out that way. You've only done it one other time.*

"I figured yelling might disrupt other dragons. And I had been meaning to try it." Gaea was the only dragon Evander could reach with his thoughts. He said it was an effect of sharing his magic. They were bonded in a way Evander never would be with another dragon—something Forrest had been incredibly annoyed by, when he'd tried and failed to hear Evander's thoughts after learning this.

You did well, Gaea rumbled. *Now, what do you need me to do?*

"Remember the dragons we discussed when Chief Stewart dropped off this box? Each one needs a ribbon. They just need to keep it close, for the second round of the trial. And they need to stay in the same relative location. No long flights or anything until the trial's over."

I'll absolutely bring them the ribbons, but I can't handle them outside the box.

I can!

Forrest zoomed into view with a triumphant cry.

Just finished a quick inspection. All the hatchlings are doing well. Looks like I'm just in time to save the day! I can handle the ribbons!

Evander placed the box in Gaea's mouth, where he held it lightly between his front teeth, and turned to Forrest with a smile. "You're a life saver, Forrest. Thank you."

A shiver of pride went through Forrest, and he puffed out his tiny chest. *I <u>am</u> the assistant keeper of the sanctuary.*

"That you are."

Forrest seemed to grow, though it was only his ego that increased. *Let's go, Gaea! We have work to do!*

Evander watched him fly off, and felt a laugh in his chest when he noticed Gaea's eyes roll before Gaea moved to follow him. Gods, he loved these dragons.

The only real task left for him to complete before the trial now complete, Evander walked from the sanctuary with a hurried step. Time to see Finlay and Elsie make their dream a reality.

Chapter Thirteen

All these years wondering what lay beyond the wall, and Finlay would see the Knights' compound twice in the same day.

The trial itself took place behind the tall walls, without spectators other than the chief, Moira, Evander, and the current Knights and hopeful recruits. Finlay knew it would be several minutes before they actually started, with opening remarks. Then several more minutes before the official start, within the compound. So much ceremony. Too much for her eagerness tonight.

Graham's stand and chair had been moved, somewhere out of sight. The open space between the village and the compound, where they currently gathered, was now decorated. Lengths of rich golden fabric framed the entrance to the compound, trailing against the ground. Torches had been lit and placed in sconces on either side, and in posts spaced from the wall to the edge of the village, providing flickering illumination in the fading daylight. A sturdy wooden platform stood just in front of the entrance.

The chief had to welcome everyone and introduce the Seer Sisters. That had to happen soon. Almost all of their population of a few hundred people had been gathered, standing in a loose crowd, for several minutes already. Finlay could see the three women, hoods drawn around their heads, standing off to the side with their heavily-tattooed-hands linked. The sight sent a prickle of unease through her. Something about them never felt quite right. She couldn't see the chief.

"Why are you craning your head around so much?" Elsie asked.

"I'm trying to figure out how long we have to wait," Finlay said. "Looking for the—there he is." She spotted Chief Stewart coming from the back of the crowd, his dragon calmly following. The chief met her eyes and altered his course, walking over.

"Good evening, Finlay," he said with a smile. He glanced at Elsie. "Elsie."

"Good evening, Chief Stewart," both said.

The chief stepped closer and lowered his voice. "I wanted to make sure you're all right, Finlay. Between your understandable grief over the dragon's death several days ago and Evander's accident today, no one would blame you for not participating in the trial."

Finlay set her chin up. "I'm ready to take the trial, sir, and I'm ready to pass it."

He studied her, one hand on his rounded belly, and nodded. "You're made of strong stuff. Let's get started."

Chief Stewart strode to the front of the crowd and stepped onto the wooden platform, turning with raised hands to signal for quiet. A hush fell, and his soft voice rose over everyone.

"Welcome, everyone, to another trial to determine who among our brave members qualifies to serve as a Dragon Knight! Well we all know why it is our sacred duty to partner with dragons, but recent events prompt me to revisit it tonight. The royal crown did not used to be run by dragon murderers. In the past, the monarchy urged peace with the dragons who share this land as their home. When one queen, jealous of the innate power the dragons contained, killed a dragon during a festival, the world changed.

"The queen found herself filled with the magic of the dragon she had killed. She became the first Mage we know of, though certainly not the first in existence. The peace with the dragons was ended in one night, as several of her warriors also attacked and killed dragons. They became lords and ladies, claiming titles and land, wielding their power over the common folk, and instilling a legacy of killing dragons to have power humans are not meant to possess.

"There were many who opposed killing dragons. I, among with others here, vowed to do everything possible to stop the practice of the Mages. This included leaving the domain of the current queen. Our community exists to oppose the monarchy, and to protect the remaining dragons in our land. Our Knights, hand-chosen by a rigorous trial, are our fearless protectors, who will one day be able to face the Mages traitorously tainting the throne, and return the country to what it should be.

"I remind you of our history now because we have seen more signs of Mages encroaching on our borders, and fewer dragons, each year. The call to action grows closer, and may sound before the next trial. To that end, we must ensure we have as many efficient young Knights as possible. Would those eligible and willing to compete please come forward?"

Elsie nudged Finlay and led the way. The eight hopeful Knights lined up behind the chief on the stand. Finlay and Elsie were definitely the youngest, both only eligible by several weeks, but Finlay recognized three who'd competed in previous trials, all within four years. The oldest of those she recognized was a boy she believed was named John, and he was twenty-three. The remaining hopefuls weren't familiar, and it was difficult to tell their ages.

Chief Stewart walked down the line, inspecting them. Likely also checking that all were of age. Last trial, a seventeen-year-old had tried to compete. The chief had an excellent memory regarding those of age, though, and caught her. Finlay realized the same girl stood in the line now, one of those she hadn't immediately found familiar. Now, she recognized her raven hair.

The chief finished his walk before the hopefuls and turned back to the crowd. "Now, without further ado, let us hear from the Seer Sisters!"

He stepped off the wooden stand, and motioned for the hopefuls to move to the opposite side. The three women, still holding hands, took to the stage. They wore matching cloaks black as pitch, and Finlay had never seen them take down the wide hoods that stopped just above their eyes. Beside her, Elsie fidgeted. Finlay wasn't the only one the Sisters made uncomfortable.

The Sister farthest to the left spoke first, in a whispering rasp:

> *"Blood and bone from many rent*
> *Countless lives to heaven sent*
> *One with false face wore the crown*
> *The trust with dragons forever struck down."*

Before Finlay could comment to Elsie how uplifting that bit was, the Sister in the middle began to speak. Her voice carried clear and strong:

> *"False hearts now lead in light of day*
> *We hide the truths we fear to say.*
> *Against a rapid many row*
> *Fighting fate bidding them go."*

And the third Sister began, higher-pitched than the others, an unsettling immaturity in her tone:

"The world on dagger's balance rests
Its fate tied to the one who bests.
A storm approaches in crying call
In dragon fire we rise and fall."

Complete silence marked the end of their speech. Finlay stared at the Sisters, unmoving. They'd looked at her.

The Sisters were known to have hazy sight at best. They rarely looked straight at a person, eyes roaming their surroundings; their normal vision was impacted by their sight into the past, present, or future, as the dragon that they shared their powers (yet they never appeared) with, could. Finlay knew she wasn't mistaken in thinking the last two had stared straight at her when they spoke. Their milky eyes had focused, if only for an instant each, on her.

It made an itch beneath her skin that no movement would scratch. The exact wording was slipping away from her more each second, but select parts remained firm in memory: fate, mentioned more than once, and the last line in its entirety: in dragon fire we rise and fall. The line rang in her ears, fixed with the image of those milky eyes locked on her, and a weight crept onto Finlay's back.

She startled when a hand rested on her shoulder. Elsie's touch drew her back to the present moment. There wasn't time to puzzle over it. She would have to settle with asking if Elsie had noticed it too, when they walked into the compound. Chief Stewart was already stepping back onto the stage, thanking the Sisters for attending another trial and inviting the current Knights to lead the hopefuls into the compound for the trial itself.

"Hey, did you notice anything weird about what the Sisters said tonight?" Finlay whispered.

"Everything they say is weird. They're weird."

Finlay bit the inside of her lip and nodded. She hadn't expected Elsie to have noticed, but it would have been nice if she had.

"I'd worry less about them and more about yourselves," Isla said, looking over her shoulder. "You never know which one of us you'll end up fighting."

Torches lit the way to the smaller pavilion where Isla had told them the Knights sparred without dragons. "All right," Chief Stewart said, when everyone stood at the pavilion's edge. "The eight of you have decided to try to join the noble ranks of Knights. To do so, you must prove yourself warriors. Show your mettle in single-combat with an existing Knight. If you pass this stage, you'll show your ability to work with dragons."

Chief Stewart looked at Finlay, and then all eyes were on her.

"Finlay McDonough, you will go first."

CHAPTER FOURTEEN

"You may choose a weapon from our selection," Chief Stewart said.

"I'd like to use my dagger, if it's all the same to you."

A slight twitch in one eye suggested he didn't love the idea, but he waved his hand to grant permission. "Moira will prepare it. Your opponent will be Meric, and the fight will begin in three minutes."

Finlay reached under her cloak and pulled the last remnant of her family from the belt on her waist. Its blade gleamed a delicate silver, offset by the gold of its hilt. A rounded stone she believed to be a ruby was inset on the pommel. In the light of the torches, the weapon was contradictory beams of moon and sun, all around that bloodied gem.

"It really is a beautiful blade," Meric said, walking over.

Finlay looked up at him, preparing herself. Meric was probably the most capable Knight, when it came to single-combat. His massive build gave him one advantage. Years of study and practice with a range of weapons gave him another. That wasn't the only reason this would be tough. Meric had taught her everything she knew.

"Finlay, come here so I can treat the blade," Moira called. The healer had a table set up, covered in an assortment of weapons.

"Her concoction won't harm the blade," Meric said when Finlay hesitated before handing Moira the dagger. "It will temporarily dull keen edges. We use it on our weapons when we spar, so we can practice truthfully but not worry about seriously injuring one another. The effect wears off on blades within the hour."

"Took the words right out of my mouth," Moira said. She used a dropper to place four drops of a light blue liquid on the blade. The liquid seeped into the blade, spreading and casting a skylike sheen across its surface.

"What weapon will you use?" Finlay asked Meric.

The man studied the contents of the table before picking up a short-sword. With the length of his arms, it was as effective as a longer blade, without as much weight in the blade. His reach would be an issue. Speed would be Finlay's ally, darting in and out with quick strikes.

Moira treated Meric's weapon, and then both walked to the center of the pavilion. Meric held his short-sword loosely, standing several paces away. "Show me I was right when I said you're ready," he said, giving her a fleeting half-smile.

"The first person to arrange what would be a fatal wound, or force the other to surrender, wins," Chief Stewart said. "Begin!"

Finlay altered her grip on the dagger and ran forward. Meric raised the flat of his blade to deter her. Finlay ducked and rolled, springing up beneath his extended arm and swiping with her dagger. Meric was prepared for this move, and used his free arm to knock hers aside and keep the blade from touching him. Finlay thrust upward with her other hand, striking his arm with the edge of her palm to keep him from reaching for her, and retreated, recalculating.

For several minutes they took it in turns to lead the offensive, neither truly gaining the upper hand.

She'd done this with Meric so many times over the years. In the first few days after she'd lost her family, when she wouldn't speak to anyone and wouldn't let the dagger fall from her grip for an instant, Meric had been the one to take her aside and ask if she knew how to use it. He'd been the one to offer to show her.

Her dagger had seemed longer, then. Something foreign and clumsy in her hand if she tried to use it as a weapon. She spun it in her grip now, the movement fluid. It was an extension of her hand; nothing less. Meric had given her that.

She had to repay him in the only way they would both accept.

He must have seen something change in her expression. His stance shifted, broad shoulders spreading, and he lunged with a wide sweep aimed to unbalance her. Finlay skirted to the side and used his extended arm as a focal point. She gripped it with her free hand and focused on speed in her steps, relying completely on her grip on Meric to keep her oriented. She swung around in that way, lurching forward, tensing her legs, and released Meric's arm before leaping onto his back; in seconds she had gone from being directly in front of him to close behind.

The impact staggered Meric but was far from enough to knock him down. Finlay used the moment he staggered to press her advantage, wrapping her legs around his torso and one arm around his neck. With her dominant hand she held the dagger, its tip resting over his heart.

Meric froze. Finlay waited, breathing heavily and wondering if this was enough.

Meric's laugh told her it was. She repositioned her dagger and dropped from his back. He turned and extended his hand. "I've never seen you use that move before."

Finlay grasped it and felt a laugh bubble inside her and spill out. "It would only work against someone as massive as you!"

Meric pulled her against him. Chief Stewart announced Finlay as the winner, but Finlay was more focused on Meric's voice, softly saying, "I'm so proud of you."

Tears pricked at her eyes when they broke apart, but quickly faded when Elsie ran forward and trapped her in a bear hug.

"Yes, congratulations!" Chief Stewart said. "Finlay, you will proceed to the next round. Our next match will have John fighting against Lachlan!"

Finlay hastened to the side as the others prepared for the second match. Elsie was bouncing in excitement next to her, either not having anything to say or so focused on winning her own match that she couldn't.

Evander showed his pride in a different way, calmer and more direct. His mouth tugged up as she approached, and it was the morning sun over a blooming garden: warm, bright, and promising joy to come.

"Well done, Finlay."

How many times had she blushed around him lately? Apparently not enough, because her cheeks warmed noticeably at his praise. Standing there, a best friend on either side, Finlay let herself relax while the rest of the hopefuls competed. The truth of it was settling in. She'd done the hardest part. Meric said combat is the first stage, connection with a dragon the second. Since Finlay visited the sanctuary almost every day, she wasn't worried about navigating it.

She cheered when Elsie faced against Bridget and won, with her favored weapon: a war hammer, the impact softened by Moira's salve. Years apprenticing at the forge had given her a crushing swing. Otherwise, the first round passed in a kind of contented blur. It had to be an hour later before all of the hopefuls had completed their matches. Five overcame their opponents: John, Blair (the girl who had tried to compete in the last trial while underage), Angus, Elsie, and Finlay.

The three who didn't pass the first round were escorted outside the compound. Once they were gone, Chief Stewart turned to the remaining five. Full night had fallen, leaving his face half in shadow from the flickering torches surrounding them. "Congratulations to each of you for making it to the next stage of the trial. I'm sure you've heard rumors about the second part. I can give you no other instruction but this: you must prove yourself to the dragons within the sanctuary and find the one I've selected for you. I'll give each of you the name of a dragon. The rest is up to you. You'll have half an hour to find your mark."

"How do I get into the sanctuary?" Angus asked. "I can't get past the crystals."

"You don't have a tattoo?" Elsie asked loudly.

Angus bristled to the top of his wedge of black hair. "I didn't get it reapplied, because I've been so busy working and preparing for this."

"Evander can reapply any tattoos needed," Chief Stewart said.

Finlay watched Evander pull out the dragon claw he'd had wrapped in his pocket, and the vial of crystal dust mixed with ink. Always prepared. He traced the dragon paw design and cut lightly into Angus's skin with the dragon claw once, and then a second time after dipping it into the crystal ink. It burned as it was applied, but it wasn't too deep. Angus's mouth wobbled trying to hide his wince. Each appliance lasted well over month, in Finlay's experience. She'd never let hers get close to that before reapplying. She saw Evander trace the scar of the pattern Angus had had before, and watched the faint white lines glow with fresh magic when he finished, darkening to a purple hue.

"Anyone else?" Evander asked. Moira wordlessly rubbed a salve over the fresh tattoo on Angus's hand.

Everyone responded negatively. "Excellent," Chief Stewart said. He gave them the names of the dragons they were to find in reverse order, so Finlay heard hers last. "Jupiter," the chief told her. He studied them all. "Good luck."

Recognizing it as a sign that their time was now being measured, Finlay left the compound at a jog. They hadn't said anything was against the rules, other than asking Evander for help. She could ask a dragon like Forrest, or Gaea, and find Jupiter in no time. She knew a lot of the dragons, but honestly had no idea which type Jupiter might be. Evander was right to say their dragon population was booming.

Elsie jogged by her side, her heavy footfalls and even breathing filling Finlay's ears. Stealth was definitely not Elsie's forte. Finlay had a mild confidence in her own stealth ability, moving forward with a light but steady tread. The others jogged just behind them, with varying levels of noise. They slowed as they approached the sanctuary. Finlay transitioned to a run, the dragon-paw tattoo on the back of her hand flashing when she crossed the barrier.

Forrest liked to stay in Evander's cottage. He was probably already there, so Finlay headed to the little building immediately.

"Forrest, have you heard of a dragon called Jupiter?" she called upon opening the door.

A snore was her response. Evander had left a candle lit on the floor near the beds. Finlay sighed and went over to the bundle of blankets near Evander's cot, reaching out to shake Forrest's shoulder. He startled so much a wisp of smoke flew from his nostrils. *Give a dragon a little warning!*

"And how do I warn you I'm going to wake you up without waking you?"

Forrest blinked, then very intentionally blew out a puff of smoke. *You could have been a little gentler.*

"I'm sorry, Forrest. I'm in a hurry. Do you know where I can find a dragon called Jupiter?"

Forrest jumped to his feet, spreading his wings. *Storm dragon. Likes to nest higher up. Gray and gold scales. His nest was near the big crack in the mountain.*

If Jupiter stayed near his nest, it would explain why Finlay hadn't seen him. She knew immediately where Forrest meant. It was difficult to access without wings. The dragons that liked the protection of the sanctuary but preferred to be left alone stayed up there, and Evander made it a point to give them their space.

She leaned forward to kiss the top of Forrest's head. "Thanks, Forrest!"

It wouldn't do to find Gaea and ask him to fly her to the nest. If Jupiter nested up there, he didn't much care for humans, and might take it as an insult if she caught a ride. Climbing up herself might warm him to her; it would show him that she was serious about finding him, at any rate, and willing to work to do it. She estimated she had just enough time if she ran to the base of that section of the mountain.

It was a good thing Finlay wasn't scared of heights. She never would have been able to climb down from the border territory to find Aerouant Glèidh all those years ago, even in the numb state she'd stumbled here. She'd never leave the valley now. The idea of scaling down the mountain elicited more adrenaline than the idea of climbing up, yet in both cases it was an eager thrumming of her heart that resulted, not a palm-slicking fear. Dragons and riders had to be comfortable in the air, at all different heights. She only wished she could ascend and descend with the speed and grace of the dragons. The only time she'd come close was falling off the cliff that time, watching Isla and Muir train.

Near the base of the behemoth of rough gray stone, small foot-paths with slight elevation could be followed. Higher up, those paths became scarcer. She found natural footfalls and hand-holds, scaling between ledges and boosting herself up.

The crack in the mountain was level with the tops of the trees in the forest. A jagged, deeply indented mark against the bleak stone face, everyone said it was gouged there by a massive dragon over a century ago. Finlay wasn't sure what had caused it, but she could imagine a dragon inflicting the damage.

"Jupiter?" she called when she reached a landing above the treeline. The edges of a nest made of branches and grass hung over an outcropping just above her head. "My name is Finlay. I'm supposed to find you. Can we talk?"

She was just starting to think the dragon belonging to the nest either wasn't there or wasn't going to respond when movement from above reached her ear.

A mottled gold and gray snout appeared, and amber eyes beneath a heavy scowl. The dragon paused and cocked his head to the side, peering down at her from the ledge. His baritone voice held a grudging curiosity.

Human, but the life force of a dragon burns within you.

Finlay's mind went blank. Thoughts of the trial, Evander, everything—gone. Those words spun around in the emptiness, refusing to take meaning.

"What?"

The dragon stared at her, spreading his wings in a slow stretch. Gray, feathered wings . . .

A cry escaped her. Flashes of fire played before Finlay's eyes. Feathery wings of gold and red beat against her memory. Her breaths came and went much too quickly, panic setting her heart to a frantic pace. She bent over with her hands on her knees. Only an extremely small percentage of dragons in this part of the world had feathers in their wings instead of scales. To be paired with another, after what she'd done—was she being punished?

She'd put out the phoenix dragon's fire. It hadn't burned, like her family all those years ago, but fire was still at the source of its death . . . as was Finlay. Her fault, her own terrible, unforgivable fault . . .

The dragon's words floated around in her mind, soft against the grating anxiety. *The life force of a dragon burns within you,* he'd said. Burns, as in the present moment?

She couldn't fall back like this. There wasn't time for this panic that never actually solved anything. Though she couldn't think what at the moment, she knew she had something she needed to do. With great effort, she steadied her breathing. She tightened her hands into fists against her legs and forced herself to stand up straighter.

Do you not know?

Finlay shook her head, looking back to the dragon above her and forcing her mind to cooperate. "What do you mean, the life force of a dragon burns within me?"

Exactly as I said. A dragon has bound itself to you.

Meaning finally broke through, however hesitantly. "Do you mean . . . the dragon is still alive?"

The words were too much to hope for. Had whatever the phoenix dragon tried to do in those final moments actually worked?

The dragon above her huffed. *Yes. Only a phoenix dragon could survive the process of fully binding to a human. Merging with it. It won't impact your human lifespan, but she lives within you now. How did that happen?*

She was alive. Relief made Finlay lightheaded. She hadn't killed the dragon after all. The burning she'd felt for hours after the incident, Evander's comment about her feeling feverish . . . the phoenix dragon had been inside her the whole time. How, indeed . . .

Are you going into some kind of shock?

Finlay opened her mouth, closed it, and laughed.

Are you having a mental breakdown?

She recovered herself and straightened. "I'm fine. Just completely taken by surprise, confused and happy. She's really alive?"

The dragon gave a long-suffering sigh. *I see we'll need to take this slowly. Yes, the phoenix dragon is alive. I can feel her energy, overlapping with yours. Tell me how all of this started, and I can attempt to help you understand.*

His condescension barely registered, Finlay was so desperate for an explanation. She told him everything from dousing the phoenix dragon's healing fire to experiencing the fugue nightmare and feeling off afterward. He stared down at her from his perch the entire time, his gaze stern but interested.

As I said before, only a phoenix dragon could survive the process. I've never heard of any attempt actually succeeding.

You were as responsible for our bond as I was.

Finlay jumped. That second comment hadn't been from the grumpy dragon looking down at her. That had been a feminine voice she'd only heard once but would recognize anywhere. It had come from completely inside her head.

An inward pulling sensation hooked Finlay from the belly-button, and several disorienting seconds later, she found herself in a different place: a meadow, with tall green grass and blooming wildflowers. A familiar, gray-tinged sky spread above her.

Finlay.

She turned. The phoenix dragon sat regally just behind her. The dragon's sunset scales were as vibrant as Finlay remembered, radiating warmth and light. She stared at Finlay with lamp-like orange eyes.

I've been calling to you. I guess you needed to know I was alive to hear me.

Finlay dropped to her knees. "I still can't believe you're alive."

As much as you are. That has more to do with you than you think. But before we discuss that, let me introduce myself properly. Finlay McDonough, I am Aithne.

Finlay repeated the name in wonder. It was perfect for the dragon before her.

Aithne laughed. **Not the most original name, is it? Fire. But it suits me, I think. You thought phoenix dragons were a myth. My kind are very close to becoming one. Few remain today. The war between the dragons and the phoenixes was devastating, and when the dragons realized by dousing healing fires, phoenixes couldn't recover . . . I'm not sure if true phoenixes survived at all. I hope so. I find peace in the thought that even if there aren't any left, some of their legacy, their fire, still exists in my kind. The dragons who realized they could mate with phoenixes,** both being creatures of fire, allowed that to happen. I am one of their descendants.

I am fully tied to you now. The phoenix becomes flames before it's reborn. In that instant that I was a spark, even a fading one, I moved inside of you, fusing us together. If my lifeforce magic fades, I will die, but I was able to replenish much of it. I told you I saw your intentions were pure. I also recognized the strength inside of you, and knew we could both survive the binding. I didn't anticipate the strain it would put on your mind and body, and started to withdraw, but you kept me anchored, and our energies merged. I owe my life to you.

Finlay shook her head at the misplaced gratitude in Aithne's voice. "I'm the one who put you in this situation. You can't make a new body from fire, can you?"

I could try, but if the effort used all of the magic I have left, it would kill me. It would likely kill you as well, since our energies have combined so thoroughly. I'm content as I am now. This mindscape expands as much as I wish, so I still have the sensation of flight, and I experience what you do.

Finlay couldn't hold herself back any longer. She ran forward, throwing her arms around Aithne's neck. Her scales were warm to the touch, soothing as a loved one's embrace. "I'm so glad you're all right!"

Aithne angled her head down and put it on Finlay's back. **And I you.** She lifted her head. **You have a trial to complete, Finlay. I'm always with you. We can talk again whenever you like.**

Finlay held onto her for another second and then sighed. The trial. She imagined that jerking feeling in reverse, and found herself pulled out of the mindscape, standing back in the dragon sanctuary with the grumpy dragon's face inches from her own. She jumped again.

You were just conversing with the phoenix dragon, weren't you? You adopted a very blank expression.

"Are you Jupiter?" Finlay asked.

He dipped his head. *The one and only.*

"Can you help me pass the trial?"

Jupiter sighed. Was that his favorite sound? *I was going to deny whichever human your leader decided to pair me with on principle, if he ever asked me to participate in your trials, but you've captured my interest. My curiosity isn't satisfied yet. So yes. I can and will help you.*

Finlay smiled. She was beginning to see why she'd never even heard of Jupiter before. Still, he was helping her. "Thank you."

He reached down and pulled a ribbon from around his rear left leg. *You'll need this as proof you found me in time, and that I support your efforts.*

She knew she couldn't have much time left, but she had to ask one more thing. "How did you know Aithne was alive?"

As I've said twice now, I could feel her energy alongside yours. Intertwined with yours, really. Any powerful dragon could tell.

I'm happy to keep talking with you and get the information I seek, but you seem invested in the trial, and your time is running short.

Finlay wrapped the ribbon around her wrist. It extended up and covered half her forearm before it was secured. "You're right. Thank you, Jupiter. I'll come back soon."

He made a sound somewhere between a grunt and a har-rumph, and flapped his wings to carry himself back up to his nest. Finlay focused entirely on descending the mountain and dashing back to the entrance of the sanctuary.

Chief Stewart, Evander, Moira, the current Knights, Elsie, John, and Angus stood in a loose gathering near the protective barrier. Chief Stewart held an hourglass in one hand. Finlay reached them, short of breath, and watched the last grains of sand fall from the top half.

"Finlay, you cut that so close!" Elsie shouted.

"But she did make it," Evander said.

"Did she?" Chief Stewart asked. "Did you find the dragon I assigned you, and obtain proof?"

Finlay held up her left arm, showing off the ribbon wrapped securely around it.

For an instant she thought she saw anger in the chief's eyes, but in the next was sure she'd imagined it. A beaming smile bloomed on his face. "Then four of the five who advanced to the second round passed. The trial has now concluded. The four of you will train to become true Knights!"

Chapter Sixteen

The rain had started by the time Finlay woke the following morning, and continued throughout the day in a forceful downpour that shrouded the world in gray mist.

The dismal weather couldn't begin to drown Finlay's spirit. She and Elsie had stayed up late celebrating the outcome of the trial. Finlay couldn't believe it was over. The recognition feast would occur at midday, rain or shine. Word was spreading. It was already official. Chief Stewart had called a brief gathering immediately after the trial to announce the four who had passed. She and Elsie were really on the path to becoming Knights.

Finlay had also told Elsie about Aithne, and sworn her to secrecy—though both knew Finlay would tell Evander in the very near future. ("You have a freaking dragon inside you! And it's a fire dragon! That's so amazing! Evander will freak out too. Can I be there when you tell him?")

Once Elsie had fallen asleep in Finlay's armchair, after a long discussion of the little Finlay knew about Aithne being tied to her, Finlay had gone to her bed and reached out to Aithne. She'd found herself back in the mindscape, and told Aithne the good news. The phoenix dragon already knew, of course, but Finlay delighted in being able to see her and interact with her. Aithne also approved of Finlay telling Elsie about her, which was an added relief.

All through that next dreary, rainy day, even the littlest things made Finlay smile. She found herself humming while she worked with Moira. When she noticed the sun peeking through the gloom after the feast late in the afternoon, glowing behind the still-falling rain, a giddy delight ran through her. She became soaked in the first minute of being outside, after the day's work was done, and she didn't sulk. Far from it, she flung her arms out, spun like a child, and ran to the dragon sanctuary with a renewed energy.

Someone's in a good mood, Forrest greeted.

Finlay laughed and scooped him up, trapping him in a hug. "You've got that right."

Too tight! Evander, help!

Evander peeked out from his cottage and smirked. "Seems like you're stuck, Forrest."

Forrest wiggled, pushing against Finlay's chest in his attempts to get free. *Traitor.*

Finlay let him go with another laugh, looking to Evander.

"Traitor?" Evander scoffed. "Hardly. I think being trapped in Finlay's arms is the best kind of trap you can find yourself in." Steady brown eyes locked on hers. "Frankly, I'm a little jealous."

A charge filled the air, which was silent aside from the sound of the falling rain.

Are you two finally admitting what I think you're admitting to each other? Or is this another flirt and skirt around it, oblivious-to-the-other's pining kind of thing?

And the charge vanished. Finlay and Evander both turned on Forrest, Finlay with shock, Evander with a scowl.

Forrest started retreating. *Guess you can fill me in later. I should go check on Jasper, make sure his hard head hasn't broken too much today.* He spread his wings and flew away at record speed.

Finlay watched him leave and swallowed heavily before looking at Evander once more. "Evander . . ."

Evander stared in the sky in the direction Forrest had flown. "He has a point," he said in a low voice. "I don't want to skirt around this anymore." He turned and strode to Finlay's side, closing the distance in four determined steps. His eyes shone dark and forceful as he reached up and swept a wet, tangled strand of hair from her face, tucking it behind her ear. "I don't want to fight this anymore. When I said I didn't want anything to ruin our friendship, it was true, but I want—"

"I want more," Finlay said, overlapping with him.

His breath caught, and the desire that appeared wasn't just a glimpse in his eyes—it was written in his entire body. Finlay saw that clearly, as she felt it gather in her stomach and spread to her fingers and toes. One hand went to the small of her back, and Evander stepped up close.

"I'd like to kiss you," he whispered, his lips barely a breath away, trembling with the last of his restraint.

She knew how hard it was for him to stop himself and essentially ask her permission first, when she could feel the want in him, but it was so like him to do so. "I'd very much like you to kiss me," she replied in a rush, before kissing him herself.

Sensations flooded Finlay. The damp, heady scent of the trees around them. The warm pressure of Evander's hand on her back. The singing patter of raindrops on leafy branches. The softness of his skin where she palmed it, behind his neck. Above all, the taste of his lips on hers, rainwater and sunlight and love.

Finlay pressed her forehead to his, her arms loosely wrapped across his shoulders, hands clasped behind his neck; dizzy with all of it, drunk on him and him alone.

"I was right," Evander murmured. "Being trapped in your arms is amazing."

"So you didn't regret that night?"

"The only thing I regret is making you think I didn't want you like this. I was an idiot."

"You were a gentleman," Finlay said. She bit her lower lip. "Maybe a bit of an idiot. But then I was too."

That maddening dimple appeared when he smiled. "We have to balance each other, remember? We can't both be idiots at the same time."

Finlay kissed him, right over the dimple. "We'll take it in shifts, then."

"Probably best if we try to avoid being idiots at all, but that sounds more realistic." Evander ran his thumb across her cheek. "Gods, you're beautiful."

Finlay brushed his wet bangs out of his eyes.

Evander frowned slightly and reached for her hand. "Your hands are warm. As long as I've known you, your hands are always freezing. I figured yesterday they'd warmed from holding my hand, but it's raining now. When they have a reason to be cold, they're not. Are you all right?"

Finlay nodded. "I'm pretty sure I know why I'm running warmer than before. Let's go inside. I have some news."

He followed her into his cottage, lit a lantern, and set some water boiling for tea, then sat across from her at his small table and listened. She took off her dripping cloak and set her dagger on the table—something that always made Evander brighten, though she doubted he realized it. It was adorable, really, how he didn't overlook the gesture. Even subconsciously, he understood exactly what that dagger meant to her—what putting it in the space between them meant.

When she'd finished, after their steaming mugs had mostly been emptied and her hair was halfway dry, Evander regarded her with a kind of awe.

"That's amazing."

Finlay searched his expression. "You believe me?"

"Why wouldn't I?" His hand sought hers, across the table. "Aithne. I wish I could meet her."

"Maybe you can," Finlay said. She tightened her grip on his hand, closed her eyes, and felt for Aithne's fire inside her, willing herself to sink into it, along with Evander.

He yelped and jerked his hand free seconds later. Finlay's eyes snapped open. "What's wrong?"

Evander laughed weakly. "Your hands warmed up a bit more than I expected." At Finlay's demanding expression, he shook his head and continued. "It's not a big deal, but your hand started to burn me. A little."

Finlay drew her hand back to her lap with a trace of horror. "I burned you?"

"No!" Evander said quickly. "No, you didn't. A bit of a glow appeared on your hand, though, and it got really warm. I think when you connect to Aithne, you access her powers. I can't go into your mind and see her with you without being burned."

Finlay stared at her hands, clenched in her lap. "I need to talk to Aithne." Without another word she focused on that internal flame. When the disorienting hook around her middle stopped and she found herself in the grassy mindscape, Finlay walked over to the phoenix dragon, who looked at her expectantly.

You have questions, Aithne said.

"I can use your powers?"

Aithne nodded once. **You know dragons can choose to share their magic with humans. The bond between your Knights and dragons is great. Ours is something greater.**

Finlay took a step back. "Evander said I almost burned him. That means I must be able to start fires, right? I can't be able to start fires."

I thought you would be happy with the ability. Fires forge new life.

"Fires destroy everything!"

Finlay stared at Aithne, her yell reverberating in her ears, her breathing unsteady. Aithne studied her with calm orange eyes. **You've lost much,** the dragon said after a moment. **I understand the tragedy left you fearful of fire.**

Finlay swallowed heavily. Fearful was almost an understatement. She couldn't go near the forge, knowing the bonfire that blazed inside. The one time she'd tried, after Elsie had started her apprenticeship there, she'd seen the waves of red heat just inside the doorway and run to hide in the dragon sanctuary. It had taken hours for her to be able to face anyone. Hearth fires, torches, candles—those were fine. Anything larger brought her back to that night, almost as powerfully as the nightmares she couldn't escape.

"I can't be able to start fires," Finlay said again, taking great effort to keep her voice steady. "What if I start one accidentally? What if it spreads? I can't lose anyone else to fire. It terrifies me, Aithne."

Aithne stepped closer. **You see only the destruction of the flames. Look at them now, and see also the creation.**

The landscape changed. Meadow grass and flowers were replaced with dark, mountainous terrain, veined with crimson light spilling upward. A volcano rose in the distance, smoke pouring from its top. The veins in the ground burst, rock tearing apart as molten hot material surged upward. Plants caught fire, red washing over everything in sight.

Aithne must have been watching Finlay, or perhaps she could sense the scream building in Finlay's throat, because the explosion stopped. As if time sped by faster than normal, the aftermath of the volcanic eruption became clear. Where lava had run in a horrifying river before, it rose now in spurts from the volcano's mouth, droplets flinging up and falling like snow, dazzling and playful. That sped by as well, and the image settled on a calmer scene. Ash and soot. Murkiness. A line of charred earth where trees once stood. Finlay saw it, and in the next several seconds she saw it change. Saw the ash drift away in the breeze, the soot and debris wash away in the rain; saw shoots of green in the dark ground, filling the cracks and rising from the former site of the trees. Change played before her eyes, at a pace that could only be obtained through memory. Within minutes the site had completely altered, trees once more standing tall.

The landscape returned to the meadow Finlay found familiar.

Fire can be deadly, Finlay. It can also be renewing. The environment around that volcano was suffering, too many living things competing for limited space and resources. The fire cleansed it, allowing life to thrive there once more.

Finlay stared at Aithne with widened eyes, unsure how to process.

Her sunset-colored wings grew more vibrant. A low hum filled the air, then a faint popping sound, and mild flames crested Aithne's wings. Slowly, Aithne spread her wings to their full span, and then began curling them inward.

Trust me, Aithne said, as her wings surrounded Finlay.

Shaking, Finlay gritted her teeth and stayed in place, closing her eyes instinctively. Warmth surrounded her first. Softness followed, as Aithne's burning wings enveloped her. Finlay sucked in a staggering breath when she realized she didn't feel any pain. If anything, energy seeped inside. Aithne tucked Finlay against her chest, her warm scales to Finlay's front, cozy feathers to her back. Finlay's trembling stopped, and she dared to open her eyes.

Fire will never hurt you again.

The block of grief in Finlay's chest that she'd thought immovable shuddered and split apart, pieces breaking off and crumbling into ash. Finlay threw her arms around Aithne's neck and clung to her, basking in the warmth of the phoenix dragon's flickering flames.

What was either moments or hours later, Finlay blinked and found herself back in Evander's cottage, sitting across from him at his table.

"Finlay?"

Evander had moved his chair next to hers, and studied her. "I'm all right," she told him.

He reached up and framed her cheek. "You looked so blank, but you were crying."

She touched her other cheek and realized it was wet with tear tracks.

"Talk to me, love," Evander pleaded in a soft voice.

Finlay leaned into his warm, rough hand. Then she held up her hand and thought of her connection to Aithne's fire. To *her* fire. An orange glow formed around it. She heard a hum, and the tiniest of pops, and a spark traveled across her fingers and settled over her palm before growing into a miniscule orange flame.

"I got something back," Finlay told Evander, who looked from the flame to Finlay's face with more than a trace of shock.

"You're not scared anymore?"

Finlay watched the tiny flame ripple. "I'll always be scared," she admitted. "Fire took too much from me for me to ever fully trust it." She met his gaze in the wavering light, struck to the core by the devotion in his eyes. Amazed at the slight increase in her heart rate, but the steadiness of her breath—a physical testament to her words. She would always have this fear. The nightmares wouldn't suddenly stop. Still . . . "I may not be able to stop it, but I can't let that fear rule me anymore." Her gaze returned to the tiny bit of energy burning in her palm. "I won't let it."

Chapter Seventeen

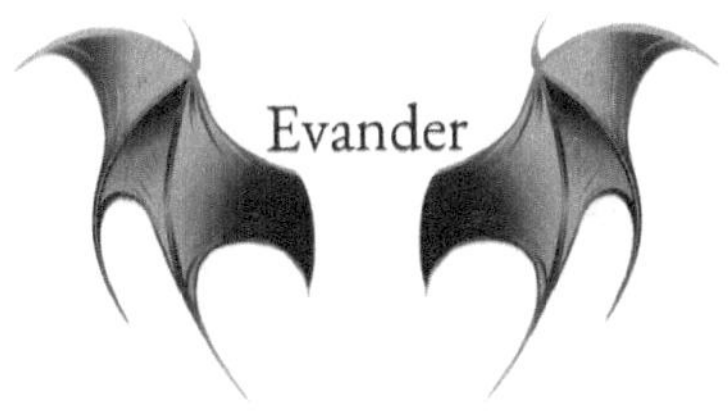

Evander

Evander had met many brave people. Tending to the dragons, and frequently interacting with those that worked
with them as partners, he saw courageous acts all the time. He
doubted he'd met anyone braver than Finlay McDonough. He
couldn't think of a better word to describe her in this moment—sitting next to him with a fire in her hand, admitting
that she would always be, understandably, scared of fire, yet
determined to face it and even wield it—than brave.

If he hadn't thought it before, he certainly would after everything that had happened tonight. Watching her in the first round
of the trial, when she'd faced Meric with her trusted dagger, he
hadn't been able to look away. She'd practically flown, jumping
onto his back with her finishing move, when she touched the

blade to his neck. There had been this energy about her, focused and sharp and impossible to ignore. Her desire to succeed was clear, and despite his slight nerves on her behalf, Evander didn't doubt she would.

And the second task, finding a specific dragon in the sanctuary. He didn't realize until Chief Stewart said the name of her dragon that she would face one with feathered wings. They had so few with feathers. Chief Stewart had chosen the dragons that would have the ribbons, and matched each potential Knight with one. Had he done it randomly, or had he chosen Jupiter for Finlay on purpose? Maybe testing her ability to recover?

Maybe it hadn't been an issue at all, and he was overthinking it, but he thought Finlay might have been stunned when she saw Jupiter's wings. He suspected it was why she'd come so close to missing the deadline for the task. Something about her had seemed a little different.

He knew now that she'd discovered Aithne was alive, bound to her in a way he hadn't known possible. More closely than he was bound to Gaea.

Finlay let the candle-sized flame diminish and disappear, her eyes on her dagger where she'd set it on the table between them. All the places he'd sat with her, spent time with her, and only in her own cottage and in his had she taken to letting the weapon out of reach, even for a short while. He'd realized it years ago, but now, the extent of her courage and strength freshly appreciated, his heart swelled. She trusted him. She felt safe, here. He knew she did it to show him that. Evander breathed out low. "You're incredible. Do you know that?"

She blinked. "I don't—"

"Love," he interrupted, and a thrill went through him that he could finally call her that. He'd slipped and said it before she'd answered his concerned query, after her talk with Aithne, and he'd seen a flicker of a smile when she heard it. He saw that flicker again now, and reveled in it. *Love, love, love.* He'd never tire of calling her that.

"I'm glad we're done dancing around each other," she said, drawing her mostly dried cloak over her shoulders again.

Some of the bravado he only felt in Finlay's presence let him speak his next thought. "We could dance a bit more, if you'd like. Together this time."

She'd been about to reach for her dagger, to replace it on her belt, and maybe leave. She didn't hesitate to change her course of movement. Evander rather thought she'd been hoping for an invitation to stay a bit longer.

Finlay slipped her hand into his and pulled him to his feet, standing with him. He still wasn't used to her hands not being freezing, but their shape, their feel, was wonderfully familiar. "I'd love that," she said, "but there's something I'd like even more right now. Some music, like we used to do."

She walked over to the trunk he kept near his bed. Their shared space, where she'd kept many of her things before she had a place of her own and when Elsie's home was full to the brim with children and belongings. He'd offered it to her all those years ago, and even now, when only his belongings remained because her few possessions were in her own little cottage, he'd insisted she had free access to it. He supposed he didn't want that piece of their childhood to be gone. It was why he kept only blankets and clothing and books in there. And something else, which he hadn't thought of in months: from inside, slightly buried beneath the thick blanket they'd picnicked on last winter, she pulled out his flute.

He breathed out a laugh. "I am seriously out of practice."

"You haven't played for me since last summer."

"I haven't played at all since last summer." The summer he officially became keeper of the sanctuary, when Rubeus retired. Though in all honesty, he'd been doing the work of the keeper for at least two years prior to that point. Last summer he'd come of age to officially take control, in the chief's eyes, but everyone had been calling him keeper since he was sixteen. Even Rubeus.

"Fix that. Play something for me now."

Evander accepted the sleek wooden instrument from Finlay, wet his lips, and gave a tentative exhale over the hole near his mouth, to blow out any dust that had accumulated. A small puff of dust emerged—not nearly enough to make him self-con-scious—and before Finlay could say anything he took a deeper breath and started to play.

A delighted, almost childish glee lit Finlay's face, making Evander's breath hitch in the middle of a note. She clapped and spun and danced around him, brushing against him teasingly and darting away, and he entered the whirl, moving up and down with his own hops and steps, as he knew they would make her laugh. The small space within his cottage meant they pressed close together frequently, though much of it was purposeful.

His playing was far from perfect, but he recalled her favorite jaunty tunes, and played them passably. And when Forrest flew in and accompanied her in the dance, twisting and flying close, Finlay's movements loosened further. She moved with the fluidity of a dragon, so that despite not having wings of her own, she seemed to fly as she and Forrest twirled around Evander. Her cloak spread behind her, adding to the impression that she danced in the air itself, as Forrest did.

Evander feared he would never be able to stop playing, seeing this unbridled joy before him. He only stopped a significant amount of time later, when he was running out of music he'd memorized and Finlay's face was thoroughly pinked.

Man, that was great! Forrest cried.

Finlay gave Evander a look that made heat rush to the back of his neck. He brought his hand to it, in case she could see the blush that crept to his cheeks as well. "I should really get home and sleep," she said. "I'm meeting Elsie early tomorrow." She took her dagger and tucked it in her belt, hand resting on the hilt a beat longer than necessary.

He was positive he could hear the reluctance in the first part of her statement, but he could also detect the excitement in the second. She would begin her training tomorrow. "You'll have to tell me how everything goes."

She gave him that look again—something that managed to convey pleasure, eagerness, and affection, and that all three were directed at him alone. The look drew him closer and he sought her lips with his, unable to watch her go without a kiss. It was brief and sweet, in contrast with their kiss in the rain maybe an hour or two ago, but no less passionate, and it took him several heartbeats to think properly after they separated. Judging from the way Finlay's lips stayed parted in that time, she felt it too.

"Sleep well, love," Evander said.

Finlay cast him a soft smile. "Until tomorrow."

She walked out of Evander's cottage. Evander hadn't realized the rain had slowed to a trickle until he looked after her, through the open door. Forrest settled over Evander's shoulder. *You two are going to be sweet like that from now on, huh?*

Evander reached up to scratch under Forrest's chin in the way he liked. "Absolutely."

Forrest leaned into Evander's hand and sighed. *With the two of you I can stomach it. You have the dragons' approval.*

Evander chuckled as he shut the door. "You're speaking for all the dragons on this?"

You might be bonded with Gaea, but you're bonded with me, too, pal. I know you, and what's best for you and this sanctuary. That's the same thing. That's you, and Finlay. Together.

Evander reached for Forrest and lifted him off his shoulder, setting him on his pillow. "Thank you, Forrest."

Forrest yawned, already curled up into a ball. *I can speak for the dragons sometimes. Especially when I know I'm right.*

Funnily enough, Evander believed he was entirely correct in this instance. The thought warmed him as he changed into nightclothes and got into bed beside the snoring forest dragon.

133

Finlay

The Seer Sisters stood in a line just inside the Knights' compound, three figures hidden in cloaks of midnight blue. Chief Stewart stood in front of them, having a hushed conversation with them.

"They're just so weird!" Elsie whispered—far too loudly, so Finlay was sure John and Angus, standing next to them, could hear—in Finlay's ear. The group stood several feet away, awaiting instruction. They'd been told at the feast to report to the compound that morning. Finlay and Elsie had arrived just after dawn.

"They really have to talk to us individually?" Angus asked, his voice a little higher with nerves.

"It's a tradition," Finlay said. She recalled Meric's words at the feast the day before, when he'd taken her aside and told her of this part. He'd warned her it could be confusing, and a bit alarming, but that it would be over relatively quickly. Finlay decided not to share that part with the clearly nervous boys, focusing on the positive aspect Meric had mentioned. "When the Seer Sisters have direct contact with us, they get a clearer view into the future. It's supposed to help us as we train, to motivate us."

"You know a lot about it," John commented.

"I knew it too," Elsie put in. "Isla told me."

Chief Stewart walked over to their group. "Good morning, future Knights! I trust you're all ready to begin your training, but before we can do so, the Sisters would like to speak to each of you individually. You are free to watch the others train while you wait for your turn, or explore the compound."

"Angus will go first," one of the Sisters said. The one with the raspy voice.

Angus squeaked when he tried to respond, cleared his throat, and nodded bravely, walking to the trio with his shoulders back.

"Want to find Isla?" Elsie asked. "She's not by the water today. She could show us around."

Finlay agreed. They found Isla in the pavilion, where it seemed she'd been waiting for them. She sat by Muir, who had his head resting across her lap. "Took you long enough," she said. She kissed the top of Muir's snout and stood. "I figured I could show you the armory. You don't have your training gear yet, but you'll get it soon."

"They took our measurements yesterday," Elsie said.

Isla led them past the pavilion, where they saw pairs of Knights sparring with weapons Finlay now knew to be magically blunted. Several Knights soared overhead, practicing aerial combat and combinations with their dragon partners. Excitement sped Finlay's pulse.

"We get to find our dragon partners soon, don't we?"

Isla smiled at her over her shoulder. "Very soon." She stopped in front of a building hewn from gray stone. "Everyone has an assigned storage section. Once you have it, you'll store your gauntlets, boots, uniforms, and personal weapons here."

Taking them inside, Isla showed them the sections they would be using. The interior of the building was sparsely furnished. It was arranged in a long, narrow shape, reaching deeply back before veering to the left to have another corridor of storage sections, all of which stood on the same side of the hallway. This left a relatively narrow walking space, with the line of somewhat private storage sections taking up most of the space. Wooden slats separated assigned sections, extending from the wall about three feet. Two thick, dark, wooden shelves had been mounted in each section, and a coat rack stood in the corners.

Walking by the occupied sections, Finlay spotted the heavy cloaks of the current Knights occupying many of the coat racks. She saw pairs of boots and tunics and pants, some neatly folded and placed on shelves, others more haphazardly strewn within the section. Many of the storage sections had weapons on their shelves: small shields and daggers, some bows and arrows, several swords. She recognized Meric's iron staff, and his deep gray cloak, even before she saw his name.

Each section had the owner's name above it, carved beautifully on a thin board mounted to the wall. Finlay suspected Moira had done them. She was surprised to see a name plate for herself already posted above an empty storage section, after they passed those currently in use.

"These are yours," Isla said.

Finlay walked into her assigned storage section. It wasn't much, really, especially not at the moment, empty of any special materials, yet a sense of awe made her pause. With how quickly they'd made the name plate, she predicted it wouldn't be long before she had her uniform. She could picture her cloak on the empty coat rack in the corner. She would bring the book Evander had given her—the one he'd written for her, detailing different types of dragons—and put it on her shelf. She would leave her uniform beside it. This space would be hers.

The only thing she wouldn't leave here would be her dagger. Her hand swept past its hilt in an automatic gesture, where it rested near her hip. She couldn't be separated from it, even knowing it would be safer here than anywhere else she could store it.

No one would take issue with her keeping the dagger on her person, especially now that she was both of age and in training as a Knight. When she'd first arrived at Aerouant Glèidh, after she'd clutched it so tightly in her grief that she'd bled, several people had tried to take it from her. For the first several months they'd tried, since children weren't allowed to keep such deadly things within reach unsupervised. After that, after they'd realized she simply needed it near, even if she didn't do anything with it, no one even tried to dissuade her from keeping it. Meric, her champion from the first week, encouraged her to keep it, realizing it gave her strength.

No, she wouldn't be leaving her dagger anywhere.

Motion behind them made Finlay turn. Cormac, Aileen, and Angus walked up, each holding a wrapped bundle of items.

"Inspecting your storage sections?" Cormac asked.

"Our training gear is ready!" Angus said. His voice had returned to its normal pitch, and he looked much more relaxed.

"How was it with the Sisters?" Finlay asked, at the same time Elsie asked about the gear.

"It wasn't so bad," Angus said, looking to Finlay first. "They're creepy, that's for sure. Their eyes . . ." he shivered, then continued. "Gave me some things to think about. Showed me some things, too. I don't think I got half of it, it was so fast. But I saw myself fighting a Mage. You were right. It was inspiring. The Sisters are talking to John now, so you two should be soon." He looked at Elsie. "I haven't looked at the gear yet. These two just told me it's arrived, and asked for my help bringing it in."

"It's just training gear, mind," Cormac said, setting down his bundle. "You won't get your heavy cloaks until you complete the training, and once you do, you'll get nicer gear as well. This will do for now, though, and it's been fitted to your measurements."

Aileen set her bundle in front of Finlay. "This one should have most of your things, Finlay. I was starting to sort them when Cormac decided to blindly grab things and shove them in bags."

Cormac looked down so his bangs hid his eyes. "Thought they'd like to see them as soon as possible, Aileen."

"You thought right!" Elsie said, opening up the bag he'd brought.

Finlay pulled the gear from the bag by her feet with a kind of reverence. The boiled leather armor was polished, clearly new, and had a faint shimmer within the dark leather that Finlay knew resulted from the salve Moira created from ground dragon scales. This armor was almost as strong as metal, with the salve added while the leather cured.

She inspected each item in turn: the cuirass that would protect her torso, front and back, slightly different than those the boys wore to ensure full protection and range of motion; pauldrons that would protect her shoulders, rounded close to the body; slender bracers for her forearms, and tassets for her thighs; thick but supple boots. Beneath all of this equipment she found the sturdy belt to fasten around her waist, with a fitted sheath to connect to it, and her hand went once more to her dagger. This would be the finest sheath it had ever had. If her family could see her. . . .

"You all right, Finlay?" Isla asked.

Finlay blinked forcefully and gathered up her materials, walking toward her storage section. She thought she heard Isla give a short, knowing laugh, but by the time she'd stored her gear and turned around, her adoptive older sister looked completely serious again.

"You want to wander on your own, right?" Isla asked.

Stunned, Finlay nodded. She forgot how well Isla knew her, sometimes.

"Try not to go too far," Isla said. "The Sisters will be ready for you soon."

"They'll find you," Angus said, in the process of putting on his cuirass. "They were the ones to recommend we take time to look around, instead of all waiting around while they talk to one at a time. They said they'll know where we are."

Finlay made her way out of the armory. She saw the Sisters, still shrouded in their cloaks, heading toward the building, and paused, but they shook their heads. The motion was eerily synchronous, and slow. "Not yet," the one with the clearest voice said.

Elsie, then. Finlay looked over her shoulder while the Sisters went into the armory, wondering what they would tell her. She sighed and set off toward the dormitories, eager to explore the housing in which, in the very near future, she could choose to reside. The solitary walk also let her not have to worry about schooling her expression. She knew her default expression bordered on melancholic. Elsie often puzzled over the grief even she could see in Finlay's brown eyes, and Elsie rarely looked at a person's expression closely enough to read their emotional state. Finlay wasn't absorbed in grief, but given how quickly her thoughts were moving, she was sure she looked it. The thoughts about how her family would react to seeing her like this hadn't helped.

The dormitory resembled the armory, though its stone walls reached half again as tall, and it didn't veer sideways. It was the largest building in the compound, because it had to have enough room for all of the Knights, and it also contained the war room, or so Finlay had heard from Meric.

Wandering inside, she quickly became turned around. So many closed doors in nondescript passageways. She couldn't go into any of the rooms without permission, and everyone was either training or fulfilling other obligations in the village. Deciding to retrace her steps using the wooden labels atop each door, knowing if she found Cormac's, she was near the entrance, she hesitated for a second to adjust her dagger by her side. In that instant she paused, a low sound hit her ear.

She stilled, listening hard, and heard it again several seconds later. A low, pained sound that could only come from a dragon. Barely discernible, and only then when standing still.

Finlay hastened in the direction of the sound, winding deeper into the maze of rooms until she came to what she guessed to be an old storage room, from a faded label above it. Heavy pieces of lumber had been nailed in place over the door, with a sign across the entrance proclaiming it unsafe, forbidding entrance.

A muffled roar from a dragon sounded again, much closer. Finlay didn't hesitate, gripping one of the boards and pulling to wrench it from the doorframe. There had to be another way to reach the dragon, but she wouldn't waste time searching for it. Making a gap large enough to shimmy through, Finlay took a candle from the nearest sconce and slipped into the room. Broken mops, buckets, and chairs littered the floor and other debris rose in piles all around. The floor had a chunk missing near the back. Shifting some of the debris around, she used the candle to search around the space. There had to be something here . . . another room, somewhere that the dragon was crying from . . .

The floor was curiously sturdy to have such a wide hole in the far corner. Finlay crept closer with light footfalls, holding her light out. She moved a chair broken in two pieces from in front of the hole in the floor and narrowed her eyes. It was jagged on the side nearest to her, but perfectly smooth on the opposite side, and certainly wide enough to pass through without touching the jagged bit. The rungs of a ladder, rusted with age, peeked out from the neatly-cut side.

Another agonized draconic groan jolted Finlay from her analysis. Hooking the candle base around her thumb to free most of her hand, Finlay descended the short ladder as quickly as she dared, and passed through a crudely fashioned, narrow corridor, to a large wooden door. She walked through, then turned to take in her surroundings.

All she noticed, however, was the large dragon chained to the ground several feet in front of her. A very familiar dragon with purple eyes.

Chief Stewart's dragon.

CHAPTER NINETEEN

"Ghillie," Finlay gasped.

The dragon lay on his side on the floor, one wing tucked beneath him, the other spread wide and limp. The braces that usually covered parts of his legs glinted in the corner. Thick metal manacles wrapped around his legs, connected to chains bolted to the floor. A bulky collar encircled his neck, also linked to a chain to restrict movement.

Finlay's hand crept toward her mouth, bile stuck in her throat. "Ghillie, what happened to you?"

Ghillie raised his head slightly off the floor and looked at her, and his gaze made Finlay's stomach clench. There was a dullness in his eyes, as if they couldn't focus on her, but even within that glaze Finlay could see glints of pain, cracking through. He groaned again, a dull, low, horrible sound.

Finlay walked over and set down her candle, kneeling and placing one hand on his snout. "Ghillie, say something," she whispered, stroking his head.

Can't . . . Finlay? . . . Can't . . . . . . think . . . pain . . .

Finlay flinched. Each word had come across so labored and slow. He'd been given something to keep him quiet. That much was clear. Those wretched manacles were digging into his scales, hurting him. Finlay touched her head to his. "I'm going to get you out of here, Ghillie," she said in a low voice.

How could Chief Stewart have done this to his own dragon? How long had it been going on? Did anyone else know?

No. She couldn't accept anyone else knowing, could barely accept that the chief had done something so horrid. She could process it later. Those manacles needed to come off. She could free Ghillie and bring him to the sanctuary, and Evander and Gaea could help him heal. That had to be her first priority.

Would Chief Stewart keep a key to the manacles down here, or only on his person? She picked up her candle and scoured the walls, looking for a hook or shelf of some kind. The ground was flat, but gradually inclined toward the back. Up to ground level. A large barn door loomed above her, at the top of that incline, feeble hints of daylight glowing in the gaps. That was the chief's private yard, if she wasn't mistaken, connected to his room on the other side of the building. When she didn't find anything of value in her quick inspection, she went to the manacles on

Ghillie's front legs, feeling all around them. Her dagger wouldn't be of any use here. Could fire . . . ?

A banging sound like wood knocking against wood made her jump. Her eyes fixed on the barn door just in time to see it swing open on one side. Light entered the room unopposed, lending the space a half-lit quality. Chief Stewart stood in the half-open doorway, clearly able to see Finlay as well as she could see him, something like shock on his frozen face.

"What are you doing here?"

Finlay straightened to her full height. "I heard Ghillie in pain. How do you explain this?"

Chief Stewart strode forward. "You heard him?" He stopped next to Ghillie, and then kicked him in the stomach. "You disloyal brute!"

"Stop!" Finlay yelled, and ran forward to shove the chief away from the dragon. Ghillie's grunt of pain echoed in her ears. Though the chief was more solid than Finlay, she caught him by surprise, and the man staggered backward.

"How dare you strike him?" Finlay demanded. "How dare you treat him this way?"

"How dare I?" the chief snarled. "I can do anything I please with my own dragon."

"He's your partner, not your slave, and you're hurting him!"

His hand came flying up out of nowhere, his knuckles cracking against Finlay's cheek. Finlay spun to the side from the force of the strike, pain blossoming in her cheek. Stars popped before her eyes, a dull ringing filling her ears. It took several seconds for her to realize she was on the ground. Chief Stewart crouched beside her, grabbed her by the arms to hoist her upright, and slammed her against the wall. He placed one arm across her throat, his eyes bulging out in fury.

"Quiet," he warned, "or I'll make you be quiet."

Finlay trembled but forced herself to keep her chin out, clinging to her anger instead of her fear. "You're not bound to Ghillie anymore, are you? You don't share his power. You don't keep him from flying because he's weak, but because you drug him so much he can't!"

He looked at the dragon over his shoulder, and Finlay surreptitiously began reaching for her dagger. "You put that together quickly. You heard him from the dormitory? I must have given him too little last night, for it to have started wearing off. I'll have to be heavier-handed tonight."

"You're disgusting," Finlay spat, gripping the handle of her dagger and pulling upward.

The arm against her throat pressed tighter, restricting her air, and the other slammed against her wrist. Pain radiated along her arm. She dropped the dagger before she could fully remove it from her belt. She leaned into the wall automatically when his arm pressed on her throat, struggling, and despite herself, a whimper escaped her. Chief Stewart's lip curled up. "So you do realize how powerless you are right now. Good." He leaned in close. "Have you ever met an elf, Finlay? I have. They mostly live in the desert regions, but I've run into a few nearby, and I learned something important from them."

Finlay squirmed.

He spoke in a language Finlay didn't recognize; the words sent a tingle through her, and made her nerves stand on end. She stilled. Something wasn't right. A sick feeling was rising in her gut . . . The chief's smile deepened, even as he touched his head with a momentary wince. "It isn't the elves that are magic. It's the language they discovered. Try to come here again and it'll be the end of your pathetic life. Similarly, if you breathe a word of this to any person, you endanger yourself and others. Tragic accidents do happen to Knights, after all."

Finlay hoped he could see the rage mixed in with the fear on her face. Hoped he could sense exactly how much she hated him. She didn't have enough air to give it voice.

"You do know how to be quiet. Excellent."

He dropped his arm, and Finlay took in a wheezing breath. The sick feeling in her gut increased, painful and sharp—spreading.

"Best get that ugly look off your face. And you'll need to make an excuse for the bruise."

He stood, arms crossed over his large stomach, and Finlay knew he meant for her to leave first. She walked over to Ghillie and rubbed her hand along the top of his head, not daring to stop but slowing her step to do so. "I'm so sorry I couldn't free you, Ghillie," she whispered.

She walked back up the ladder and out of the dormitory with the same slow step. Each step decreased the sick feeling inside her gut that resulted from whatever magic Chief Stewart had spoken. She took it as proof she couldn't physically move to free Ghillie. It wouldn't let her get near him again, especially now that she'd left. She had a feeling the pain would be worse next time she strayed too close to the dormitory, and that the only reason it hadn't been debilitating this time was that the spell was cast while she was still within its borders.

All of the excitement she'd felt that morning had been tainted. She'd wanted to look into staying in the dormitory. That could never happen. A dragon was suffering beneath the noses of most of the Knights. How could she work with Chief Stewart at all? Would anyone believe her if she told them? She knew two would. Evander and Elsie. But could she risk telling them, and putting them in danger as well as herself? Did the spell Chief Stewart had cast only keep her from physically coming to Ghillie's aid, or would it strike if she spoke about his fate as well? She could take that risk for herself, but if he targeted Elsie and Evander . . .

She couldn't make the decision now, and wanted nothing more than to go home and curl up on her bed, kidnapping Forrest on the way and holding him close when the tears she knew were coming broke through.

She paused at the dormitory entrance, pulled from woolly thoughts by the sight of three heavily cloaked figures standing just outside, staring at her. She doubted she reacted externally, but her heart gave a leap of fright. Just what she needed right now.

"Finlay McDonough," the Sisters said, their mismatched voices in foreboding cadence. "It is time to see."

"Your past," the ancient voice one rasped.

"Your present," the clear voice intoned.

"Your future," the youthful voice chirped.

They led her to the courtyard, past the pavilions where Knights and dragons trained, to the back wall of the compound. Vines crept over the wall in this section, flowers blooming in the cracks. There was a bench facing the pavilion, and had she been able to appreciate it, Finlay would have marveled at the beauty of the little spot, with its clear view of humans and dragons working together in the distance. When they directed her to sit, she felt very little, and looked at the Sisters expectantly.

"Hold out your hand," they said together.

Finlay did as they said. The Sisters stepped forward, reaching out with their hands, and Finlay obtained her first true view of their faces. She'd glimpsed the milkiness of their eyes before. She hadn't absorbed how extensive it was. All three had hazel eyes, so the pale splotches created a stark contrast with the fragments of darkness. Finlay at once had the feeling they saw everything and nothing.

They extended their tattooed, olive-toned hands, the one with the raspy voice gripping her forearm near the elbow, the one with the childish voice gripping closer to her wrist. The one with the clearest voice took Finlay's hand.

The world shuddered around Finlay when their skin touched hers. Her body froze, her eyes widening and her mouth opening. She couldn't see the courtyard or pavilions anymore. A rush of fragmented images dominated her sight, real and seeming immediately in front of her, accompanied by sounds: Michael preparing to deliver a killing blow with a stick sword in their yard. Flames spreading across her body. Elsie pulling her back from the cliff's edge with a laugh. The border of the dragon sanctuary. Her father's dagger. Lightning illuminating a dark night, crackling but not managing to drown out the piercing scream. Da singing her to sleep. Her own pale hands, covered in blood. Meric, fighting her in the trial. Three burned husks in an ashen field. Aithne flying with fire rippling along her wings. A man with dark hair and unshaved cheeks, standing on the mountain. Jupiter flying with her on his back. Evander kissing her in the rain. Ghillie crying out. Herself looking out of a high tower in a castle.

Amidst the flurry of images and sounds, the Sisters' voices said things. Snatches of their words filtered through the images, though in the midst of it, she couldn't separate their voices.

"Betrayal's bite is fatal from loved ones.
Hardened by loss, braced for the fall.
A new era will burn away the old, or fall to ashes before it takes
hold.
Fate taken into undeserving hands rebels against them.
Flames will change the kingdom whole, sparked by the girl with
the dragon's soul."

Past, present, and future crashed into Finlay, overwhelming her senses. The Sisters lifted their hands from her skin, ending the torrent of images. Finlay swayed and gripped the edge of the bench, sinking onto the seat. "What was that?" she asked in a rough whisper.

"Your path," the Sisters said in unison. They stared at her for a long moment with their mottled gazes before turning on their heels and walking away.

"Wait!" Finlay called. "I need you to explain!" She stood and went to follow, but stopped when a wave of dizziness hit her. She closed her eyes and took in a steadying breath that helped immediately.

"It will pass," the clear-voiced Sister said.

"Farewell, Finlay McDonough," they said together.

Finlay watched them walk away, heart still pounding in her chest. Meric had said it would be disorienting. She hadn't expected it to be so overwhelming. She went back to the bench and closed her eyes again, focusing on the fire that let her find the mindscape. Aithne was expecting her again, sitting upright, distress clear in her orange eyes.

"I know you hear and see everything I do in the real world," Finlay said. "Did you see what the Sisters showed me, even though it was in my head?"

I did.

Finlay sank down on the grass and drew her knees to her chest, wrapping her arms around them. "We can piece through it after. First priority has to be Ghillie."

You worry others know what your chief has done. Why do you think the man was so determined to convince you to keep quiet?

"He probably hasn't told anyone else," Finlay said. "I know that, but I can't trust the man who's leading us . . . how can I trust that what we've been doing is right? He's not the leader of the Knights, but Calum usually defers to him. Does he hate dragons? It seems like he hates the Mages, but if he can do that to Ghillie . . . someone else must know, right?"

Don't let this betrayal make you paranoid, making enemies out of allies. There is no point in questioning everyone's motives right now. I would guess the Knights know nothing of the mistreatment. It sounds like the chief has a system in place to keep Ghillie quiet during hours he might otherwise be discovered. Aithne's fire flared. **To confine a dragon like that, and dull his spark so much! It's horrible cruelty!**

Anger focused Finlay. "I need to free Ghillie."

Absolutely, but you have to proceed with caution. The chief will be watching you closely from now on.

"If I go to Meric and others now, before he has a chance to change anything—"

You were with the Sisters for a longer time than you think. Anyway, you'll need proof to convince the Knights.

"The proof is how weak Ghillie is! He can barely think straight!"

Just as there are ways to restrain Ghillie, there are ways to make him appear unaffected. Without knowing how the chief is doing it, we can't count on Ghillie being able

to corroborate our story. He might have a way of swaying Ghillie's thoughts.

Finlay wanted to retort that it was ridiculous, but she remembered one dragon who could enter dreams. He'd been able to put such powerful visions before sleeping minds that people couldn't tell if it was a dream or another reality. He'd left shortly after arriving at the sanctuary, when his growing abilities scared many of the humans and dragons. That had been years ago. Maybe the chief had taken some of his power? Maybe he didn't even need to. Who knew how much of the elven language he'd mastered, and how many spells he could weave with it?

Finlay groaned, abandoning that line of thought. "You're right. So we need to prove he's abusing Ghillie a different way. But it can't take too long. I can't let Ghillie keep suffering." She met Aithne's eyes. "Evander or Elsie might have a better plan."

Aithne let out a weighted sigh. **You must decide for yourself. I can't be of any true help outside of discussing with you and helping you master my abilities. I believe the chief will threaten anyone he believes you would confide in, and take no remorse in acting to hurt them to send you a message. Or silence them if he thinks they would reveal him. And this spell he's cast . . . I don't like it.**

Finlay didn't mind the risk for herself, but again, she paused thinking of what could be done to her loved ones. Could the spell hurt them, too? Or was it Chief Stewart who would do that? Could she ask for their help and free Ghillie with a full guarantee of their safety?

If the spell hurt them . . .

Even if it didn't, if she did tell them, Elsie would want to storm into the cellar and break Ghillie out immediately, proof or not. If the chief had a way to disrepute what Finlay said, it could end Elsie's career as a Knight before it began. Evander . . . Evander was a different story. It would cause him legitimate pain to think of a dragon in danger. He would absolutely believe Finlay, and it would make him hate the chief. But Evander couldn't hide that kind of strain on his soul. It would be obvious something was wrong, and the chief would know Finlay had told him. That would just put him in danger.

She had to figure this out on her own.

Chapter Twenty

Finlay

Familiar black eyes stared at Finlay when she left the mind-scape, close to her face, and she jumped more from surprise than fear.

Elsie backed away while Finlay muttered a curse under her breath. What was it with others getting so close to her while she talked to Aithne? First Jupiter, now Elsie. She knew she hadn't been talking to Aithne that long.

It wasn't just Elsie standing before her. Isla was there as well, along with a twenty-something man Finlay could name but didn't know well: Calum, leader of the Knights for the last few years. She'd overheard many people discussing Calum, fawning over his ash-blond hair and strong jaw, the splash of freckles over his nose that was more apparent because of the fairness of his skin. She supposed he was handsome. She'd also never really noticed anyone but Evander.

Finlay had seen Calum lead nighttime patrols many times, having watched the Knights leave almost every night for years. She hadn't heard much about him, though. Apparently he was a private person—a belief that made his admirers fawn over him even more as they wondered about his secrets, making up stories to fit whatever type of person they hoped him to be.

"You took a really long time to respond, Fin," Elsie said. "Thought the Sisters hurt your brain or something."

"You could say that," Finlay said, standing. "It was a lot to process."

Elsie raised a brow in a silent question, and Finlay nodded as minutely as she could to tell her yes, she had been talking to Aithne. Another flickering expression told Finlay Elsie expected details later.

"Best way to get over it is to dive into something else," Isla said. She stood behind Elsie, scrutinizing Finlay. Though she had the same dark hue to her eyes as her sister, there was always something else in Isla's gaze. Finlay was certain Isla was questioning the bruise that had to be blooming across her cheek as well.

"What are we diving into?" Finlay asked.

"You can't train as a dragon Knight without a dragon to call your partner," Calum said. "It's time to go to the sanctuary and find that dragon."

Finlay couldn't help but stare at him for a second, hearing his voice. It was one of the loveliest voices she'd ever heard, ringing with a gentle strength. So unlike most of the authoritative voices she'd heard, which made efforts to be loud or grating or packed with energy.

"You'll each have a mentor for the next two months, while you train. We'll show you what we know, and help you forge a bond with your dragon partner while you hone your skills."

"We?" Elsie asked.

"I'm yours," Isla told her. "I didn't want anyone else getting stuck with you."

Calum met Finlay's eyes. "I'll be your mentor, Finlay."

Elsie frowned. "I thought Meric would jump on the opportunity to mentor you."

"Meric was a mentor for the last batch of Knights," Calum said. "We have a rule that you have to alternate trials in which you can mentor, to give everyone a chance to work with a future Knight. Everyone has something to give to future generations."

"I'm honored to have you as my mentor, Calum," Finlay said.

Calum's shoulders shook in a brief laugh, though it seemed like he tried not to react. "Yes, well, we should get on with it. I'm sure the others are already at the sanctuary."

Finlay didn't need to be told twice to go to the sanctuary. She practically led the way, each step closer to the sanctuary allowing her to push the Sisters' visions, and Ghillie's plight, to the back of her mind.

Aileen and Angus were near the front of the sanctuary when they got there, Angus bravely trying not to flinch as Evander drew his permanent tattoo on his hand. Evander paused when he heard them approach, eyes darting over to them, and flashed that dimpled smile at Finlay before turning back to applying Angus's tattoo.

"Almost done," he said in a low voice.

"Is John already searching for his dragon partner?" Isla asked.

"Yes," Aileen said. "Cormac and I brought the boys over together. John had his mark applied first, and he barely gave Evander his hand long enough to finish, he was so eager to go find his partner."

"Those willing to work with Knights will be in this general area," Evander told them. He lifted the claw he used to apply the tattoos from Angus's hand, scooped a smear of a pale lotion onto his fingertips, and swept it over the back of Angus's palm. "That should help with the pain, and make it heal more quickly. I can bandage it if you'd like, but it should dry soon."

"I'll take a bandage," Angus said quietly.

"Not a problem," Evander said, and secured a cotton pad over the area. "You are all set, Angus."

"Elsie, you can go next," Finlay said. She wanted a moment with Evander.

Finlay waited while Evander applied the permanent tattoo for access to the dragon sanctuary to Elsie's hand, watching the process closely. The sharpened dragon claw he used to cut into the skin wasn't the only way to apply tattoos, but it had been ceremonial for years. The mixture of ink and finely ground crystal retained the pale purple and blue coloring of the solid crystals at the borders. The temporary tattoos put crystal dustings just within the surface of the hand. The permanent ones had a higher concentration that would never fully fade, imprinted more deeply into the skin.

Try as she might to focus on the process, her attention did keep moving to the young man himself. Her eyes followed his steady hands up to his slender but strong arms, the broad curve of his shoulders and slope of his neck, coming to rest on his face—his head was angled down slightly while he leaned over Elsie's hand, giving a clear view of his golden lashes.

"You want me to wait for you?" Elsie asked when Evander finished with hers.

"You go ahead. We have to separate anyway, to find our dragons."

Finlay sat down in the seat Elsie had just occupied and held out her hand to Evander. He hesitated to take her hand, looking at her with drawn brows. "You don't seem as excited as I expected you to be," he said quietly. "And is that a bruise forming on your cheek? What's wrong?"

Everything. "I fell when the Sisters showed me things," she lied. "And I'm just being reflective today. Help me get out of my head?"

He cleaned the dragon claw in a dish of water, wiped the tip, and dipped it in the bowl of ink. "How would you like me to distract you? Forrest's latest adventure with Jasper? The riveting tale of how I made my breakfast?"

A laugh bubbled in Finlay's chest. Evander must have seen it in the twitch of her lips; he had a growing grin when he took her hand and started applying the tattoo. "Breakfast, then. It was an arduous journey to retrieve eggs . . ."

"You got eggs?"

He blinked at her. "Did you not?"

"I ate bread with a bit of jam."

"Well, that doesn't seem right, being your first day training as a Knight. I'll have to make it up to you with dinner."

"Except you can't cook."

He smiled. "Who said I would do the cooking? Just you wait, Finlay. But anyway, back to my heroic quest for breakfast this morning . . ."

Water over a burn. That was Evander in those moments he applied her tattoo and told her a dramatic tale of barely edible (once he'd cooked them) eggs. He couldn't heal the wound she felt inside, but he could soothe it, because he could soothe her. He wrapped her hand with both of his after he finished with the tattoo, cradling it with a feather-light touch.

"Something's bothering you," he whispered. "You don't have to tell me. But if you decide to confide in me, I'll gladly listen. Either way, meet me here when you're done for the day."

Finlay knew Calum was watching. She didn't care, and leaned forward to kiss Evander. When she pulled back, Evander had a dazed look on his face, and a loose upturn of his lips. "For being you," she told him before he could ask why she'd kissed him. Heat bloomed in her cheeks. "And because I couldn't resist."

Calum cleared his throat. Finlay choked back a snort of amusement at how uncomfortable the man looked, standing nearby and pointedly avoiding eye contact. "We should really get going. You don't even know which dragon you'd like to ask to be your partner."

Finlay stood. "I think I do, actually."

Calum studied her, something approving in his gaze. "Go ahead, then. I'll wait here."

She set off at a light jog, ignoring the faint prickling on the back of her hand when she moved it. Moira's salve was already numbing the area. A few minutes at this pace brought her to the base of the mountain, and she climbed the same way she had during the trial to reach Jupiter's cave. It was easier this time, without the fear of running out of time weighing her movements.

Humans are so loud. Are you back to give me more answers?

Finlay stopped below the ledge of his cave when he peeked his head out. "Yes. And to ask a favor."

Bah. I just did you a favor, helping you pass the trial. What else could I possibly do for you?

"I need to find a dragon to act as my partner. When I complete my training, there will be a ceremony, and I'll be bound to that dragon. You and I both know that can't happen, though. Please consider being my partner, Jupiter, and pretending to share your powers with me."

He leaned down so far over his ledge Finlay half expected him to fall over. *Why?*

His baritone voice demanded the answer be a good one. Finlay knew she would lose him if she didn't capture his interest now. "You said I hadn't sated your curiosity yet. I'll give you more answers now, but you must be curious how Aithne and I will work together. If you agree to be my partner, you can have all the answers you want, immediately."

But I would serve a human.

Resentment dripped from his voice. Finlay shook her head. "You would work with a human. Not serve one."

Cooperation so quickly devolves into hierarchy and abuse, with humans.

An image of Ghillie, wincing as Chief Stewart kicked him, made Finlay look away. "Maybe with some." She straightened. "Not with me. I would never do anything to harm a dragon. If you agree to be my partner, you'll truly be my partner."

He stared at her with huge amber eyes, and then snorted. *Not much of a wordsmith, are you? I would say you're merely another skilled actor, but your dragon agrees with you.*

"You can hear her?"

I don't need to hear her to know she agrees with you. Your energies flared when you were making your passionate—though basic—appeal. In harmony. If the phoenix dragon supports what you are saying, I have no reason to doubt you. I will be your partner.

Finlay smiled.

Jupiter shook his shoulders cockily. *I may be the only dragon capable of convincingly acting like we've bonded. I'm a cut above the rest, as I'm sure you realize.*

Finlay did her best to keep her smile. He and Forrest would get along well . . . This would be interesting, that was for sure.

They didn't do much that first day, after finding their dragon partners. No official training, at any rate. The four mentors: Calum, Aileen, Isla, and Cormac, encouraged Finlay, Angus, Elsie, and John to spend time with their partners in the compound. They stayed in a loose group, sometimes in the air and sometimes on the ground, getting to know each other and familiarizing themselves with each other's dragon partners.

Elsie found a sturdier, non-water dragon, as she'd hoped: Kenna, a dragon that resembled the magma in which she thrived with her black and molten orange tinted scales and had a tremendously hot fire, and a ridiculously hot head, from the brief conversation Finlay had with her. Angus paired with a gentler dragon by the name of Fern, a calm voice of the forest. John asked Jasper to be his partner. Finlay would have whistled to herself if she could have whistled when she recognized him. Forrest would have some things to say about this later. She might never hear the end of it. So much dragon drama, between this and her own partner!

Sure enough, Forrest flew to her as soon as she slid off Jupiter's back after he flew them back to the sanctuary that evening. Forrest flapped his tiny wings to hover in front of her at eye level. *Someone really picked Jasper?* he demanded.

"John did. The new Knight a few years older than me." Finlay looked around to make sure Jasper wasn't near enough to hear. "I think John has as hard a head as Jasper. And almost as big."

Forrest had been whipping his tail back and forth, but the motion lessened with Finlay's comment, and he snorted. *Guess that makes sense.*

"I thought you'd be happy Jasper won't be around as much. He won't break as many things."

He'll manage. He'll probably reenact training exercises for his adoring fans.

Finlay pulled Forrest close and held him for a second. "I'm a fan of yours, Forrest. Always and forever."

He rubbed his snout along her neck in a nuzzling gesture, then pushed free of her grip. *Evander is waiting for you with a surprise you'll like. You kissed since last night?*

"Forrest!"

That's a yes!

"Oh, you go on," Finlay said with a sweeping gesture, cursing the warmth in her cheeks.

Forrest laughed and flew off. Finlay found Evander near his cottage, standing next to Gaea. Her heart picked up its tempo at the sight of him, doubling its rate when he saw her and lit up in the way he only ever did for her.

"What's this?" she asked.

Evander picked up a wicker basket. "I told you I'd handle dinner. How do you feel about eating in the sky?"

Finlay looked to Gaea. "You're going to take us for a flight?"

You're at home in the sky, he said in his deep rumble. *Evander thought you'd like this.*

"Evander was right to think so. Thank you, Gaea."

So it was with more than a trace of excitement that Finlay found herself high above Aerouant Glèidh minutes later, safe on Gaea's back with Evander holding her at the waist. Gaea took them above the inky clouds, where they could see the sun shining in its evening glory.

"You got permission to leave the village?" Finlay asked over her shoulder.

"I didn't have to. We're only flying above it, not past it." He breathed out in mild amusement. "Funny how we all think of it with a name, but pretend it's still unnamed some of the time."

"Meric told me they purposely left the settlement unnamed, because they don't want it to be permanent. Incentive to take back the throne and rejoin Alocasia, and all that."

"Even Meric calls it Aerouant Glèidh," Evander said. "It has to have been here for twenty years, anyway."

Finlay looked down at their home through a gap in the clouds. "It does seem like past time to make it official." She didn't say what she was really thinking: if they were waiting to have a large enough force of Knights to move directly against the Mages, it could be decades before they took action. Unless they found other allies . . .

The truth of what needed to happen whispered in the back of her consciousness, as if stirred by her encounter with the Sisters. Having someone inside the castle, who could help dismantle the

Mages from within their ranks, would be the best way to topple the throne. One person . . . but they would need a way to gain access . . . Finlay blinked hard to push the thought away. Not a concern, at the moment.

Evander loosened one arm from around her waist. He handed her a sandwich from the basket he'd brought. "I'll have to make you eggs another time."

Finlay's neck heated. Eggs. Breakfast. Breakfast with Evander, which would likely happen after spending the night together . . . . after they'd maybe . . . she quashed the thought down, though the thrill it sent through her remained. It had taken them days to work up the courage to kiss. It would be a while yet before they reached that point. Maybe.

Finlay unwrapped the sandwich and gasped. "There's so much meat in this!"

She felt Evander's laugh against her back. "I convinced Marge I needed a picnic feast to celebrate your first day as a Knight. She snuck me an extra ration of meat."

Finlay had already taken a massive mouthful. Thick, soft bread, a true layer of beef (which she only had every few weeks), a creamy sauce, spinach . . . "This is amazing," she said between bites. Part of her knew she should set it down and talk to Evander while they ate. Eat it more slowly, at least. Her appetite overrode propriety, and the hearty sandwich was gone very quickly.

Evander laughed again when she finished and leaned against him with a contented sigh, swallowing his own last mouthful and wrapping his arms around her middle. "You should have regular portions of meat now, if you take your meals in the dining hall in the compound. Most of what the farmers raise goes to the Knights, so they stay in peak condition."

Finlay tilted her head to look up at him. "Can you take your meals there too? I know you never really have, but could you, if you asked?"

"I get a bit more than most, but no, I don't go to the compound that often. I've never thought to ask. I don't deserve special treatment."

Finlay put her hands over his. "You certainly do."

They flew high above the borders of the village, coasting above the thick line of clouds until well after the sun had disappeared. The moon shone scarcely a sliver in the dark skyline. Unfortunately, the heavy clouds obscured the stars when they landed near the lake's edge.

They slid off Gaea's back and walked a short distance away. Evander turned to her and, taking a small breath, straightened his shoulders and offered one hand, palm out. "May I have this dance?"

Finlay took his hand. "I didn't expect to dance so soon."

"I didn't want to make you wait too long. But Forrest has been my only real dance partner, so you'll have to bear with me."

Forrest was an excellent dancer. Still . . . "We've danced plenty of times, Evander."

His hand applied a gentle pressure to hers. "I've always had a flute in my hands. Not you. This is different."

It was, she realized, returning the pressure to his hand. In the best of ways.

"What will we dance to?" she asked.

His eyebrows furrowed. "I may have neglected to think of that."

She slid her free hand onto his chest, feeling the steady beating of his heart beneath her fingertips. Its pace quickened at her touch. "We can dance to our own music," she said. She moved her hand up to his shoulder, his skirted down to her waist, and they moved to their own heartbeats on the water's edge. Slow rotations, sideways steps. Front and back, gliding fluidly in movements that matched no proper dance, but couldn't be called anything less. Evander lessened his grip on her hand and raised his arm to spin her out. Finlay paused when their arms were fully extended, meeting his warm eyes wordlessly.

He spun her back in more slowly than she'd spun out, their bodies brushing against each other before they parted to stand as they had before, resuming their informal dance. A low heat simmered where it had only sparked before, spreading by the second and drawing them closer; each motion closed the distance between them, fabric to fabric, skin to skin, as they instinctively moved to hold each other and sway in one spot. She rested her chin on his shoulder, and heat raced through her veins when Evander's hand trailed up to the small of her back, nestling her body against his. Her fingers scraped against his shirt as she clutched him in return.

She leaned into his collar, her lips whispering against his neck. "Evander."

His breath shuddered in and quickly out, stirring her hair back. She wasn't sure who moved first, or if they perhaps moved at the same time, but in an instant they were kissing, soft and deep and slow, and nothing else mattered. It was the volcanic eruption Aithne had shown her: an awareness that the land around them was shifting, breaking, heating—and that they were the cause, burning away the old to give life to something new—something stronger, between the two.

Evander's breath was warm on her lips when they separated to breathe. "Finlay."

She caressed the back of his neck, fingers twisting through his hair. "Yes?"

He smiled. "I just needed to say your name. My Finlay." He sucked in a small breath, moving to back away with widened eyes. "I didn't mean to say you're mine."

Finlay held him close, with a breath of a laugh. "I am yours, Evander. I always have been."

The tension melted from his body. He kissed her again, light and sweet. "You know you have my heart, Finlay. You have everything I am."

She rested her chin over his shoulder, leaning fully against him and breathing in his scent of soil and sweat and *Evander* and closing her eyes. Let herself forget everything, for a moment, and bask in his warm embrace as they swayed once more in the silent spring night.

"I love you."

171

"I love you."

After several days that seemed to stretch into an eternity, the next month passed by in a moment. Finlay trained with Jupiter under Calum's guidance from early in the morning to almost twilight. She took an hour midday to rest and eat lunch with Elsie. Each night she ate with the other Knights, trying to gather as much information as she could that might help her free Ghillie.

Aithne had been right to reassure her. Finlay doubted any of them knew what Chief Stewart was doing to Ghillie. She grew to know several of the Knights well, often sitting in a group with Elsie and Isla, Aileen, Cormac, Meric, John, and Angus. Calum even joined them sometimes, which Meric told Finlay she should take as a sign of encouragement that he liked her, if he wanted to be near her more than the hours they trained each day.

Many nights, after dinner, she would go to the healing den to scour Moira's books, studying the herbs and creations she'd worked with for years in a way she never had before in the hopes of finding something to help Ghillie. Something to counteract anything the chief would give him that might impact his perception of things. Something to pull him from the stupor in which he lived daily. Moira seemed to think she'd finally realized she liked working in the healing den. Finlay pretended to have a new fondness for it for her sake. It would keep suspicion from her activities anyway, if Moira spread word that Finlay was a late bloomer when it came to 'the healing urge' as she called it.

The fact that even if she found something, she wouldn't be able to bring it to Ghillie, didn't deter her. Finlay did try walking to the dormitory again, a few days after finding Ghillie. She could go into the main doorway, but each step beyond that point brought that painful, sickened feeling to her gut, and she'd abandoned the effort about halfway to Ghillie's prison.

Her training regimen and study at the healing den left little time for leisure, and after going nearly a week without significant time there, Finlay made herself take a break every other day to go to the sanctuary and spend time with Evander. All of the dragon eggs had hatched, and Evander was busy making sure they had all the love and care they could want during the day, in addition to his normal responsibilities. Finlay went with him to play with the cuddly creatures when she first reached the sanctuary, on the nights she visited.

Most nights she did this she was so tired they would barely go for a walk after playing with the dragons before she was ready for bed, but the bit of time she spent with him—quietly, just the two of them—restored her soul in the same way sleep restored her body. The stress of knowing Ghillie was still suffering but being unable to do anything, seeing the chief's nearly constant looks, drained her almost as much as all of the physical training. She needed the time with Evander, and sometimes Forrest. Those stolen moments with Evander . . .

"Finlay? You asleep with your eyes open?"

Finlay blinked and came back to herself at Angus's question, lifting her cheek from her hand. The dining room had mostly emptied. Finlay hadn't realized she'd gone so far into her thoughts. Last time she'd paid attention, their table had been almost full. Now, only she, John, Angus, and Elsie remained. "Sorry. No, but I am tired."

"My da slept with his eyes open sometimes," Angus said. "Not very often, but it was unsettling."

"You think everythin's unsettlin', worrywart," John said.

Angus shrank a little in his seat.

"Today marks a month since we started training," Elsie announced.

"One more month and we're full Knights," Finlay said, meeting Elsie's gaze with a trace of a smile.

"We don't need another month of trainin'," John said. "We're ready to go on patrol now!"

"They know what they're doing," Angus said.

"Do they? Or do they just want to keep us from outshinin' 'em?" A glint entered his eyes, and he stood and leaned over the table, palms flat on its surface. "I've heard the chief talkin'. He says we're among the strongest to be trained. If he's sayin' it, what's to keep us from becomin' full Knights now other than a silly ceremony?"

"We still have more to learn," Finlay said.

"We'll always have more to learn," John countered. "There's a time when the best learnin' comes from action. Now's that time. I'm goin' out on patrol."

Angus stood, sending his chair skittering back. "You can't!" It was the loudest Finlay had ever heard him.

John walked around the table and moved up close to Angus, towering over him. "You gonna stop me?"

Angus swallowed hard and opened his mouth to answer. Finlay rushed to stand at his side, as did Elsie. "Angus is right," Finlay said quickly. "You can't go on patrol by yourself."

"Never said I'd be goin' alone. I expect you lot to come with me."

"Why would we do that?" Elsie asked.

"Because you want it, too. You want to be out there, makin' a difference instead of just trainin'. I see the way you act when we practice. You want this just as much as me, only I'm the one willin' to break a rule to do it. To prove we can help fight against those good for nothin' Mages now, instead of bein' left behind another month."

"But it is breaking a rule," Angus said.

John stared at him. "Some rules are meant for breakin'. A true Knight would feel the same."

Angus flinched as if struck.

"Tonight, at midnight," John said, looking from Finlay to Elsie. "They'll be back from their patrol and long since in bed, none the wiser to what we're doin'. Are you comin' with me?"

Finlay was the one to respond first. "Yes."

Angus looked at her with shock, and more than a little betrayal. Elsie patted Finlay's shoulder. "I always say it's better to ask forgiveness than permission. I'm in too."

"Why?" Angus asked Finlay.

"Because she's not a ruttin' coward," John said. "I expect you to keep quiet, Angus."

Angus had his shoulders squared but looked down under the force of John's gaze. Apparently pleased, John relaxed his tense stance, told Finlay and Elsie he'd see them soon, and left.

"You're not a coward," Finlay told Angus.

Angus wouldn't look up from the floor. "Maybe I am."

"I think you're brave in a different way than John," Finlay continued. She touched his arm. "Don't let him make you think you're not a true Knight."

He walked away with a mumbled acknowledgement and a quick stride, and Elsie turned on Finlay as they headed out of the dining hall. "Okay, why do you want to do this? Normally I'd be convincing you."

Elsie couldn't know the real reason: that Finlay hoped to find a solution for Ghillie outside the confines of the village. The knowledge that it had been a month since she'd seen him, that he was still suffering . . . she had to take some kind of action, and knew storming into Ghillie's chamber wouldn't solve anything. If there wasn't some kind of immediate solution outside the village, maybe the change of scenery would jog something in Finlay's brain. What if what the Sisters had shown her could help? She hadn't pieced through most of it yet.

"You're really quiet again. You keep doing that lately. Talking to your inner dragon?"

Finlay breathed in slowly. "No, but I think she'll agree this is necessary. I've thought it through. I think it's the right course of action. Calum said he's been seeing more activity near the border. He isn't positive it's Mages, but if it is? It's best if we prove we can help defend against them."

Elsie's lips tugged up. "Absolutely."

There was almost no moon in the sky above, everything covered in an inky blanket, save where starlight pierced through. Finlay used to love nights such as this, rare as they were. Everything on the ground became harder to see, but the stars never seemed

177

to shine as brightly as when the moon stepped back from her spotlight. It was the clearest the night sky ever was, and without the heavy clouds usually hanging overhead, she could appreciate its beauty from the ground.

Finlay left for the sanctuary a bit earlier than she thought Elsie and John would, knowing she had a greater distance to cross to find Jupiter. She actually summoned a spark to help light her path, holding it in her palm. She'd conferred with Aithne minutes before, and walked with greater confidence knowing the phoenix dragon supported her decision. Aithne was as anxious to find a solution as Finlay.

You have a special assignment? Jupiter asked once Finlay found him, woke him, and asked for his help. He seemed particularly grouchy at having been woken in the middle of the night.

"You could say that," Finlay said.

You did say that.

"And you could say it too."

Feeling cheeky tonight, aren't we? So why are we breaking the rules?

Finlay took that as confirmation he would take her, and climbed onto his back. "I can't tell you yet. Just in case it hurts you. But trust me when I say it's crucial, and it's for a dragon's benefit."

Finlay had puzzled over the chief's wording particularly hard that day, tired of her lack of progress in freeing Ghillie, and found a potential loophole: he'd said she couldn't breathe a word to another person. He never said anything about telling a dragon.

She wasn't sure, though, and wouldn't risk hurting Jupiter or another dragon. She could, however, let Jupiter know she was on a mission.

They met Elsie and Kenna and John and Jasper. Elsie tossed her the bag of training gear she'd taken from the armory. It had been agreed upon that, since Elsie and John both slept in the dormitory, they would sneak into the armory to grab their gear, and Finlay's as well, just before meeting at the sanctuary. Finlay hastened to get everything on, touched the dagger at her side, and held on tightly as Jupiter took flight.

You can't tell me exactly what's wrong, because you think it might hurt me. I'm not sure what kind of magic is involved there, but I understand your reluctance to test it. What do you need me to look for?

Finlay strained her eyes, looking at the ground below. "I wish I knew."

Insightful as ever.

The remark didn't contain the sarcasm it usually did. They scoured the mountainous terrain, eyes on the ever-changing line where land met sky in the search for something out of the ordinary. They flew for what had to be over an hour, Finlay's frustration climbing with each minute a solution eluded her. The only thing they spotted were the hulking forms of a few mountain trolls, looking for food.

Jupiter's voice broke the silence. *Fire.*

Finlay and Jupiter had taken the position on the right. The faint glow of a fire showed in one of the caverns far to the right—probably as far inside as whoever had lit it dared, but still close enough to the outside world to vent properly. On a night cloudier than this, it probably wouldn't be noticed.

"I know that," Finlay said to herself. That cavern seemed familiar.

Should we tell the others?

"I think it's better to avoid any confrontation if we can help it," Finlay whispered.

"Mages!" John hissed.

Finlay swerved and looked in the opposite direction, but barely had time to spot anything before John and Jasper took off in a dive. She forced down an exasperated sigh. "Jupiter, follow them, please."

Adrenaline coursed through Finlay with the steep dive that sent her stomach up near her throat and her hair flying back. It wasn't purely the good kind, though, anxiety paling the excitement. John jumped off Jasper's back the instant he touched the ground, reaching for the sword in his scabbard. The five people sleeping near the smoldering remains of a fire, four men and one woman, jumped upright with a start.

Up close, Finlay took in the fine clothing they wore. Her eyes went to their hands, where she spotted golden rings glinting on the fingers of four of the people: three of the men and the woman. The fifth member of the party, a teenage boy who looked no more than fourteen, had a thin necklace around his throat, with a golden ring hanging from it. They were definitely Mages. Was there a difference in their ranks, for some to wear the rings on their fingers, others strung on necklaces, or was it merely personal preference?

Finlay doubted John had known for certain that these were Mages before he'd dived into an assault. He clearly had an attack in mind.

"What is this?" the woman asked.

"Looks like they brought Robin a dragon to slay," a man probably close to Meric's age said with a grin.

John raised his heavy, two-handed sword threateningly. "You don't want to be tryin' that. We've come to tell you to get lost, or we'll make you."

"We've done nothing wrong," the woman said with a sneer.

"You've murdered dragons!" John roared. "Innocent creatures that trusted you!"

"We follow our queen," the oldest man said.

"We follow our hearts," Elsie countered, gripping her weapon tightly.

Finlay's hand hovered over her dagger.

"Your hearts told you to ambush us?" the woman asked.

"They tell us to protect dragons," John said. "If that means gettin' rid of disgraces of human beins' like you lot, I won't lose any sleep."

He lunged before fully finishing his statement. The oldest man stiffened when John's sword pierced his gut, face slackening. Finlay's mouth dropped. John yanked his sword free when the man started to fall, and in seconds the man's lifeless body slumped to the ground.

Finlay lost track of everyone's movements after one tense, frozen moment. She blocked a heavy blow from the burly man who'd stayed silent throughout the exchange, and knew Elsie and John clashed with the other two Mages. The boy stayed back.

"Who's a murderer now?" the man who had charged Finlay cried. He lunged at her again, fingers bared like claws. Finlay had thought in the split second before she'd gone to block his first blow that he was so enraged he forgot his weapon. But he didn't need one. Purple haze coated his fingertips, more dragon-like than human, the short, rounded nails now long, sharp claws. The claws slashed against Finlay's bracer, leaving gouges and a hissing purple smoke.

This Mage had to have killed some type of poison dragon. One wound from those mutated claws could be deadly.

Finlay staggered backward, reassessing. She didn't want to kill anyone. She also couldn't let herself be killed. Not only did she really not want that to happen, but she was the only one who knew about Ghillie. There were ways to fight without killing, but John had killed one of them without warning. These three, or at least the one fighting Finlay, wanted blood in return, and likely wouldn't be turned around easily.

Finlay's hands warmed, the fire in her veins rising to the surface, and her hand shook over the hilt of her dagger. The warring instincts to use fire or her dagger cost her precious seconds.

The Mage thrust his hands forward, and a jet of poisonous spray shot from beneath his claws. The dragon beside Finlay lunged forward, jaw open wide, bright fire rising in the back of his throat. The air shimmered with the heat, and Finlay watched in a stunned kind of amazement as the torrent of flame he breathed obliterated the poison meant for her.

The Mage shrank back, arms raised to keep the fire from reaching his face. Jasper looked at her with one eye, the fire calming in his throat.

"Thank you," Finlay told him, voice shaking.

He dipped his massive head and turned, and Finlay turned with him to see the others. The blood on John's claymore gleamed a red-black in the night. He whirled against the female Mage like a vicious hurricane, more strength than finesse. She seemed an equal match with her own blade. Elsie had her war hammer in one hand, shield in the other, and had been forced into a defensive stance by the other fighting Mage—she had to keep her shield high to fend off the blue flames he breathed, preventing her from getting in close and striking.

So much fire . . .

The man who'd attacked Finlay was on the ground, moaning and staring at his severely burned arms and hands. Finlay ran around him and came up behind the Mage fighting Elsie, drawing her dagger in the process. The man saw her but couldn't do much, with the fresh bout of fire he was breathing toward Elsie, and failed to block the pommel of Finlay's dagger. It collided with the top of his head in a heavy downward blow, and he toppled to his knees, his fire sputtering out with a wheeze. Elsie ran forward and smacked him in the face with her shield, and he dropped the rest of the way to the ground, out cold.

The one with the poison dragon powers staggered to his feet, and Elsie went at him from one direction while her dragon partner, Kenna, approached him from behind. They definitely had that handled. The boy with the Mages rested on the ground near the one John had killed, visibly shaking. He didn't have a weapon drawn, and Finlay hesitated when she stood before him. "You don't seem like a killer to me. Don't let them make you one."

Jasper roared at that moment, and Finlay spun with a sickening dread twisting her gut. The storm John and the female Mage had been in with their swords, which had prevented anyone from getting close enough to help, had calmed in the worst way. What Finlay could only describe as a shadow surrounded John and, in an instant, sank inside him. John gave a strangled gasp and fell back, his sword falling from his grip.

The shadow rose out of John and whooshed back to the female Mage, who smiled at him sadistically.

She didn't have time for more than that before Jasper lunged forward and snapped her in half. Finlay rushed past the feet that were all that remained of the Mage, sliding to her knees by John's side. "What did she do?" she demanded.

John was awake, his mouth parted. His limbs twitched. He stared at Finlay with blown pupils, horror in his eyes.

"You'll never recover from that one," the last Mage said through a bruised, swollen face, where he lay on the ground. "Shadow soul attacks on the inside."

"We need to get him back!" Finlay yelled to Elsie, ignoring the Mage.

"Are you coming with us?" Elsie shouted at the boy.

"What?"

"You haven't killed a dragon. You don't have to be our enemy. But you need to decide now!" Finlay cried, hooking her arms beneath John's shoulders to pull him toward Jupiter.

"Don't be a traitor!" the Mage said.

I'll take him, Jasper growled.

Finlay pulled John the extra foot to Jasper instead of Jupiter. The giant dragon reached his long neck back and gripped John's sleeve with careful teeth, helping Finlay pull him onto his back.

"What do I do?" the boy asked, standing by Finlay's side.

"Get on Jupiter's back, and hold on," Finlay directed.

"Didn't see it coming," John said in a labored whisper.

Finlay made a shushing sound and pulled him close. "It's all right, you'll be fine."

"So dark," he breathed. "No point. No reason . . ."

Finlay held him tightly as they ascended on Jasper's back, both to keep him from falling off and in an attempt to soothe him. He was limp aside from the trembling of his limbs that she doubted he could control. She'd wanted to scold him for his impulsivity, but all she found herself doing as they flew was murmuring reassurances that everything would be fine. She couldn't see anything wrong with him physically. Even when he stopped talking, and his shaking slowed and ceased, she cradled him against her, whispering and staring down at his face.

She barely realized when they reached the village, and wouldn't have if the boy hadn't cried out when they tried to go past the borders of the sanctuary. She heard Elsie tell the dragons to bring them to the compound instead, and felt Jasper land on the ground minutes later. At that point, still staring at John, Finlay let herself take in the vacant glassiness of his stare, the perfect stillness of his chest.

"Finlay, how is he?" Elsie asked.

Finlay couldn't look away from those unseeing eyes. "He's dead."

CHAPTER TWENTY-TWO

Elsie tried to pull John from Finlay's grasp, and Finlay automatically tightened her hold on his arms.

"Let go."

Finlay forced herself to look away from John, and found Elsie standing right next to her. She wasn't entirely sure why she couldn't let John go. She knew she couldn't do anything to help him. She'd gotten to know him over the last month, as they'd trained together, but they hadn't been particularly close. He'd been a bully to Angus, arrogant and sometimes mean, and so rash. Diving down to that group, murdering a Mage and starting a fight . . .

The night's events wouldn't release her thoughts. His final words echoed in her ears, unrelentingly.

"Jasper, help them down."

Jasper angled his body, and Finlay slid off his back and onto the ground, pulling John with her. Elsie sat down beside her, knocking against her shoulder

"It's okay," Elsie said in a surprisingly gentle voice.

Jasper stood and spread his wings. *I'll go get Evander and Moira.*

"It's my fault," Finlay said once the buffet from his wings was gone, again in that deadened voice. It fell harshly over her ears, and understanding dawned on her. Understanding didn't make her feel better. If she hadn't agreed to go, maybe he wouldn't have gone out. She could have asked Angus to tell others, just after they left, so they would be caught. There were so many things she could have done differently. She didn't kill John, but she was absolutely responsible for his death.

"No. It's that Mage's fault. And John's, for picking a fight in the first place." Elsie was quiet for a moment. "What do you think she did to him? Scare him to death?"

Finlay shook her head numbly. "He was scared, but it was more than that. The fear faded. Everything faded. It was like he lost the will to fight, or do anything." *No point. No reason.* "Like he lost the will to live."

Elsie shivered. "I'm not upset Jasper ate her."

A savage part of Finlay agreed with Elsie. She sucked in a breath and looked around, remembering the boy. He stood off to the side, under Jupiter's watchful eye, standing as small as he could.

"Was I right?" she asked him.

He swallowed hard and nodded. "Catherine killed a shadow dragon. Her shadow soul drains a person's life force and makes them want to die. With their life functions so low, their readiness to die makes it happen."

"That's despicable," Elsie said.

His voice bordered on musical, high and light. "I didn't know her long, but I could tell she wasn't a good person. She could have used it differently if she'd wanted to."

Finlay slid John's body from her lap, cushioning his head to lay him flat on the ground. "That fight shouldn't have happened."

"It absolutely shouldn't have," a stern voice said. Chief Stewart was jogging over, belly bouncing with each step, dressed in nightclothes with a robe uncinched over them. Several Knights followed just behind him, also looking as if they'd come straight from their beds. Angus stood in the back, horror clear in every aspect as he saw John's prone figure on the ground.

"What happened?" Meric asked.

"Let's wait for Evander and Moira, so we don't have to explain twice," Elsie said, pointing. Jasper was about to land.

"Finlay?" Evander called. He jumped from Jasper's back before Jasper fully stopped and ran to her side, agitation clear.

"I'm not hurt," she reassured him, and he kissed her forehead with a sigh of relief.

Chief Stewart cleared his throat, pulling his robe closed and crossing his arms. "Your explanation, girls. Now."

Finlay let Elsie do most of the talking, only really chiming in to describe how she did everything she could for John while they flew back. Everyone listened intently, Evander standing beside Finlay with his warm, calloused hand gripping hers, Moira kneeling by John's body to inspect him.

"You claim it was John's fault the fight happened?" Chief Stewart asked once they'd finished.

"John was impulsive," Cormac said, separating himself from the group of Knights. His voice was thick with grief. "I knew he was frustrated that he couldn't be made a full Knight sooner. I'm sure he thought this was the fastest way to prove his worth."

"It was foolish," Calum said. "On all of your parts. Angus, I understand your reluctance to get your friends in trouble, but you should have come to us sooner than you did. Finlay, Elsie, I can't begin to understand the recklessness you displayed tonight." He paused, the sting of his calm voice worse than if he'd shouted. "Because of your actions, though, it might be best to consider making you full Knights earlier than usual."

Chief Stewart whirled. "You want to reward them?"

"Absolutely not. But they've been punished enough. They have to live with this guilt for the rest of their lives. We've been noticing more scouts near the border. They say they fought a band of five. Four," Calum amended, looking at the boy still standing meekly beside Jupiter. He looked back to Chief Stewart. "The fight we've been preparing for is coming. We should use all the resources we have."

Evander's hand tensed in Finlay's.

"We'll discuss it. As for the young Mage," Chief Stewart said, taking a step toward the boy.

Fear flashed in his eyes. Something almost maternal rose in Finlay, and she moved in front of the boy. "He hasn't killed a dragon. He didn't raise a hand against us. I offered him safety."

"Which wasn't yours to offer," Chief Stewart said. Silence. "You may stay on a probationary basis. But it will be on Finlay's watch. If you do anything to harm someone here, you'll both face the consequences."

Finlay met the cold eyes with a steady gaze. He would find some reason to make the boy leave, she was sure, and in doing, he would make Finlay leave. He would use this situation to get rid of her, and make sure his secret remained intact.

"You can stay with me," Finlay told the boy.

"Go rest," Moira directed Finlay and Elsie. "I'll help Kyle prepare John for the ceremony of life."

"We'll pick up training mid-morning," Calum told Finlay. "Everyone, back to bed!"

Elsie went over to Isla, who motioned for her to talk. Finlay didn't envy Elsie that conversation, and feared she would have words from Isla the next day. Evander walked with Finlay to Jupiter and the boy. "I'll go back to the sanctuary with the dragons. Do you want me to come after?"

Finlay leaned in to kiss Evander's cheek. "No, thank you. But I'm glad you offered."

I'm sorry I didn't help, in the fight, Jupiter said. *I froze. I . . . I'm not even sure why.*

A fresh batch of concern piled onto the heaping amount in Finlay's thoughts. Jupiter, showing regret? Admitting a mistake? "I froze too," Finlay told him. "Please, just get some rest."

He dipped his head, let Evander climb onto his back, and took off, Kenna and Jasper flying behind them. Finlay faced the boy, who'd been silently staring at her. He was slender and slight, about a head and a half shorter than her, and Finlay was decently tall herself. It was his face that made him look younger, with smooth, youthful warm beige skin. Big, dark eyes, with a slight curve to them. Fine cheekbones. Raven hair, a bit long, overhanging his forehead. She'd guessed him to be fourteen, but upon closer inspection, she had no idea.

She made her voice as gentle as she could. "Follow me." They walked toward the compound entrance. The clarity of the stars was fading; daylight would overtake it soon. "What's your name?"

"Robin."

"I'm Finlay."

"I thought they were good people," Robin said in a small voice. "I've been looking for so long . . . I thought they could be good, if they tried."

Finlay looked at him out of the corner of her eye. "How long were you with them?"

"A few months."

"And where were you before that?"

He stared straight ahead. "A lot of places."

They reached Finlay's cottage, and she opened the door to let him walk in first. She had to try one more question, and broached it as carefully as she could. "When you said you'd been looking for so long, what did you mean? What were you looking for?"

He sighed. "Home."

Finlay's heart constricted as she lit the candle by the door and went to start a fire. "You can stay here as long as you'd like," she said with her back to him. "Okay? You can use my bed, too."

She stood and went to turn around, but froze before she could when Robin came up and hugged her from behind. Finlay put her hands over his, feeling the way he trembled. He stilled, seeming to relax more, and then drew back, retrieving one of the two blankets from her bed, bringing it to her cozy chair, and curling into a ball atop it, nestled in the blanket. Finlay thought he was asleep in seconds.

She put her cloak over him as well, noticing that with the blanket beneath him it didn't fully cover his torso. Then she changed out of her gear and into nightclothes and got into her bed, fully expecting her numb mind to slide into sleep immediately. Except it wasn't numb. It was . . . warm? Her hands warmed as well, steadily, and it took her several seconds to realize Aithne must be trying to get her to visit the mindscape.

"I didn't realize you could communicate with me like that," she said once she appeared there.

Aithne shook her head. **It's just the feeling. I can't make you produce fire. But it got the point across. We need to talk.**

"I know it was a lot. I'm still kind of processing everything."

Not about the fight, Finlay, though I do regret not realizing what was happening sooner. It's possible my magic could have helped him, and even saved him.

Finlay's mouth went dry. "Are you serious?"

It's possible. But don't think on that. We need to talk about the boy. He is not as harmless as you believe.

That protective instinct swirled again in Finlay's gut. "What makes you say that?"

Aithne fixed her glowing orange eyes on Finlay.

He's a faerie.

CHAPTER TWENTY-THREE

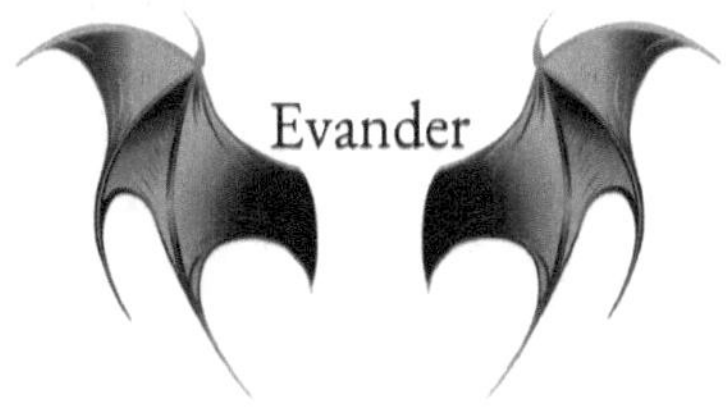

She could have died.

The horrible reality of the events of that night crashed over Evander in a relentless wave, as he and the dragons returned to the sanctuary. John was dead. Elsie and Finlay could easily have met the same fate.

No, he told himself sternly. They were too strong for that.

But John had been strong as well. Death didn't care about a person's strength. It claimed the strong and the weak in equal measure, and everyone in between.

He shook his head to rid himself of this dark line of thought. He was just anxious after the fact. Worried about Finlay, despite knowing she was safe now. And, if he was completely honest, a bit mad at her, for taking this risk. Something was going on with her lately. Something was bothering her, weighing her down, and she wouldn't tell him what it was. He knew whatever the cause, it had something to do with her decision to sneak out tonight. She would have had a plan of some sort.

He just wished she would confide in him. He doubted it was a lack of trust that kept her silent about whatever it was. In his experience, she tended to think she had to shoulder things alone, to keep burdens from falling on others. He was sure that was what she thought she was doing now.

Do you have a crate of ale you can spare? Jasper asked once they landed.

Evander left one hand on Jupiter's neck and turned to face Jasper. The hard-headed dragon—both literally and figuratively—didn't seem at all like himself, sorrow drowning his words.

"I'll see what I can find," Evander promised. "Give me a moment."

I'll be going back to my nest, Jupiter said. *Don't know why I didn't . . .* he trailed off, though Evander suspected he'd been speaking to himself even before going silent. He flew off without another word. Kenna motioned to Jasper, to tell Evander she would stay with him, and Evander raided his pantry for all the ale he could find. He would have to check on Jupiter in the morning.

He found two jugs in the back of his cupboards and poured them into Jasper's mouth after confirming the dragon wanted it. Such a small amount in the massive dragon's body wouldn't do much to dull his pain, but it might make him drowsy enough to sleep right away. That promise met, and after seeing Kenna and Jasper fly back to their respective nests, Evander walked away from his cottage. He needed to hold a baby dragon. He needed to see something innocent and light.

Hey, I thought you were coming back in! Forrest called, flying out of the cottage and staying level with Evander as he walked. He'd woken when Evander searched for the ale.

"I will soon."

Evander felt Forrest's concern, and it warmed his core. When he reached Soren's nest and saw the mother dragon curled around Aerie, that warmth reached his thoughts. Soren stirred at Evander's steps, opening her startling silver eyes.

Is something wrong? she asked.

Aerie shifted, lifted his tiny head, and yawned, pink tongue lolling out in the process. He blinked at Evander and made a cooing sort of sound.

"No," Evander whispered. "Nothing to bother you with right now, anyway. I just wanted to check on the two of you."

Aerie stood and stretched his wings, then stumbled sleepily to Evander, who crouched and held out his hands. The youngling was smaller than Forrest still, more the size of a kitten than a cat, and would be for at least a few more months. He settled in Evander's arms with another loud yawn, laid his head against Evander's chest, and breathed out slowly, going back to sleep.

Evander closed his eyes and cradled the baby dragon for several long moments, Forrest and Soren watching with care. Holding a baby dragon didn't magically negate the bad things from that night, but it reminded him of the good.

Sometimes, that was all he needed to be okay.

Chapter Twenty-Four

Finlay

Finlay's breath left her in a rush. "He's a faerie? How do you—?"

When you touched his hands, I felt his energy. Magic sings in his veins. It's unmistakable.

Finlay sat down on the grass and raked a hand through her hair. She'd heard of the fae before, but they were so secretive that she'd never even glimpsed one. "So he has magic. Do you think he's a threat?"

I don't know anything about him, but I'm sure he would glamour any human or dragon he perceived to be a threat into thinking he was harmless. It would be easy for him, with an instant of eye contact.

"He didn't glamour me," Finlay said.

Aithne lay her head down beside Finlay and flared her fire, warming her. **I think he glamoured Jupiter, during the fight. Jupiter said he didn't know why he froze. If the boy thought Jupiter would attack him . . .**

"Wouldn't Jupiter sense he was a faerie? He flew Robin back here."

Not if he is still under the effects of a glamour. With prolonged contact like that, it could take several hours for it to fade.

Finlay leaned against Aithne's neck. "I don't like thinking like this, Aithne. He seems like he just needs some support. I don't think he's planning to hurt anyone. He could have ended our fight before it started, glamouring everyone there, but he didn't."

Maybe not, but it is important to be aware of his abilities.

Finlay nodded, but couldn't bring herself to share Aithne's suspicions. Other than Jupiter being glamoured. That made sense, as Jupiter would very easily have looked like a threat. Finlay didn't think Robin saw them as a threat anymore. He'd certainly seemed grateful when Finlay offered him sanctuary.

Now that we've addressed that, is there anything I can say to help you deal with what happened tonight?

"I went looking for a solution for Ghillie and helped get John killed. He couldn't have known they were Mages, but he saw people there . . ." Finlay sat upright. "I saw a fire, in one of the caverns. Not far from where we fought the Mages."

Aithne blinked and the landscape around them altered, becoming the stretch of mountains Finlay recalled. **It's familiar,** Aithne said.

It clicked. "It's one of the places I saw in the visions the Sisters showed me!" Finlay stood, walking closer to the cavern with smoke trailing from its entrance. "There's something important about that cavern, Aithne. Maybe I did find a solution for Ghillie, and it's in that cavern!"

The flames along Aithne's wingspan danced higher. **It may be time to involve Elsie and Evander. I know,** she said quickly, when Finlay turned with her mouth open, **I'm the one who encouraged you to keep silent. But I have a feeling you'll need help for this to go smoothly. We both agree it's taken too long already.**

Finlay stared at the cavern image, determination stewing inside her. "I'll free Ghillie within the week."

Another thought murmured at her. A grander thought. *Don't forget the greatest mission,* it said. Ending the rule of Mages. In her determination to help Ghillie, everything outside the settlement became less important. Now, believing she had the start to a solution for Ghillie, that mission rose up again.

Images the Sisters had shown her that day swirled on the outskirts of this thought. The one of herself standing in the castle showed clearest. If someone went to the Mages and infiltrated their ranks . . . could it be her fate to do so? Or was the image of her standing in the castle something in the distant future, after other events had led to the end of the current rule?

You need to sleep, Aithne said. **Let your mind work things out as you rest.**

Finlay sighed. "Goodnight, Aithne."

"Good morning, sleepyhead," Finlay said when Robin stirred.

The boy sucked in a breath and bolted upright. "How long have you been awake?"

"Just a few minutes. I have something important to tell you. A secret. I think you have one too."

Panic crept into his tone. "Look at me, Finlay. I haven't lied to you."

Finlay partially smiled, but didn't meet his eyes. "I know you don't want to hurt me, or anyone. The only reason I know you have a secret is because of mine: I have a dragon living inside me. A phoenix dragon. She sensed your magical energy when you touched me."

In her periphery, she watched the boy's reaction. He stared at her, open-mouthed. "You have a dragon inside you?"

"It sounds strange, but yes. And no one but you, Elsie, and Evander knows. I'm trusting you to keep it a secret, and hoping you trust me to do the same for you. Can I . . . can I see you as you truly are?" she asked more quietly. "No glamour to make you look fully human?"

His breath hitched again. "You really do know."

Despite the fact that he hadn't promised, Finlay brought her gaze to his. Sapphire blue glowed at the edges of his black eyes, blending into the midnight center in a starburst fashion. Definitely not human eyes. The pointed tips of his ears peeked from beneath his hair. Robin didn't seem to breathe while she looked at him, fear and uncertainty in his youthful brow. Finlay didn't look away, and spoke in her most reassuring voice. "I trust you. I want to help you. And I think if we're fully honest with each other, we can do something good."

He swallowed hard. "I didn't do any other kind of glamour on you. Just the light one I do on everyone, to hide my eyes and ears. I didn't make you protect me."

"I know."

"You couldn't know. You wouldn't remember."

Finlay touched his arm. "But I trust you, Robin. Sometimes you meet a person and know right from the start they can be trusted."

He searched her face with those intense blue-black eyes, and then stepped closer and held her tightly. "I thought the energy I sensed from you was just because you're so in tune with dragons. I didn't know humans could bind with them. You're incredible."

Finlay allowed herself to hold him back, wondering if it was Aithne's influence that let her seem to sense Robin's character. Dragon intuition, perhaps, paired with human sentimentality. Something deep in her gut told her she could trust this faerie boy, and whatever concerns Aithne harbored, Robin didn't instill them in Finlay in the slightest. "Special circumstances. I'll tell you the story while I make breakfast. Then we have to find my friend Elsie before training. I need help from both of you."

Robin moved to eat the runny eggs and wheat toast Finlay put in front of him timidly, despite the eagerness she'd seen in his eyes when he saw the steaming food. That changed when he saw her take a giant bite, and he ate with greater gusto and a grin after that. He wiped the back of his hand across his mouth when he was done and chuckled nervously. "That probably wasn't the best manners on my part, but I was starving," Finlay said in response, grabbing both of their plates and bringing them to her washbasin.

"Me too."

"I didn't used to get to eat eggs very often. My rations increased when I started training as a Knight, so I can have them every morning, if I want."

Robin took his plate from her and pumped for her to draw up the water, and washed his plate beside her. "The Mages are all well-off, so they had plenty of food whenever they wanted it. Their breakfast didn't taste as good as yours."

Finlay knew that couldn't be true, since she was only slightly better at cooking than Evander, but the compliment heated her cheeks anyway. Robin dried the plates and put them on her shelf. Finlay took care of the water. That done, Finlay led Robin to the tree where she and Elsie always met. Though they didn't watch Elsie train each morning anymore, they continued meeting at that spot before walking into the compound together for their own training.

Robin fidgeted when he recognized Elsie. "She's my best friend, and I promise you can trust her," Finlay said in a low voice. "But I won't tell her about you. You can decide."

"You took your time," Elsie greeted.

"She made me breakfast," Robin said.

"I was going to make myself breakfast anyway. You didn't make me late for anything." Finlay stepped closer to Elsie and lowered her voice. "Can the three of us talk for a minute?"

Elsie nodded and motioned for them to sit down. The grass was slightly damp from early morning rain, so Finlay spread her cloak—the lighter one she only used to be able to wear in the tail-end of spring and through summer, because she always used to be cold, which was now the only cloak she needed due to hers and Aithne's fire—as wide as she could so both she and Robin could sit on it. The boy didn't have anything with him, having forgotten his pack in the commotion the night before.

Elsie tore off her own shawl and sat down on it. All three faced the lake, as if admiring the view. It lent them the closeness Finlay needed to speak without fear of being overheard.

"Elsie, this is Robin. I told him about Aithne. He can keep it a secret, but I needed him to know. I have something very important I need to tell you." Finlay took a deep breath. "There's a dragon that's really in need of help. No one else knows. I've been trying to figure out how to do that, and I might have a clue, but it'll mean leaving Aerouant Glèidh again. Tonight. I'll need the two of you to cover for me."

"What do you mean, a dragon in need of help?" Elsie asked. Finlay winced at her volume, and Elsie lowered it to normal speaking tones, still louder than Finlay's hushed words. "Is this why you wanted to go with John last night? How long have you known about this dragon?"

"It is, and since we started training."

Elsie studied her, for a moment seeming much more like Isla than herself with the scrutiny in her gaze. "And you can't say more, can you?"

An inkling of relief trickled down Finlay's spine as she shook her head. Elsie understood something bigger was going on. "I can't."

Robin frowned. "Why can't you say more?"

"Finlay likes to keep the weight of things to herself as much as possible," Elsie told him.

Robin stared at Finlay, and his eyes widened. "There's magic involved."

Finlay wasn't sure if he could somehow sense it, or if he simply guessed, but she nodded.

"How can you—never mind," Elsie said. "What do you need us to do, Fin?"

"Just stay at my cottage tonight. Robin, you would be there anyway, but Elsie, I need you to stay there too. Spend the night."

Elsie nodded. "Okay, but I don't get how that helps. I'm thinking you want to make sure no one tries to check you haven't snuck out again, but if someone comes to check that we're both still here, they'll know I'm not you."

Finlay glanced at Robin, whose mouth opened almost comically as he understood what she would ask him to do in that situation. When Finlay returned her attention to Elsie, she found her looking between Finlay and Robin with suspicion. "I won't be long," Finlay told them. "I just need to check something, and I'll come right back. Hopefully with a plan."

Elsie sighed, apparently deciding she didn't need to know whatever was going on with Robin at the moment. "All right."

They stood and walked to the entrance of the compound, waving to Graham as they passed him at his station. Robin snuck to Finlay's side and whispered, "Do you really need Elsie there tonight? I can glamour anyone who comes by into thinking you're there more easily without her."

"It'll throw suspicion off," Finlay whispered back. "And like I said, I really hope to have a plan when I get back, and I'll want to tell the two of you immediately so we can set it in motion."

"You *better* tell me immediately," Elsie said, brushing past Finlay to jog and meet a very irritated-looking Isla. Calum stood near her, standing calmly with his arms loosely crossed over his chest.

"It's been decided," he said without preamble. "We'll have John's ceremony of life at twilight tonight. You'll train harder than ever today and tomorrow. Tomorrow, we'll have your recognition rituals, to bind you to your dragons and mark you as full Knights." He looked from Finlay to Elsie. "Don't make me regret pushing for this to happen early. I believe you're ready. Prove it to the others."

Calum wasn't kidding when he said Finlay and Elsie would train harder than they ever had. Robin ran alongside Finlay when they were directed to run the borderline of the dragon sanctuary first thing. Robin was slight, but kept up with a graceful kind of ease Finlay wasn't sure whether she should attribute to his faerie nature or his physical prowess. There had to be out-of-shape faeries. Probably his personal physical prowess.

To Finlay's great surprise, Calum and Isla ran with them as well. Elsie glared at her sister from the halfway point on—Elsie hated prolonged running. Finlay kept her gaze trained ahead. She deserved to feel this burn in her muscles, and the silent weight of Calum's disapproval. Part of her wished the run fatigued her more, as it had the first several times they'd done it in training, but regular meals packed with nutrients and proteins had allowed her to gain a little muscle mass on her slender frame. The run was tiring, but not exhausting.

They had a few minutes to inhale lunch late in the afternoon. Then they returned to training, meeting with Aileen and Angus—who was remarkably pale and withdrawn—and spending a few hours working on aerial maneuvers with their dragon partners before sparring with their weapons magically blunted. Robin watched them closely all the while.

Dinner was a subdued affair, and almost as fast as lunch. Calum called all the Knights to attention shortly after they'd all seated with their plates full of meat pies and vegetables. "John's ceremony of life will start shortly," he announced. "You have fifteen minutes to finish eating and dress in your gear. We're going to honor John's memory as if he were a full Knight. Meet at the compound entrance."

CHAPTER TWENTY-FIVE

Finlay stood next to Elsie and Angus, slightly apart from the other Knights, who were all dressed in their gear and solid cloaks. The three stood in the front, with a close view of the funerary scene.

Many people had come for the ceremony of life. Robin stood near the back. Jasper crouched amidst the crowd, his eyes closed. Evander stood next to him, hands clasped in front of him, head angled down. John lay on the bier several feet away, his training cloak draped over his body like a shroud. Strong-smelling herbs and flowers were woven into the bier and placed around the body. The little Finlay had eaten for supper sat like a brick in her stomach, grief and anxiety knotting inside her. John had been killed in battle. A bright flame, snuffed out, Chief Stewart would say. He would be a bright flame once more, his body cremated after words were spoken, stories shared. Knights were rarely killed, because they rarely saw combat with Mages, but this was always the way when the tragedy did occur.

Angus trembled, his arm brushing Finlay's. "This is my fault," he said, in a voice so low Finlay barely heard it. "If I'd gone to Aileen sooner, or done something to stop him myself—"

"He would have gone another night," Finlay said. "And I would have gone with him. You don't hold any blame, Angus."

She glanced at him and saw tears already falling down his cheeks. "I didn't want him to die."

A large hand came to rest on Angus's shoulder. A familiar hand, dark, scarred, comforting. "It's all right to feel grief," Meric said, leaning closer. "It's all right to show it." He put his other hand on Finlay's shoulder. "That's why we're here tonight. To grieve, and remember."

Chief Stewart stepped forward, Cormac next to him. Meric pressed reassuringly on Finlay's and Angus's shoulders before stepping back into his place.

"It is never a good thing that brings us to this ground, where we say a final goodbye to those we've lost, yet tonight it seems unusually cruel. John O'Rourke was a spirited young man, with a promising future as a Dragon Knight. Cormac, his mentor, would like to say a few words before we proceed."

Cormac's eyes were rimmed in red, his bangs disheveled, his cheeks bright. He stood next to the bier and stared at the shrouded body atop it for several long seconds. "John was ambitious.

He was daring, and courageous, and probably a bit too self-confident. Gods know I was when I started my training. But he would have made a damn fine Knight. I'd say he was a damn fine Knight. And if those responsible for his death weren't already dead, I'd be hunting them down myself." He took a slow breath and looked at everyone. "But we shouldn't be angry right now. So I'd like to tell you a few stories about the training I did with John."

Cormac spoke for several minutes. Then John's father. Then Calum. Then, to Finlay's great surprise, Angus asked to speak. His voice was small but sincere. "I didn't know John well before we started training. He was a bit older than me. We didn't agree on a lot, and sometimes he could be . . . he could be cruel. But I know he helped me grow, too. I'm not saying cruelty is all right, but I think, in his way, he was trying to make all of us the best Knights we could be. Me, Finlay, Elsie . . . John wanted us all to be able to make a difference. He wanted to make a difference. He was dedicated to fighting the Mages, like all of us should be."

He cast a quick look at John's body before ducking back to his spot next to Finlay, shoulders hunched.

"Would anyone else like to speak?" Chief Stewart asked. Finlay wanted to say something. She knew it had taken a lot of bravery for Angus to speak up, to honestly say how John hadn't always been pleasant or kind but had still been a decent, mostly good, person. She wanted to say how strong John had been at the end. She knew her voice wouldn't reach far enough if she tried.

"You're braver than I am, Angus," she whispered, taking his hand. "I can't say what I know I should. So thank you for saying what you did, for all of us."

Angus applied gentle pressure to her hand.

"If everyone's shared what they wanted to, it's time to say goodbye. This young man's life was cut shorter than it should have been, his inner flame snuffed out. Jasper was John's partner. He's asked to generate the flame that will spark inside John one last time."

Jasper stood and walked closer to the bier. Bagpipe song began. Finlay tensed but still flinched when Jasper opened his mouth and breathed a column of fire, lighting the bier in an instant. The cloak shrouding John and the wooden platform were lost in seconds, indistinguishable from the mass of writhing yellow-white flame. Dragon fire burned hotter and faster than any fires humans could light. A wave of heat emanated from it, burning against Finlay's collar and up her face.

The instinct to step back, to cower behind Meric and wrap her arms around her knees or be wrapped tight in Evander's arms until the raging flames were gone, was strong, especially as her pulse hit an erratic beat and the heated air seemed to choke her. Angus's gentle hand on one side kept her frozen. Elsie's hand on the other side, gripping her hand firmly the second Jasper breathed the fire, kept her stable. Not entirely whole, facing the largest flame she had in years, but able to stand her ground in the face of it, despite her trembling.

It was over in moments, the force of dragon fire reducing the bier and the body atop it to ash swiftly. The strong-smelling herbs and flowers masked other unpleasant scents that would have drifted from the flames, the air heavy with them in a medicinal perfume. When the fire was mostly out, Chief Stewart thanked everyone for coming, and people began walking away. Angus delicately slipped his hand from Finlay's, saying goodnight to her and Elsie and walking with a quick step.

"I better stay with Jasper," Evander said, walking over and taking Angus's place next to Finlay. "He'll need company." He brushed a strand of Finlay's hair back, tucking it behind her ear. His hand lingered on her cheek a few seconds before he drew it back. "Elsie, I assume you're keeping her company tonight?"

"You bet."

Evander smiled lightly. "Good."

Elsie linked her arm with Finlay's as they walked at a more natural pace back toward the main village. Robin waited until they got closer and then walked on Finlay's other side. "You're really pale," he told her. "Are you extremely sad?"

"Finlay doesn't love fire," Elsie said.

Finlay forced her lips to twitch up into something vaguely like a reassuring smile when she looked at Robin. "I'm fine."

Judging from his expression, he knew she was lying, though he didn't press her. They walked back to Finlay's cottage and straight inside, where Elsie insisted on making some tea before Finlay even thought of leaving.

"I can steady your nerves, if you'd like," Robin whispered while Elsie set water to heat over the fire. "A mild glamour."

Finlay's smile wasn't as forced this time. "Thank you, Robin, but I'll pass for now." She went to the kitchen to get cups ready.

"You didn't freak out as much as I thought you would," Elsie said, filling one of the offered cups and handing it back to Finlay.

"I've been working on it with Aithne," Finlay told her.

"Good on you," Elsie said.

The tea was a little too strong for Finlay's liking. She drank it all anyway, and the anxiety that had been roiling within her had mostly faded by the time she finished it. What little remained was due to her plan to go see whoever was in that cavern. Elsie whiled away the time talking to Robin, telling him stories of past adventures she'd had with Finlay—ending with the time Finlay leaned too far over the edge watching Isla train and fell into the lake.

"That's becoming your favorite story, isn't it?"

Elsie smiled at her. "You have to admit it's a good one. I haven't heard of anyone else falling into the lake."

Finlay chuckled. "That's true." She looked out the window and took in how dark it had gotten, and how still. "I think it's safe to go now."

"You're still determined to go alone?" Elsie asked.

Finlay nodded and reassured them she would be back as soon as she could. Putting her gear back on, she drew her summer cloak tight about her and walked to the sanctuary.

The night was warm, as though some of the blazing fire earlier had seeped into the air and saturated it, but fully dark. Finlay didn't see anyone as she made her way. She climbed to Jupiter's nest, whispered her plan to him, and accepted his grumbling complaints wordlessly as he stepped out and let her climb onto his back. He ascended with quiet strokes of his feathery wings, each motion a soft beat against the warm air.

You're sure this is the wisest decision? he asked after he stopped grumbling about how insensitive she could be to his need for sleep, several minutes later.

Finlay laid a hand on Jupiter's neck. "I wouldn't ask you to bring me otherwise."

He increased his speed, bringing them to the cavern they'd spotted the night before and landing at its edge. Smoke drifted from the entrance again, though in more of a wisp than before. Faint firelight rippled inside.

"Hello?" Finlay called, pausing just inside. "Anyone here?"

"Did you bring me a dragon to slay?" A masculine voice replied.

Finlay drew her dagger and crept into the cavern, skirting along the stone wall with it bared in front of her. "Try and you'll regret it."

"All right, all right," the man said, as Finlay rounded the curve and entered the widest part of the cavern. He raised his hands placatingly. The light of his small fire let her see him clearly. He had shaggy black hair down to his chin and stubble lining his jaw, and the palest green eyes Finlay had ever seen. "Had to check, didn't I?"

Finlay kept her dagger ready. "No."

"What's a Knight doing here?" he asked in a casual voice, as if Finlay didn't have a blade pointed at him.

"I'm not a Knight. Not yet. What's a Mage doing here?"

A crooked smile. "I'm not a Mage. Not yet." He moved one hand to hold up the gold ring on a cord around his neck. "Probationary. Haven't killed a dragon yet. Not letting myself go back until I do." His eyes raked over her. "You said you're probationary too. What do you have to do to become a full Knight?"

"Maybe I have to capture a Mage."

"Somehow I doubt that, but if you do, capture away." He let his hands fall to his sides. "That's a fine weapon. Where'd you get it?"

Finlay lowered it slightly, disliking the familiarity in the way he looked at it. "It belonged to my father."

The man sat down and poked his dying fire with a stick, stirring the embers. "Then you should listen to me when I tell you you're on the wrong side."

Finlay stepped closer, still tense. "What do you mean?"

He threw the stick aside, and it clattered on the stone floor. "I mean, a dagger that fine is recognizable. Daggers are presented to those eligible to be in the queen's inner circle when our rings are inscribed, after we've killed a dragon. When it's official. Your father must have been a Mage."

Steeled as Finlay was determined to be, his words cut through to her core. Da's face flitted before her eyes, with the crinkling lines around his eyes from laughter. There was no way her father had killed a dragon. Unless . . .

Vague, blurred recollections of another home before their cottage in the miles of border space between Alocasia and her settlement now flashed across her mind. A finer home, with thick stone and carpentry. It was insubstantial as mist, shrouded enough to be a dream, yet Finlay did know she hadn't been born in that small cottage on the border. She knew Michael had remembered a different kind of life, had noticed that, though both worked very hard, their parents hadn't had the appearances of their few neighbors: the calloused, scarred hands from working all their lives, the firm musculature of their bodies and toughness of their skin—they hadn't shared those characteristics from the start. Meaning they must have come from a different situation. They never talked about their past, aside from short stories about how they courted.

Da always had a smile, except when he talked about dragons. Finlay had never understood why his smile lines vanished when he talked about the magical creatures, because it was clear he loved them. Her grip on the pommel of her dagger tightened. If he'd killed a dragon in his past, that guilt-ridden love made sense. As did the nightmares that would shake him some of the time—those that killed dragons suffered from regular nightmares.

"You didn't know, did you?" the man asked, in a different voice than before.

Finlay struggled to find her voice. "It may be true, but it wouldn't sway me to join the Mages' side. If anything, it should persuade you to abandon them, as my father did. He must have realized he was in the wrong, because as long as I knew him, he spoke against killing innocent creatures." Her voice strengthened. "He would have become a Knight, I'm sure."

The man studied her. "So you don't think dragon murderers are irredeemable."

"I don't know that my father was a dragon killer, but I think most people deserve a second chance."

"A noble sentiment. Speaking of noble, though, I've always wondered something. How can you call yourselves Knights when you broke from Alocasia, and carved off territory in the process? You don't have a kingdom."

Finlay's answer this time was immediate, and charged. "We do have a kingdom. We just need to rid it of the killers who've soiled it and reclaim it."

He rubbed a hand along his jaw. "I can see neither of us will be able to sway the other to change sides tonight. A shame, really, but I'm always up for a challenge. I'll sway you to my side yet. If we ever meet in battle, I won't try to fight you. Can I expect the same courtesy from you?"

Loathe as she was to seem to agree with anything this arrogant man said, Finlay nodded. "I won't fight you."

Her heart beat faster. A probationary Mage, clearly attracted to her . . . she could use this. She could use this, for Ghillie, and for every dragon. But Ghillie first. The other step required more thought.

"I actually have a proposition for you. Don't even think it," she warned, raising her dagger again when she saw a suggestive upturn of his lips. She wasn't normally so quick to violence, but something about this man grated all her nerves. She had to put up with him for a bit longer. "I think we can help each other," she continued several seconds later. "You want to prove yourself as a Mage. I won't help you kill anyone, dragon or person. But making the Chief of the Knights lose his position would benefit you, wouldn't it?"

He quirked one eyebrow. "I wondered why you sought me out. Why would you want to do that, probationary Knight?"

"You have bad leadership. I do as well. How long would it take you to get a few other Mages here?"

"There are many Mages. One with a rather handy method of communication lives not far from here—because of you and your Knights, of course—and can spread word to get a sizable group here within a day." He leaned closer. "You want me to gather Mages, but you don't want us to kill anyone. How does that solve anything?"

Finlay ignored his last question and looked away, hating the guilt creeping like vines around her heart. This was a treasonous plan. Even knowing she had no loyalty to Chief Stewart, the idea of setting up a confrontation between Knights and Mages constricted her chest. "I'll get him to lead tomorrow night. You need to have Mages you trust ready to ambush, but it's only a display of force. No action." She forced herself to meet his eyes. "Is that something you can agree to?"

"I can try to keep my more violent allies from coming."

"Not good enough. I want your word you and your allies won't kill."

He placed one hand over his heart, an infuriating tilt to his lips. "So you'll have it, my beautiful, dangerous lady."

"I'm not your lady."

He looked at her with a straight face. "Maybe not. But you could be, someday."

She turned to leave, but paused at the cavern entrance when he asked her to wait.

"May I know your name? I'll share mine first, but I have to know. I'm Alistair."

She looked over her shoulder to see him standing, looking at her with a bit of eagerness in his pale green eyes. Her irritation faded, for a moment. "Finlay."

He smiled, and Finlay swept from the cavern without another glance. Jupiter crouched to let her climb on without pause, and Finlay could tell he had something he wanted to say. He waited until they were safely in the air before he spoke. *This is dangerous.*

Finlay's confident façade vanished. "I know."

Why do you trust him, even a little?

The Seer Sisters' vision played before her eyes. She'd seen that cavern, in the mass of images and sounds, but she'd also seen a face. His face. Alistair. "The Seer Sisters let me glimpse him, that first day of training, but it's also . . . this feeling I have. I don't trust him, exactly, but I think in this case, he'll stay true to his word because it benefits him. He'll get a positive reputation if he can say he organized a display that crippled the Knights."

You don't think you're rushing into things, doing this tomorrow?

"*I've known about the dragon for a month, Jupiter!*"

The words ripped free of her chest in a snarl that made both Finlay and Jupiter flinch. Finlay's eyes widened, and she took a breath to calm her voice. "I can't let him suffer any longer. I'll go mad, thinking about it."

Jupiter was silent for so long Finlay was certain he was mad at her for her outburst. Then he spoke, in a surprisingly gentle tone. *I was wrong to ever have doubted your sincerity.*

Finlay squeezed her eyes shut tight. The tears broke through anyway, trickling from the corners of her eyes. She hated those tears for falling, hated herself for being selfish enough to cry about it, but there it was, all the same: the day she'd been dreaming of for years, in which she finally became a Knight, was in reach, and she still wouldn't be able to catch it. She could have told Alistair to have his fellow Mages ready in two days' time. She could have let herself go through the binding ceremony and accepted the rank of Knight, and celebrated with Elsie and Evander.

She really couldn't, though. She'd let this go on for too long already. If she didn't become a true Knight, so be it.

Easy to think. Harder to accept. Hot tears flew from her cheeks as Jupiter brought her home. Finlay let them, silently letting the grief ease. These tears needed to be gone by the time she and Jupiter reached the settlement. There wasn't time to wallow. Elsie and Robin would expect to hear her plan, and she needed to be fully confident when she shared it.

Her fingers grazed the jeweled pommel of her dagger, and she took in a final shuddering breath as Aerouant Glèidh came into view. In twenty-four hours, Chief Stewart would be exposed as the dragon-torturer he truly was.

CHAPTER TWENTY-SIX

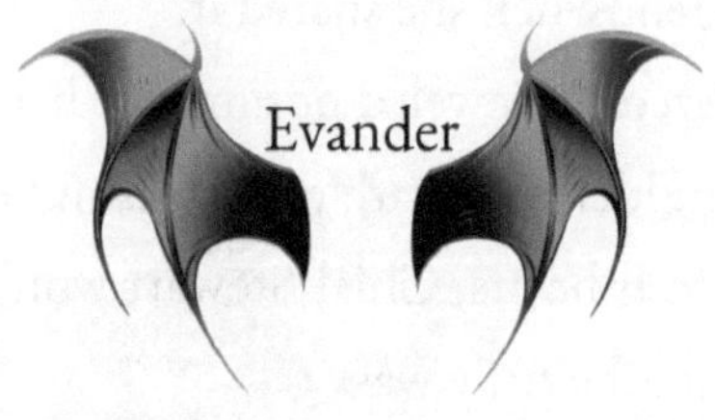

Evander didn't think he would see Finlay most of the next day after John died. He remembered Calum saying they would be training hard all day, and knew the ceremony of life would take place that night. He would be able to check on her there, and rest easy in the meantime knowing Elsie was by her side, making sure she didn't drown in guilt.

He had several things to tend to, himself, the first of which being checking on Jasper, Kenna, and Jupiter. "Ready, Forrest?" Evander asked after putting his porridge bowl in the wash basin.

Forrest licked a speck of porridge off his snout while Evander took his smaller bowl. *Daily rounds, plus a bit extra, here we come!* He paused, lowering his head slightly. *Is it wrong to not be overly sad today?*

"Things always look better in the morning," Evander told him. "What happened last night was a tragedy, but we move on. It's the way of the world. Having energy and enthusiasm doesn't mean you're not a little sad inside. I think it's helpful if you go about with your usual smile, Forrest. Jasper will definitely need to see it."

Forrest flew in close, landing on Evander's shoulder and nuzzling his face, and flew to his side again. Jasper nested near Gaea and a large cluster of dragons, near the base of the mountains. Evander and Forrest approached quietly when they saw his immense form lying still in his nest, even in the bright midmorning light. Evander paused when he heard slow, rhythmic breathing, and saw the rise and fall of Jasper's chest.

"Let's not wake him," he whispered. "We don't know how long he was awake."

Much of the night, a feminine voice said. Turning, Evander saw Kenna walking near. *He didn't want my company, but I watched from a distance until he finally passed out.*

"How are you doing?" Evander asked.

I'm bitter I didn't get to burn the Mage that did it before Jasper ate her, but I suppose Jasper needed that closure himself.

Let us know if you need anything, Forrest said.

Kenna nodded and walked away, and Evander set his sights up the mountainside. "Now to check on Jupiter." He'd only made the climb to Jupiter's nest a few times, because he knew the dragon wasn't overly fond of other dragons or of people. Finlay said he was growing on her, but still seemed to prefer his distance from just about everyone. That was fine—as long as Evander was sure his mental state was all right after the events of last night, he would leave the dragon in peace.

"Jupiter?" he called minutes later, standing on the ledge below the storm dragon's nest. "Are you in there?"

His mottled gray and yellow snout appeared, and he fixed sharp amber eyes on Evander as he leaned his head out of the nest. *About time you came.*

You could have come to us, Forrest grumbled.

"What's wrong?"

I was hoping Finlay would be with you if I waited for you to come to me. She needs to know as well. Remember how I said I couldn't think why I froze last night? Evander nodded, and Jupiter continued. *It took several hours away from his influence for it to wear off, but I'm certain now: that boy who came back with us is a faerie.*

Forrest had been hovering in the air near Evander's head, but at these words the regular flaps of his wings faltered, and he dipped level with Evander's stomach before he recovered himself. *A faerie?*

Evander frowned at Jupiter. "What makes you so sure?"

Some dragons are sensitive to the magic in others. It's how I sensed Aithne living inside Finlay when we first met. I felt the magic inside that boy. He cast a glamour when we first looked at him, to make him appear human, and I'm sure he cast another glamour on me during the fight, to keep me from joining. Made me believe I was too scared, or something. You can't question it in the moment, with glamours. Then he rode on my back all the way back here, and I barely had a thought in that time. He kept me from thinking about him. Glamours usually start with eye contact, and they can be prolonged through touch. It only wore off fully before dawn, when I remembered the magic I felt emanating from him.

"He looks human."

It only takes the fae an instant to cast a light glamour like that, to hide their non-human features.

"How do you know? What do you know about faeries?"

Jupiter harrumphed. *I traveled in my adolescence. I believe most faeries live across the southern sea, closer to where I hatched. That's where I've had my experiences with them, at any rate. Most are flippant regarding the use of their powers, treating humans and magical creatures as whatever they desire most in the moment: companions, playthings, or pests. Fickle as toddlers of any species, even fully grown. Suffice it to say my experiences with them were . . . informative. And destructive enough for me to leave the area completely, seeking a permanent home elsewhere.*

Jupiter had always been a private dragon. Antisocial, really. Evander jumped on the opportunity to learn a bit more from him. "You were born near the main homeland of faeries?"

No. I encountered groups of them exploring the islands. If I ever saw their true home, if they even have one, they stripped me of the memory. As it is, my time with faeries is somewhat blurred, but shaped enough to know I prefer to stay away from them.

Evander didn't share the thought that came to mind. Perhaps, if the faeries Jupiter had encountered had used their abilities to pluck memories of their home from his mind, they'd also impacted his view of them. What better way to keep outsiders away than leaving them with an impression of cruelty?

So faeries are bad news? Forrest asked, voice tight.

"You can't generalize like that."

They're dangerous. You can't argue with that, Evander.

Evander met Jupiter's eyes. "They can be dangerous. As can you. Even me."

Is he going to hurt Finlay? Forrest asked. *He went home with her.*

Evander's chest tightened, but it was superficial. He didn't truly think Finlay was in danger. "If he's really that skilled with glamours, he could have made Finlay, Elsie, and the dragons forget they'd seen him, and gone on his merry way. Something motivated him to come here."

He must want something from us, Jupiter said.

"Maybe that something isn't bad," Evander reasoned. He pushed down his concerns that the faerie boy was up to something devious. Jupiter, and Forrest, seemed inclined to think that way, and he could listen to them more later if he needed. He would rely on his usual instincts, and give the boy the benefit of the doubt until either the boy proved he deserved it, or the alternative.

We still need to make sure Finlay knows, Forrest said. He flew around and looked at Evander face-to-face, yellow eyes comitpletely serious.

She may already, Jupiter said. *If I sensed the boy's magic, Aithne might have as well, and she certainly would have told Finlay.*

Forrest's gaze didn't waver, demanding an answer from Evander. "Finlay is safe today, training with Elsie and the others. We'll check on her as soon as we can, I promise." Forrest didn't look away. "Want to go check on her now? Don't interrupt training, but just get a look at her, to ease your mind?"

Forrest softened and threw his wings back with purpose, flying down the mountainside and heading to the compound.

You're truly not worried at all? Jupiter asked.

Evander looked at him. "I'm always a little worried, where Finlay's concerned. Forrest will alleviate the bit of worry I do have."

Jupiter grumbled something incoherent. Evander stayed put until Forrest returned, what had to be fifteen minutes later, and reported that everything looked fine. *They're doing an awful lot of running,* he said. *They didn't see me. The faerie is with them.*

"Robin," Evander corrected, gentle but insistent. "Like I said, I'll check on her at John's ceremony of life," he promised.

They kept busy the rest of that day, checking on all the babies and making their usual rounds, asking if anyone needed anything, monitoring the healing of wounds, etc. Evander spoke with Jasper about an hour before they had to leave, determined he was off but not unreasonably so, and stayed with him until they went to the ceremony site, where he and Jasper stood near the front.

Evander searched the growing crowd and found Finlay immediately by her bright coppery hair. She stood next to Elsie, and in front of Meric, so although he didn't get to meet her eyes before the ceremony started, a thrum of relaxation went through him. Even with the blaze she was about to see, she would be fine.

His eyes found Robin, standing in the back of the crowd. He didn't look at the boy's eyes, but inspected him from the corner of his own. Again, doubt as to the validity of Jupiter and Forrest's fears filled him. The boy seemed vaguely like a lost kid. Evander doubted he meant any harm.

He would talk to Robin tomorrow, and find out for sure.

Chapter Twenty-Seven

Finlay had mustered her confidence again by the time she returned to her cottage. She found Elsie and Robin in very similar positions to those they'd had when she left, at least two hours before.

"Have you moved at all?" she asked as she hung up her cloak.

Robin jumped up with an eager smile. "You're back! No one came by."

"I ate most of your crackers," Elsie said. "I stood up to get those."

Finlay breathed a laugh. "Well, I'm glad you liked them. They'd been in my cupboard for a few weeks."

"I could tell."

Robin analyzed Finlay with his blue-black eyes. "You seem better than before. Did something go well?"

"You could say that." Finlay took off her gear as she explained, starting with the bracers on her arms. She undid the sturdy belt around her waist last, removing her dagger from its sheath there and hooking the blade through her belt loop, in its usual place.

"This is treason," Elsie said once Finlay finished.

Finlay stilled with her hand on the dagger's hilt. "I suppose it is."

Elsie walked over and knocked her shoulder against Finlay. "All these years of friendship, and it's only when a dragon's in danger that I see how much of a badass you are."

"I don't like doing this," Finlay protested.

Elsie gave her a wry grin. "Sometimes being a good person means breaking a few rules, skirting a few lines. You've always been okay with the little stuff, like watching Isla train. This is something more." Her grin softened. "This is being a good Knight."

"You said the man was named Alistair?" Robin asked.

He'd been silent while Finlay told them about her conversation with Alistair, and had a distant aspect, as though deep in thought. "That's what he said, yes. Do you know him?"

"I didn't have any kind of rank, so I didn't get to meet them personally, but I I used a"—his eyes flicked to Elsie, and he changed course, having been about to say he used a glamour, Finlay was sure—"used my charms to get to know some of the lords and ladies. His name was mentioned. He's one of the lords.

Late to prove himself as a Mage, apparently, but they spoke well of him."

Elsie turned her full attention to Robin. "How long were you with them?"

"A few months."

"And you decided to try to join their ranks?"

His chin jutted forward. "I don't like mistreatment of any creatures. I thought I could find enough people with similar opinions hidden within their number to make something of a difference."

"And did you find people willing to turn on the crown?" Finlay asked.

"There are always people willing to betray others," Robin said, a dark undercurrent to his youthful voice. "In this case, that's in your favor. Yes, there are people who, given the opportunity, would support a coup."

Finlay toyed with a strand of her coppery hair as she tried to process it. Maybe the day they went against the Mages really was drawing near, as Calum always said. Did he know about a support system within the kingdom, or simply trust that, as Robin said, there would always be some willing to fight when presented with the opportunity? Would it be as much of a struggle as she imagined, if they had that internal support? Many of the dragons living in the sanctuary would likely volunteer to fight as well . . . would she need to volunteer to go into their ranks, as her heart urged her to? Was it right to wait and see how things played out, with this hope, or take the opportunity she'd glimpsed in that cavern tonight?

Elsie's calloused hand lightly touched Finlay's, stilling her movement. "Don't get lost in your head yet, Fin."

Taking a deep breath, Finlay let her hand fall to her side and nodded. "Right. One step at a time."

"So we're doing this tomorrow, after the ceremony."

Finlay froze. "After the ceremony?"

"You told that Mage it would be tomorrow night, right? Well, we can still have our ceremony in the afternoon. It'll mean they have to let me come with you, since we'll both be full Knights!"

Elsie's words echoed in Finlay's ears. "The ceremony . . . is tomorrow afternoon?"

"Not everything has to happen at night. Just a lot of things, where we're concerned."

So her tears had been wasted. She would have the moment she'd dreamed of for so long. And then her chance to free Ghillie.

"You should sleep," Robin told her, reaching out to touch her arm. "Tomorrow will be a big day."

Sleep was the last thing on her mind, despite her exhausted emotions, yet Finlay did change into nightclothes and retire to her bed. Elsie climbed in with her, as they used to sleep all the time, and as Elsie still reliably did two days a year: the anniversary of Finlay's arrival at Aerouant Glèidh, and Finlay's birthday—the two saddest days of the year, as far as Finlay was concerned.

"It'll be okay," Elsie said, in her attempt at a whisper that was still normal volume.

Finlay closed her eyes. When she opened them, she found not the meadow scene she was accustomed to in Aithne's mindscape, but a volcanic scene, molten earth radiating heat beneath her bare feet. Her eyes widened, body tensing. In the same instant, that energy emanating from the ground traveled through her soles, warm and undeniably inviting. She released a slow breath that bordered on a sigh. Her heart, which had stuttered, ready to pump more furiously, remained at its steady pace. This was nothing like the funerary fire earlier.

Aithne looked at her and must have thought Finlay was stunned with fear, because she made the image shift back to the grassy meadow with wildflowers.

"Is that where you're more comfortable?" Finlay asked.

The only place I'm uncomfortable is the ocean. The meadow soothes both of us. Aithne sat on her rear, shoulders straight in a regal pose. **What's bothering you, Finlay? The faerie boy is right that you should be getting sleep.**

Finlay lowered herself to the ground and ran her hands over the long grass. "Is it wrong to celebrate, before we've freed him?"

Aithne lowered her head so she was eye level with Finlay. **There is a reason to celebrate every day, just as there is a reason to mourn—you decide which course you take. You deserve to be recognized among your fellow Knights. Elsie deserves it, and Angus. It's not wrong to want that. And you did tell that Mage nighttime, as Elsie already remind-**

ed you. Would you rather pace and worry all afternoon, and then go, or enjoy yourself first? Either way, Ghillie's situation will remain the same during the daylight hours tomorrow. Think of the next day, Finlay, when that won't be the case.

A contented sigh escaped Finlay. "Thank you, Aithne."

Aithne huffed warm air at Finlay, stirring her hair back. **I just wish I could do for you what Jupiter does.**

Finlay placed a hand on Aithne's snout. Whatever the phoenix dragon said, she would always carry guilt about this situation inside. "I wish that too."

Aithne leaned forward and touched her head to the top of Finlay's for a second before drawing back. **All right. Get some sleep.**

Finlay withdrew from the mindscape and stared at the ceiling of her cottage, listening to the deep, even breathing of Elsie beside her for a long while before she felt weariness pull her into slumber.

The inching threads of summer spun ever closer, evident in the lingering warmth in the air the following day and the bright shine of the sun. The spring chill was officially gone, and likely had been for at least a week, but it wasn't until that next morning that Finlay realized it.

Elsie offered to take Robin to breakfast at the dining hall. Finlay, too nervous to eat anything significant, let them go ahead and nibbled at some berries as she walked to the compound a few minutes later. Calum rose earlier than most of the Knights, and liked to run the perimeter of the compound at this time of the morning. Finlay found him jogging near the far wall, where the Sisters had shown Finlay her fate the day she started her training.

Calum stopped when he saw her approaching and dipped his head in greeting. "Good morning, Finlay."

"Good morning," she replied. Her hand strayed to her dagger. *Be strong. A lie is necessary.* "I have something I need to tell you."

"You seem stressed. What's wrong?"

"I didn't want to bring it up yesterday, with John's ceremony, but I found something the night the three of us went out."

Calum motioned for her to continue.

"Everyone knows we fought a few Mages. I don't know if John or Elsie saw the band of them that Jupiter and I did, in the caverns nearby. At the edge of sight, but still. Twenty horses can't hide as easily in the mountains as twenty people."

"That many?" Calum sucked in a breath. "They might have found us."

Finlay's insides squirmed at the lie. "That was my concern. They may not all be Mages, but it seemed too many to think none of them are."

He raked a hand over his ash blond hair. "We need to call a meeting." He strode to the dining hall, agitation in every movement. Almost everyone was inside, either already sitting with the hot breakfast the cooks provided or else getting their plates filled in the back. Finlay stopped just inside. Calum walked to the front of the room, his appearance making all conversation drop off suddenly. "Knights, I'm calling an emergency meeting. Thirty minutes. Meet at the pavilion. Tell anyone not here, attendance is required."

He turned and headed back out of the dining hall. Finlay followed him outside but paused when she saw him move toward the dormitory. He had to let Chief Stewart know he'd called a meeting. Finlay realized the half an hour's delay might have been purely for the chief's benefit.

"So what did you tell him?" Elsie asked, startling Finlay. Robin walked out and leaned against the wall, eating a muffin. Looking around, but surely listening.

"I didn't mention that Chief Stewart needs to lead, if that's what you're asking. It would be better if that bit came from you, I think."

"Since it's the chief's dragon that you're trying to free, and he knows you know?"

Finlay's eyes shot wide, and she pulled Elsie further aside, closer to Robin. "You knew?"

One corner of Elsie's mouth lifted in a smile. "Total guess. But it seemed weird to insist that having the chief lead us tonight would help a dragon in need. Unless it's his dragon, and you want something about Ghillie to be seen."

Finlay threw her arms around her friend's shoulders. "Elsie, you're amazing!"

Elsie's body shook with her laugh. "I was thinking 'decent at putting things together' but I'll take amazing."

Finlay leaned in close and spoke in a hurried whisper. "I couldn't tell anyone because of a spell, but if you figured it out, we don't even need to do the raid tonight! You can go and free him right now—he should still be out of sorts, so the others can see!" She pushed Elsie's shoulders back lightly. "Why didn't you tell me you knew last night?"

Elsie shook her head. "Didn't fully realize it till I sat down to eat breakfast. You know food helps you think. You can't tell Calum and the others you lied."

Finlay's thoughts raced. "I'll recommend we do a quick sweep of the area now, and say that they've gone from where they were."

"You know what this means?" Aileen said, walking out of the dining hall. Her excited, raised voice carried to where Finlay and Elsie stood with ease, though a quick look told Finlay Aileen was talking to others behind her. "A call to action!"

"It might be too late for that," Elsie said.

Desperation clamored within Finlay, and she turned to Robin. "Is there anything you can do to help?"

He hesitated. "I can try."

Elsie spun to face him. "We need to talk after, so you can tell me exactly what it is you can do."

Robin nodded. "Okay."

And they waited. Finlay even made herself annoyed by her constant fiddling with her dagger and her hair, waiting for

Calum and Chief Stewart, and any straggling Knights, to gather at the pavilion, but couldn't help it. Thirty agonizing minutes later, everyone had gathered. Twenty-seven Knights, the elected chief, and a faerie boy only Finlay knew to be a faerie.

Finlay watched Robin as Calum appeared, and saw the blue rimming his black irises spin. Her gaze darted to Calum, and with narrowed eyes, she thought she saw a glint of that same blue flash in Calum's lighter eyes. It was gone in an instant, but Finlay raised an eyebrow in Robin's direction.

"He's a little more open to suggestion now," Robin confided, scarcely above a whisper. "That should help."

Calum raised a hand to quiet the voices of the crowd and stood in front of the group, a step ahead of Chief Stewart. "We've learned of a potential threat," he began. "Everyone knows John, Finlay, and Elsie snuck off two nights ago. Finlay just confided in me that she saw a large group of Mages alarmingly near."

"You think they know where we are?" Cormac asked.

"It's possible, and given how many horses Finlay reported spotting, likely. We never see Mages in larger groups than five or six. She saw signs of at least twenty."

Murmuring broke out.

"I don't know for certain which way they were heading," Finlay said. "They could have no idea we're near, and it's possible some aren't Mages at all. A small scouting patrol would let us see if they're even there anymore."

Calum studied her with his serious blue eyes.

"Or we could surprise them and send them back where they came from!" Cormac said. His hair hung heavily over his forehead, matted and shiny—dirty, as if he hadn't washed it. Dark shadows extended from beneath his eyes. It pained Finlay to see the rage and grief so clear upon his face. "This is a chance to show them we're a serious threat!"

Calum's gaze switched to Cormac.

"A patrol could sneak up on them," Elsie said. "Ghillie has camouflaging magic, right? He can cloak a small group, to see if they're still in the same location."

Finlay's eyes locked on Chief Stewart. His neck went rigid. "I hardly think that's necessary. You know Ghillie hasn't flown a significant distance in years."

"We could ask Ghillie if he thinks he can manage," Calum said. "Camouflage would be a major advantage."

"So a small patrol?" Finlay asked, hope growing.

Calum looked over everyone, gauging their reactions to the patrol option. While it was obvious several, especially Cormac, wanted to have everyone go, most were nodding in approval. "Yes. You'll need to go, Finlay, to show us where you saw them. Chief Stewart and Ghillie will be necessary as well. And I'll go, as well as . . . Isla. It would be your night for patrol anyway, so you'll join us."

Cormac stepped forward. "Let me come too."

Calum hesitated. "Let me think about it, and we'll discuss after," he said after a moment's deliberation.

Cormac didn't look pleased, but neither did he look completely put-out.

"So we should go now, right?" Finlay asked. "With Ghillie, we won't need to worry about daylight making us easier to spot, and we can know for sure that much sooner." *And the Mages shouldn't have gathered.*

Chief Stewart raised a hand before Calum could reply. "Ghillie's camouflage works better at night. Let's wait until nightfall. That way Moira can have time to make something to strengthen Ghillie beforehand." His eyes darted over the Knights as he searched for another convincing deterrent to leaving now. "We have the binding ceremony this afternoon as well. Finlay's needed for that."

"I'm happy to delay it," Finlay offered.

Chief Stewart looked at her with a controlled expression Finlay could still easily see through. She wondered if anyone else noticed the veiled hostility in that gaze. Elsie seemed to be glaring at him, which was support enough for Finlay. "After everything you've done," Chief Stewart said to Finlay, "I insist you go through the binding with your *remaining* peers."

Finlay flinched and seethed inside.

"It appears we have a plan," Calum said, clapping his hands together. "The binding ceremony will take place immediately after lunch. Light training until then. At twilight those going on the patrol will gather at the sanctuary and scout. We'll forgo the usual moonlight surveillance."

They broke apart to attend to their training. Finlay turned to Elsie as they walked to the armory, trailing behind the others. Anxiety seemed to be making a nest inside her, at this point, taking up permanent residence. "Give me another direction to fly," she demanded.

Elsie's eyebrows pressed together. "What?"

"I can't go to the real spot," Finlay whispered. "The Mages will have gathered by then. Give me a different destination, so I can fix it in my head and don't panic later."

"How about where we saw those two trolls fighting over a deer carcass? That was a decent space away, wasn't it?"

Finlay ran through their flight path and nodded. They'd taken a sharp turn to the left after that, wary of more trolls straight ahead. The creatures tended to live in herds of up to fifty, and had a blood and battle lust unlike any creature Finlay had ever seen—best to avoid them whenever possible. Finlay nodded again. "Perfect."

Elsie gripped Finlay's arms on both sides, forcing her to stop and look straight at her. "Where's the badass you showed you have inside last night?"

Tension broke away with a laugh, and then a real smile that lingered on Finlay's lips.

Elsie dipped her head in approval. "There she is. Don't get lost in your head, and it'll be fine." She looked around. "Now where's Robin? He has some explaining to do."

CHAPTER TWENTY-EIGHT

The best way Finlay could think to avoid becoming lost in her head, as Elsie said not to do, was to lose herself in something . . . or someone. To be grounded in a moment she wanted to fully experience, with a person whose very presence anchored her and provided warmth and security.

In the hour scheduled for lunch, Finlay stole to the sanctuary to find him. She didn't even reach it before she saw him, walking toward the compound. He blinked when he saw her, and then a smile spread across his face, that adorable dimple quirking into existence. He bounded forward and stopped in front of her, looking at her as if in wonder. "Hi."

Finlay giggled and placed a palm on his cheek. "Hi."

"I was just coming to see you."

"So was I."

He leaned in and pressed his lips to hers, one hand brushing her hair back. Finlay melted at his touch, all stress evaporating beneath the simmering heat springing between them. "It's been too long since we did that," Evander whispered.

Finlay trailed her hand down his arm, her fingers skimming across his skin—it was warm enough that most people wore short sleeves now. Despite the warmth that never left her, Finlay kept her light cloak to avoid suspicion that anything had changed for her. She'd always worn a cloak, even in summer. To go without one might spur questions she didn't want, which could lead to the discovery of Aithne. It was actually quite warm, she realized, bordering on humid. Evander's breath hitched when her hand moved across his toned arm and slipped into his hand, and he let her turn him around to head back to the sanctuary.

"I'm sorry I haven't seen you as much the last few days. I really wanted to, believe me."

"I know you've been busy, love. Forrest, on the other hand, is one day away from thinking you're avoiding him."

"I can remedy that."

They reached the sanctuary, the matching dragon paw tattoos on their linked hands glowing as they passed the crystals that ringed the preserve. "Forrest!" Evander called. "Look who's here!"

A tiny green shape flew out of Evander's cottage and slammed into Finlay, who staggered and moved to catch him. *Finlay!*

"A little warning before you do that!" she told Forrest.

The dragon turned his head to face her, placing his paws near her shoulders so his face was close to hers. *Don't go so long without visiting, and I can do that.* He jerked his head in Evander's direction. *That one was getting hives, stressing about you.*

"I was not!" Evander's cheeks pinked. "I just know it's been a whirlwind, lately, and wanted to be there for you."

Finlay walked closer and leaned her head on Evander's shoulder, still cradling Forrest in her arms. "You are always there for me, Evander."

Are you guys getting all mushy already? Forrest grumbled.

Finlay's lips quirked up. "I thought you wanted us to be a couple?"

Well, yeah. You two are great together. Doesn't mean I want to see it—all the time.

Finlay kissed his head before he wriggled free. "Wait, Forrest," Evander said. Forrest paused, hovering in the air between them. "I'm going to give it to her now, and you said you wanted to see."

Forrest beat his wings harder in anticipation, buoying himself above their heads. *You're gonna love it!* he told Finlay.

Evander walked into his cottage and came out swiftly, something hidden in his hands. "It's not much, and I had some help making it, but"—he adjusted his grip so he displayed the object in his hands, rather than concealing it—"I hope you like it."

It was a circular object, rounded and flat like a button, with a shining metallic surface like gold. Smaller than Evander's palm but far larger than a button, Finlay's mouth opened when she recognized the ornamental clasp for what it was. Engraved into the face of it, etched with fine detail, a design of flames rippled.

"You'll be getting your official cloak today, to mark your recognition as a full Knight. I thought you might use this as the clasp."

Her hand shook slightly as she reached out to touch the smooth surface of the ornament. Part of her was surprised when the flame design didn't burn her. Evander took her palm, turned it over, and placed the ornament in her grip, warm hands folded around hers. "I know fire is complicated for you. I know you've been pushing yourself lately, doing everything you can to embrace it. I'm not sure you realize you already have. Acceptance doesn't mean perfection. It means growth." Steady eyes the color of loam earth met hers, tenderly demanding her gaze, and something shifted.

His voice wrapped around her, low and sweet, carving away everything around them: uprooting the ground and shoving out the sky, stilling the wind and overshadowing the sun. She wasn't left drifting in nothingness, though, searching for stability. Home was clear in his warm brown eyes, in the gentle pressure of his hands over hers. Home, and light, and love, and anything she ever asked of him.

A step brought him closer, his face inches from her own. "I see your struggles, and I see your strengths. I see *you.* Warm and bright as if you've taken a part of every flame you've ever seen and made it your own, you have no idea how strong you are. You have a spark, a radiance, nothing in the world can put out. And, love—you've burned your way into my very soul."

Finlay took a shivering breath that was immediately lost when she breathed out his name. It seemed all she could say in these moments was his name. *Evander, Evander, Evander. I love you, I need you, I want you.* It also seemed he understood what she wanted desperately to say, and heard it in those three syllables. Maybe he knew before she said anything. She'd never been very good with words.

"Will you wear it?" he asked several extended heartbeats later, his voice husky and trembling with barely-contained restraint she could also see crumbling in his eyes.

Finlay freed her hands, tearing her eyes from him with great reluctance to secure the ornamental clasp in the drawstring pouch on her belt. That done, she returned her gaze to his, taking in the gently swooping curl of his dark blond hair on his temple and feeling that blazing heat rise inside her more fiercely than ever before. "Absolutely."

Her own restraint crumbled an instant before his. Finlay looped her arms over his shoulders and pushed up against him with a bit more force than she meant, her lips flying to his. Evander caught her in a sweeping spin, hands around her waist, lifting her slightly as he turned so their kiss went unbroken by the movement.

Finlay's feet settled on the dry ground, but that didn't stop the weightless feeling Evander instilled in her, as though he was the only thing keeping her grounded. Finlay distantly heard Forrest mutter something about leaving, and felt a twinge of guilt—it was gone in the next second, as she found Evander's hair and he sighed—or was it a moan?—against her lips; whatever the sound, it conveyed a kind of pleasure that stirred something inside her, and she was pulled fully back into the kiss, lost in him once more.

Despite everything around them falling away, some part of Finlay was extremely aware of the rapidly passing minutes. She drew back, reclaiming her breath and forcing herself to come back to reality. Evander realized it too, and moved to hold her loosely, in a regular embrace. "I have to get ready for the ceremony," Finlay panted, nestling her nose against his collar. A short laugh escaped her. "Funny, I kind of wish I didn't have it now." She kissed the hollow of his throat, smiling when she felt his pulse jump, then trailed her lips across his skin and kissed his jaw, then his mouth, once more.

Evander took a few seconds to open his eyes, and then he looked at her with flushed cheeks and smiled, knowing she didn't truly mean it; at the same time, she sensed the same reluctance in him that she felt, and knew part of him wanted her to stay as well. Wanted the ceremony to be later, and to have more than the stolen moments they'd had of late. "I'll be watching in the crowd. Forrest too, I'm sure."

Finlay held Evander's gaze for a moment before turning and walking away, with a smile over her shoulder. "You both better be there. And find Robin for me?"

She jogged back to the compound after he gave a confirming shake of his head, past the slowly gathering group of Knights outside its gate, to hurry and change into a fresh outfit. Despite having about ten minutes left, Finlay was the only one in the armory. The outfit was basic, but nicer than that she'd had for all of her training: sturdy black pants that hugged her legs, tailored to her height; a fitted white tunic that extended past her waist, with sleeves rounded over the shoulder and a curved neckline; a thick brown belt over the tunic, onto which she slung her dagger; new black boots that came almost to her knees.

Looking into the full-length mirror in the front of the armory, Finlay saw the change in herself from a month before. The slender muscles of her arms and legs were apparent now, her limbs no longer stick-like. She didn't see an expression bordering on melancholy staring back at her, but a vaguely determined one—as if the grief she always carried with her, and all of her other stresses, were still there, but not things Finlay had to passively deal with and reflect on—rather, as if she was ready to take action to solve the things she could. She'd known she'd changed in mindset, but seeing this resting expression made it real. Evander had been right; Finlay had changed.

She ran her fingers through her long, coppery hair, neatening it from the mussed state it had been in after her time with Evander. That done, Finlay nodded at her reflection and ran out of the armory, reaching for a cloak she didn't have out of habit.

"Finlay!" Meric called when she ran past the gate of the compound, from where he stood with all of the other Knights just beyond it. He waited closest to the gate, facing it; no doubt looking out for her. "You're almost late!"

Finlay stopped next to him. "Sorry. Lost track of time."

She knew he wanted to look disapproving, but the scar-free side of his mouth twitched in amusement. "You look ready. I hope you don't mind that I asked to be the one to give you your cloak."

Finlay opened her mouth to respond but found words failed her for the second time that day, and instead wrapped her arms around the man in a tight hug. He laughed and held her for a second before letting go. "I don't mind," Finlay finally said. "I love that, actually."

"Fin, get over here!" Elsie yelled. Elsie stood at the front of the group, next to Angus, Calum, and Chief Stewart. Finlay made her way over to them, and Chief Stewart raised his hand for attention.

"Now that everyone is here," he said, with a pointed look at Finlay, "we can proceed to the festival grounds. The three dragons partnered with our youngest Knights are already there."

He didn't need to give any further instructions. Most of the settlement's population attended the binding ceremonies, meaning most everyone knew exactly how it would occur. Since it attracted so many people, this ceremony always had to take place in the festival grounds, the largest fertile expanse the settlement possessed that wasn't needed for agriculture. It bordered the lake on one side and the compound on the other, the mountains looming on the horizon in either direction.

The current Knights would split into two groups, on either side of the square. Spectators would line up facing them. Those about to complete the binding ceremony, Calum (or in the ceremony Finlay could remember before Calum became leader of the Knights, a retired Knight called Heloise), Moira (with a small table laden with the ink mixtures they would use and the dragon claws used to apply the tattoos), and Chief Stewart stood in the center, along with the dragon partners.

A huge crowd had gathered when Finlay and the others approached the festival grounds, numbering close to two hundred if Finlay had to guess. More than two-thirds of their entire population. The back of Finlay's neck heated when the majority of the eyes turned to look at her, Elsie, and Angus, and the ceremony began.

CHAPTER TWENTY-NINE

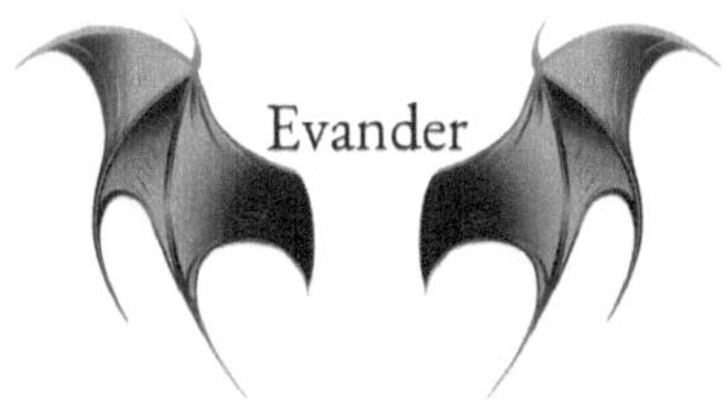

Evander

Evander's dim idea of asking Finlay about Robin faded when he saw her, and remembered just how long it had been since he'd kissed her . . . and swiftly remedied that fact.

When she remembered she had to go get ready for the ceremony—there was no way Evander could remember anything, lost in her embrace as he'd been—and asked him to find Robin, his goal to confront the boy returned to the forefront of his mind.

"Forrest, are you coming?" Evander called.

He heard the rustle of Forrest's wings, as unique a sound to Evander as the timbre of Finlay's voice, he heard it so often, and Forrest landed on Evander's shoulder, his hind feet scrabbling on Evander's back as he steadied himself. Evander knew he hadn't gone far, and had been waiting for this invitation.

"I'm going to find Robin. Don't look him in the eye," Evander reminded Forrest.

I got that, thanks.

Evander almost chuckled at his churlish tone. Nothing could dampen Evander's mood right now, even the tiny dragon's sass about being sidelined while Finlay and Evander kissed. Evander headed in the direction Finlay had, toward the compound, thinking the faerie boy might be there. He didn't have to go through the gated walls to look, though, as a large group had gathered outside it, and he spotted Elsie and Robin standing within said group.

He kept his eyes on Elsie as he approached. "Hey," he greeted. "Ready to become a Knight?"

Elsie grinned. "More than ready. But Fin just ran by . . ."

"I may have distracted her," Evander said. "She actually asked me to find Robin before the ceremony. Can we talk for a minute, Robin?"

In his periphery he saw Robin frown, probably seeing how resistant he was to looking at him, and then the boy sighed. He motioned with his hand, and Evander and Elsie followed him slightly away from the crowd. "You know, don't you?"

"How did you find out?" Elsie demanded in her loud voice.

Evander blinked at her. "You know the truth about him?"

"You and Elsie have similar timing," Robin said with a chuckle. "I just told her a bit ago. And you can look at me. I won't glamour you."

Have you glamoured Finlay? Forrest asked.

"No," Robin said. "She told me her secret when her dragon revealed mine." Robin exhaled a laugh. "Her other dragon partner told you. Hope he isn't mad I glamoured him."

Only a little, Forrest said.

Robin nodded. "Understandable. I don't expect you to believe me right away, but I feel a kind of kinship with Finlay. Like I know I can trust her. And I do. And since she trusts the two, sorry, three of you so much, I will too."

It was enough for Evander to finally look him straight-on, and he smiled when he spotted the slightly-pointed tips of Robin's ears peeking from beneath his dark hair, and the incredible blue-black of his eyes. "It's nice to truly meet you," Evander said, offering his hand.

Robin shook it strongly and echoed the sentiment. Elsie went to stand by Angus.

"I have so many questions," Evander said. "I've never met anyone like you."

"I've only met a few, that I can remember," Robin said. "I must have known more at one point, but I've got a few blanks in the memory department."

Concern flitted through Evander, but he could see Chief Stewart getting the Knights in order. They didn't have time to discuss anything else right now. "Stand by me and Forrest," he told Robin, motioning with his head for them to start walking. "We can talk after the ceremony."

Forrest glared at Robin as they walked. "You're Forrest, right?" Robin asked. "Finlay's mentioned you a few times."

Forrest's glare faltered. *She has?*

"A few times I don't think she meant for me to hear, but she was wondering under her breath what you and Evander were doing. When we were training, and before bed."

Forrest's tension melted. *Of course she mentioned us. She's crazy about us.*

Evander met Robin's eye with a darting glance and flicked one eyebrow up, to silently commend him for that. Robin grinned, then looked at Forrest with a thoughtful expression. "You have another kind of magic around you. Something . . . different."

Evander slowed his step. Forrest tensed on his shoulder. *What do you mean?*

Robin blinked several times, taking his time to answer. "I'm not sure. It's not faerie magic, but it seems similar. And it isn't a spell or anything. Just a kind of magic residue, or imprint."

Evander looked at Forrest when the dragon turned to him. "Maybe it has something to do with your time in your egg." He glanced at Robin. "Forrest isn't a pygmy dragon. I've been trying to figure out why he's stayed this size for ages, and my best theories were something about when he was still in his egg. I found it on its own, and no sane dragon would abandon a nest."

Robin sucked in a small breath. "A pixie. I'll bet anything a pixie came across your egg and sat on it. They have the same kind of magic, but much weaker, and they're tiny. They're also extremely protective of the young."

Something in his tone said pixies had helped Robin before, and more questions about the faerie boy surfaced in Evander's mind. He reached up to scratch the underside of Forrest's chin. "What do you think, Forrest? Pixie dust?"

Forrest was still tense, but did lean into Evander's affectionate gesture. *It makes more sense than anything else you've guessed. I'm still a full dragon.*

"Of course you are," Robin said, before Evander could. "If anything, this just makes you more unique."

Forrest thought about that for a minute. *You bet it does.*

CHAPTER THIRTY

The male Knights always went first, so Finlay watched as Chief Stewart welcomed everyone and Calum motioned for Angus and Fern to step forward. "Angus Russell. Your compassion and dedication have shown through in your training. Are you ready to bring those attributes to our ranks and accept the full responsibilities of a Dragon Knight?"

Angus's throat bobbed as he swallowed nervously, and then he squared his shoulders and looked Calum right in the eyes as he said, "Yes."

Calum turned to Aileen. "Do you believe your charge is prepared?"

"Absolutely," she said without hesitation.

Calum touched Angus's arm to guide him closer to Fern and looked at the dragon. "And you are willing to partner with this young man, to defend our settlement, dragon-kind, and any in need of assistance, even at the risk of your life?"

The mild-mannered forest dragon snorted, making a swirl of floral scents drift in the air. *I would consider it an honor.*

Finlay saw the proud twist that flickered on Calum's mouth, try as he might to remain inscrutable. Training with him for the last month had given her more of an understanding of the leader of the Knights. It was as if formality had been drilled into him, and he thought showing full emotion would harm him in some way. Those flickers of expression weren't much, but they were enough to let her know he cared, and was showing it in the only way he thought he could.

"You will be bound, dragon and human," Calum said, reaching to take the dragon claw Moira handed him. He lowered his voice. "I only need a few drops, and Moira will put a salve on after the ceremony to heal it in minutes." His words eased the tension in both Fern and Angus's shoulders. Calum took the tip of the dragon claw—one of the only things sharp enough to slip beneath a dragon's scales without true force—and pressed it against Fern's leg. When he drew it out, scarlet coated the ivory claw, and beads of blood formed around the entry site on Fern's leg.

Calum accepted the small bowl Moira held out for him, and tapped the dragon claw over it to spatter droplets of blood inside it. "You've said you'd like your mark on your other hand," Calum verified, stirring the mixture in the bowl. When Angus nodded, Calum held Angus's hand steady and traced the dragon claw over the back of his hand.

Warmth and pride expanded in Finlay's chest, watching Angus receive the tattoo with his shoulders straight and his expression confident. He barely flinched. When it was complete, and Moira was putting her salve and a bandage over it, the brightest smile Finlay had ever seen on Angus's face appeared. "Fern," he said in an excited whisper. "I can feel your magic!"

Fern extended her neck to press her snout to Angus's head. *And I you, little one.*

Moira took the dragon claw to clean it. Aileen walked forward, a deep green cloak bordered with brown folded neatly in her arms. Calum motioned with his head for Angus to go to her, and Angus's already bright smile grew as Aileen drew the heavy cloak over his shoulder.

"Congratulations, Angus Russell, Dragon Knight!" Calum cried.

Everyone echoed the sentiment. Angus and Fern moved to the side, and the ceremony continued when Calum looked at Elsie.

"Elsie Lee-Hughes."

Finlay watched her best friend with rapt attention, smiling when Calum commended her for her strength and honesty and laughing when Elsie's excitement made her practically yell that she accepted the responsibilities. Elsie chose to have her tattoo applied to her upper arm, just below the shoulder. In minutes Elsie too had received her official cloak, a gorgeous midnight color rimmed in orange, from Isla, and Calum turned his attention to Finlay.

"Finlay McDonough."

Calum's light blue eyes showed respect when Finlay approached, and Finlay's cheeks warmed. She doubted many could tell there was a difference in Calum's gaze, but she saw it.

"Your courage and resolve have shone clearly throughout your training. Are you ready to bring those attributes to our ranks and accept the full responsibilities of a Dragon Knight?"

Chin high, Finlay spoke clearly. "I am."

Jupiter strode forward as Calum turned to him, spreading his wings behind him in a display before folding them against his body again. Jupiter looked at Finlay as he agreed to work with her, even at the risk of his life. *Make it convincing,* Finlay silently urged him. Nothing would happen when the tattoo was drawn, but they would have to make it look like they could suddenly feel each other. A low hum escaped him, which Finlay took as a sign he remembered.

Calum pressed the freshly cleaned dragon claw through Jupiter's scales as he had the others, and asked Finlay where she would like her mark as he mixed the dragon blood with the tattoo ink. She gestured to the same spot Elsie had hers and stood still while he applied it, ignoring the light sting as it cut into her skin.

Until she couldn't ignore it. He finished tracing the outline of the dragon head, and something changed. The area heated, fire rushing through her veins. Her breath caught as a different sensation rushed through her, originating from the tattoo site. An electric charge. It met the flames with an explosive force that rocked Finlay's body, which tensed and spasmed.

Calum withdrew the dragon claw and put a steadying hand on her arm. "Finlay, what's wrong?"

Her breath shuddered as explosions went off all over her body, vision cutting in and out. A hot surge of fire caught in her chest, and the mindscape blinked in and out of view for several erratic heartbeats before she settled on the grassy meadow of the mindscape. Aithne stood directly in front of her, claws digging into the ground, sunset wings spread, feathers on end, eyes narrowed in concentration.

"What's happening?" Finlay asked, wincing.

The blood from Jupiter is trying to form a link between you. Since you and I are already more deeply bound, my magic and Jupiter's are clashing. More violently than I'd thought. It will pass in a moment. My fire is almost through it.

"But the tattoo isn't done."

Aithne thrust her wings to their widest extent. **I'll burn through it. Go back, before they think anything more is wrong.**

The words spilled from Finlay's mouth, higher-pitched than she intended. "I don't want your magic to run out!" Aithne had said if her magic ran out, she would die. Finlay absolutely could not let that happen. Not for her.

Aithne's jaw opened in a smile of sorts. **This won't come close to using up my magic, Finlay. Now go.**

Finlay forced herself out of the mindscape. As soon as her true surroundings occupied her vision, the sparking pain became prominent again, though admittedly less than before she'd spoken to Aithne. Calum and Moira stood very near her, inspecting her with evident concern. Low murmuring reached her ears, familiar voices of the Knights breaking through along with an indecipherable mix from the crowd. She knew if she looked, she would see many heads craning to look at her from behind Calum and Moira.

"Finlay?" Calum asked. Finlay guessed from his tone that it wasn't the first time he'd said her name since she entered the mindscape.

"I'm all right," she said, thinking quickly. "The magic was stronger than I expected, that's all."

I am a particularly strong dragon, Jupiter supplied in a grandiose voice.

"Please, finish the tattoo," Finlay requested. "I'm sorry I disrupted the ceremony."

"Don't worry about that," Moira said, playfully swatting the arm that didn't have a partial tattoo. "Are you sure you're all right?"

"Perhaps this is a sign Finlay isn't up to the task of being a Knight after all," Chief Stewart said from behind Calum and Moira, with a barely concealed smirk.

"Please," Finlay repeated, looking to Calum.

The man scrutinized her and then sighed and picked up the dragon claw and tattoo ink bowl he'd set on the ground. He resumed the process without a word. Finlay gritted her teeth as the mini explosions ran through her again, Jupiter's magic colliding with Aithne's. Calum lifted the dragon claw after he finished the design, his gaze snapping back to Finlay's face. She met it with her chin tilted up again, forcing her jaw to relax.

"Jupiter, your magic really is strong," Finlay said, sliding her gaze to his and feigning a self-criticizing chuckle.

Calum motioned for Meric to come forward. The robe Meric had for Finlay was deep red, with brilliant gold embroidered on the sides. He tried to smile at her as he looped it over her shoulders and joined the clasp in the front. The motion was half-hearted, worry tainting it. He swept her hair aside, letting it settle over the hood and shoulders before stepping back.

"Congratulations, Finlay McDonough, Dragon Knight!" Calum said.

Those watching echoed, but without the resounding confidence Elsie and Angus had gotten. Finlay sensed many eyes still on her, curious minds wondering what had gone wrong and why. This was not good. Not good at all. Too much unwanted attention could bring questions . . . she might have to pass it off as being weaker than she expected, loathe as she was to go through with that. Of course, they may not even ask, just make their own assumptions . . . she could hear Elsie telling someone to mind their own business, her voice barbed.

Forrest flew to Finlay's side in a rush of tiny green wings. *You all right?*

"Finlay!" Robin called, breaking through the front of the crowd when everyone started to disperse. Evander shouldered past people a few steps behind.

Finlay waited until they had all reached her, including Elsie, before answering the question she knew they all had. "I'm fine. I'll tell you about it in private."

Moira walked closer again, breaking the bubble those closest to Finlay had made that blocked out everyone else. "Let me check on you," she said.

Finlay relented and let Moira inspect the tattoo site and use her salve and bandage it, take her temperature, and ask her about what had happened. She stuck to her story about underestimating the force of Jupiter's magic, being overwhelmed by it, and Moira took her word for it, despite the scrunching of her eyebrows that said she thought there was something more. Her worried comment that Finlay seemed slightly feverish was dismissed by Finlay saying excitement and anxiety always did that to her.

That done, Finlay, Robin, Evander, Elsie, Forrest, and Jupiter went to the sanctuary—Evander had to go back to its border to give Robin his temporary tattoo first—where Finlay told them what had really transpired, in Evander's cottage.

"I guess there's a good reason we don't allow people to bind with more than one dragon," Evander said. Warmth akin to sunlight spread from where his palm held hers, the healing magic he shared with Gaea casually flowing into her. It made it remarkably easy to relax; all traces of pain were long gone, a vaguely floating feeling bordering between being drowsy and being tipsy filling her in its stead. Evander must have seen this, because he pulled his hand from hers before the feeling could coalesce.

"Did you see the chief's face?" Finlay asked Elsie.

Elsie had her arms crossed, a stormy look in her dark eyes. "I did. I also heard him try to say the pain was a sign you shouldn't be a Knight."

"He wants to kill you," Robin said. He spoke plainly. "At the very least he wants you dead."

"Because she knows he mistreats Ghillie," Elsie said.

Evander held up a hand. "Could you repeat that, and explain?"

No more worrying about the chief's spell. "I don't care if it's a risk. I want everyone to know exactly what I saw before tonight, since if there's ever a chance for the tragic 'accident' I know the chief has lined up for me to happen, it's tonight. The first day of our training, I was exploring the dormitories. . . ."

She'd imagined the look of horror on Evander's face if he found out about a dragon in trouble right beneath their noses. It was worse in reality, color leeching from his cheeks and unshed tears glistening in the corners of his eyes.

She paused when she finished, waiting for a horrible pain to start in her center. None came. Everyone around her remained in good health. A curse flew from her lips. "That spell didn't keep me from telling others. It just keeps me from going near Ghillie."

Elsie was fuming as well, the storm in her gaze giving way to a thunderclap in her booming voice. "That bastard!"

"The braces on his legs cover the scars from chains," Evander said, as if to himself. "His legs probably straightened naturally, a long time ago. It happens with humans and dragons . . . sometimes limbs are bowed and need more time to straighten. I never suspected . . ."

"No one suspected," Elsie said.

"I wouldn't be surprised if Ghillie does have a condition," Finlay said. "You know Moira looked at him when he was young, and the old keeper of the sanctuary did as well. I don't think the chief had a reason to lie about him back then; not when he was a youngling. There *is* something different about Ghillie. But I'm also sure Ghillie isn't anywhere near as weak as Chief Stewart claims."

Evander took a second before he said anything. Finlay took in the way his brow tightened, and knew he was burying the guilt inside for now. She hated that he felt it, when none of this was his fault. Chief Stewart had found Ghillie as a hatchling, years before any of them had been born. "So by having him go on patrol tonight, you want everyone to see that he can't control Ghillie's magic," he said.

Finlay closed her eyes. "I thought it would be a good way to arouse suspicion that something wasn't right with Ghillie, and the truth would come out. Now I just feel like I've done everything wrong, and it's too late to stop what I've started."

"He tricked you," Robin said with low force. "He used magic and lied about how much it could do. As far as I can tell, you did everything you thought you could. And now we'll have a backup plan. If for whatever reason his guilt isn't suspect tonight, I'll make sure his dragon is freed. One way or another."

The stubbornness, the determination, the kindness . . . Finlay's heart gave a bittersweet twist. Gods, he reminded her of Michael. She pulled Robin close. "Thank you."

This situation is so messed up, Forrest said, small and compact on the ground. His wings were pulled in tight against his body. He rubbed his head against Finlay's leg. *Let me tell you the same thing this guy said, though, from a dragon's perspective. You did nothing wrong. Now we can all help.*

A choking feeling constricted Finlay's throat, an odd burning sensation pricking behind her eyes. She stared hard at the ground until it went away, and then tentatively smiled. "Everyone else is celebrating right now, getting ready for the feast." She pulled the ornament Evander had given her from where she'd squeezed it into the sheath for her dagger and placed it over the clasp of her cloak. "I haven't eaten a thing."

"They're bound to have some delicious food there," Evander said.

"They can't celebrate the newest Knights with only one there, either," Elsie said. She looped her arm through Finlay's. "Let's go eat and be fawned over."

CHAPTER THIRTY-ONE

Twilight arrived both in a blink and a timeless void, at one moment seeming more than hours away and the next, nerve-wrackingly close. Finlay ate her fill and tried to fully enjoy herself, and had mixed results. She knew it would have been worse if her friends hadn't soothed her thoughts before.

Isla walked over to Finlay when night claimed more of the sky than day, the relaxed, content expression she'd had all afternoon and evening fading. "Time to get into gear."

Finlay nodded and followed her to the compound and into the armory.

"You haven't been as cheerful as I thought you'd be today," Isla said. "Worried about tonight?"

"Yes."

"Can I tell you a secret?" Isla didn't wait for Finlay to respond. "The first time I went out on patrol, I was sick right before we left. Tossed up my dinner. All the other Knights saw. It was humiliating, but nerves do that sometimes." She sighed. "That's the funny thing about nerves, Finlay. When you pretend they don't bother you at all, they get the best of you at the worst times. I think you're in much better shape than I am in that way. You'll be fine."

Gratitude lightened Finlay's step. "Thanks, Isla."

They went to their storage sections and put their gear on. Finlay reattached the flame-engraved ornament over her clasp when she drew her cloak over her shoulders again, fully clad in her leather armor beneath it. Isla looked at her without a word. Finlay had always thought she looked at home in the uniform of the Knights, with a confidence she was never short of, but that seemed ideally suited to, the mantle. She'd done her sleek black hair into a plait down her back, ready for a confrontation if necessary. She analyzed Finlay when Finlay stepped out from her storage section, silently asking if she was ready, and at Finlay's acknowledgement, turned and led the way back out of the armory, setting pace next to Finlay for the walk to the sanctuary.

Finlay spotted Evander first, his dark blond hair glinting in the gloam. She knew Robin was in Evander's cottage, where he could see them off but not attract attention. Evander had gathered Jupiter and Muir, and waited near them. Isla moved right to Muir's side, pressing her forehead to his—something she'd told Finlay and Elsie she did before every patrol: taking a moment to become more in tune with her dragon partner. Finlay greeted Jupiter, rubbing one hand along his neck, and watched for a second before looking around.

Calum was already there, standing tensely next to his dragon partner, Louis, a few feet away. Chief Stewart and Ghillie were there as well. The armor the chief wore was too small for his paunchy belly, and sweat beaded on his brow as he looked around. Good.

Evander pressed close to her side. "I can't look at them," he whispered. "How could you stand facing the chief and acting like everything was fine? I want to throw him from a dragon's back every time I glimpse him."

"You have a dark mind sometimes," Finlay told him. "But nothing compared to what I've imagined doing to him. Imagining it helps me pretend everything's all right in the few moments I see him."

"Ghillie is definitely out of it."

Finlay took a deep breath. "I'm going to talk to him."

Evander brushed his knuckle down her cheek. "Be careful."

Finlay ran to Ghillie, inspecting him. He sat by the chief's side, as he usually did to watch the Knights going on patrol leave. Similar to all of those evenings Finlay had seen him like that, he had braces on his legs, which she now knew covered evidence of shackles cutting into his skin. He looked at her when she approached with calm purple eyes.

Hi, he greeted.

His voice came though slightly slower, but looser than normal, ringing with warmth. "Ready to fly, Ghillie?" Finlay asked.

He hummed, his mouth open in a kind of smile. Hatred seethed Finlay's soul. Ghillie was coherent, but only just. Still entirely controllable. Still unable to voice his true thoughts. Probably just cogent enough to fly and camouflage them, but not enough to realize it was Chief Stewart the actions benefited. Surely if he could realize that, he wouldn't even consent to fly.

"He's ready," Chief Stewart said, standing immediately next to Finlay. "I'll get you for this," he hissed in her ear while pretending to lean forward and adjust the strap of Ghillie's gear.

"Funny, I was just thinking the same thing," Finlay spat back.

"Cormac?"

Finlay turned at Calum's questioning tone. Cormac appeared, a glowing crystal in his hand casting an odd sheen to his face. Even without it, Finlay knew something was wrong. There was a strange look in his eyes, and a redness around them that wasn't from grief, but something else entirely . . . A dragon walked behind him. Jasper.

"What are you doing here?" Calum asked.

"Talking to Jasper," Cormac said with a bit of a sting. "Poor dragon needed some company, see. There should have been another Knight bound today."

"We all miss John," Calum said.

Jasper snarled, sharp teeth flashing in the dark.

"His death puts things into perspective, Calum. We need to go as a group, to fight the Mages today and make the move we've been talking about for too many damn years! Before we lose more than we can stand and trap ourselves in this valley for good!" Cormac stepped backward, level with Jasper, his body rigid. Trepidation trickled down Finlay's spine. *Don't, Cormac.*

Calum held up his hands and crept closer. "We don't even know that the Mages are still there. That's why we're scouting. If they are, of course we'll plan an attack. I agree it's past time, but tonight is not the time for an outright assault. Not going in blind."

"Maybe this will change your minds." Cormac jumped onto Jasper, who pushed off the ground and firmly gusted his wings to buoy them into the air. Finlay recoiled from the spray of pebbles that flew up with the sudden movement.

"Cormac, don't!" Isla yelled.

"Cormac!" Calum called.

Jasper held himself above their heads, Cormac peeking over his flapping wings to shout to them, "Get the others if you'd like, or just follow me. Either way, I'm tired of waiting for the perfect day to take back the kingdom."

Jasper slammed his wings down, launching them higher up, and he and Cormac flew out of sight.

"What is he thinking?" Calum hissed.

But Finlay knew. It dawned on her with horrible, gut-wrenching clarity. "He's bent on revenge for John, and Jasper knows where we saw the Mages that killed him."

Calum acted quickly, mounting his dragon Louis and issuing a directive. "Evander, tell the others we need them to follow us, and be prepared to fight! We may not have a choice. Hugh should be able to track us. Everyone else, go!"

"Gaea!" Evander called. His dragon partner came out of nowhere—but no, he'd just been robed in shadows several yards away—and stooped so Evander could climb onto his back. They took off an instant after Finlay, Chief Stewart, Isla, and Calum, and their respective partners. He looked over his shoulder as they climbed into the air, his eyes flitting to Finlay's. Then they were too far for her to see his features clearly. Finlay watched their silhouettes as she and Jupiter raced in the opposite direction, and when she couldn't see them anymore, faced forward and tried to still the shaking of her legs and the roiling of her stomach. Why had she let herself eat anything? Why hadn't she talked to Cormac, when she'd known he was in pain?

She slapped her cheeks to force herself out of this useless spiral of anxiety.

I've never heard you do that before, Jupiter said.

"I needed a stern reminder not to get lost in my head, fixating on everything that's going wrong." It worked. The stinging of her cheeks refocused her and let her assess her surroundings instead of flying blindly. She couldn't see many details in the night, but with the stars and the more blue-than-black tint to the sky providing dim illumination, outlines—sharp points of mountain peaks, jagged zigzags of rocky faces, crisp lines of trees and rounded curves of boulders—were clear. A warm breeze carried the humid air to her, the familiar, heady hints of soil and minerals from the mountains below coming with it.

"Ghillie!" Calum said, at least thirty minutes into the flight, when Jasper and Cormac came into view but before they entered earshot. "Camouflage all of us, including Cormac and Jasper!"

"It won't do any good if he goes in to attack, or shouts anything," Isla said.

Calum stared ahead. "It gives us a chance, if we can reason with him, to turn around and avoid a fight. Increase speed."

Muir shot ahead the fastest, scrunching and snapping forward like a whip. Jupiter and Louis tied at a second's delay, wings going back so forcefully they were parallel to their bodies in the backstroke. Ghillie sped up several seconds after that. Cormac turned when he heard them approaching, a grin splitting his face. "Glad you caught up! Jasper says we're close!"

Finlay's heart sped. It had taken them longer last time because they'd taken a circuitous route. Now, traveling straight to that location, they really were getting close. She could see the pockmarked spots in the mountain that, closer-up, would reveal to be caverns, some natural, many widened and deepened by the kingdom over the years, to provide Mages shelter while they hunted dragons.

"Cormac, think about what you're doing," Calum urged, riding level with him. "You said losing John made you decide it's time for action. What if this costs another life?"

"It'll always be a risk, whenever we face them," Cormac countered. "At least this way anger can fuel us!" He urged Jasper to go faster, and moved too far ahead to speak without shouting and shattering any secrecy they may still have.

"Knock him out!" Chief Stewart cried. "We'll corral the dragon back and place them in lockdown."

Something bright caught Finlay's attention. A fire, on the horizon. Ahead of them, Jasper roared.

"That's not an option anymore," Calum said grimly. "Prepare for battle."

"Are we still camouflaged?" Isla asked.

"We never were," Finlay muttered. She gripped the edges of her cloak tightly as they approached the gathering of Mages. There really were at least twenty gathered, all dressed in metal chest plates and pauldrons, some with weapons at the ready, others with their hands splayed, not needing a different weapon. Was this just a small group? How many Mages were there overall? "Jupiter, I'm sorry I got you into this."

I stand by my decision to join you, he told her. *Don't count me out yet.*

Chapter Thirty-Two

Jasper let out another bone-rattling roar when he dove to confront the Mages, and Finlay watched several of them stagger, clutching their ears. Those same three didn't stay put for long. Jasper unleashed a column of flame that charred one. The fire traveled beneath the armor over his chest and enveloped him. It set the other two ablaze on their arms, making them dive to the ground in attempts to stifle the flames.

A spear hurtled toward Jasper's neck in the same moment. Cormac deflected with his sword—all he had time to do before Finlay and the others came close enough to join the fray and absolute chaos made individual movements impossible to see. The Knights were outnumbered when it came to humans, but they had five dragons on their side.

Jupiter landed with a resounding thud. He spread his wings to knock the four Mages around them back and used a breath attack: dark gray storm clouds crackled and boomed, hovering in the air near the Mages' heads.

One, a tall black woman with a golden choker around her throat, smiled. "A storm dragon." She thrust one hand into one of the gray clouds. Several sparks traveled across her. Gathering into a fully formed blast of lightning, the Mage sent it at Louis. "Thanks for the power base," she said to Finlay.

"Go!" Finlay urged, and Jupiter spun and lifted into the air again. They had to find a different target, if that Mage could use Jupiter's breath attack to fuel her own.

They landed a short distance away. Finlay dropped from Jupiter's back to fight by his front leg, dagger bared. A brawny male Mage with a mace ran toward them, noticing Jupiter snapping at another.

Finlay sprang onto Jupiter's back and flipped off his head to land on her feet behind the Mage, slicing her dagger across the back of his thigh in the same motion. He howled, turning and reaching for the bloody wound. Finlay slammed the pommel of her dagger on the crown of his head, and then bashed him with her forearm, elbow pointing out, for good measure. He sank to the ground and didn't rise.

Adrenaline lent everything a sharp focus, dulling the sights and sounds out of range and honing on those with the most potential to attack. An exceptionally pale Mage attempted to sneak up on Jupiter with claw-like fingers. Another Mage with heavy burns across his face slashed a short sword at Jupiter, feinting closer to Finlay with each step. It wasn't like Finlay saw it in slow motion, but she registered both in the same instant, even recognizing which was the more urgent concern. Her reaction was so automatic it was mindless.

She twisted, gripping her cloak and flaring it out, as the burned Mage sprang at her. Capturing his slashing sword with the heavy fabric of her cloak, Finlay held his weapon by the blade. The Mage gasped when his sword stopped mid-swing, and looked from his grip on the hilt to Finlay's hold on the blade. Finlay pressed her advantage, yanking the blade down and letting go. The Mage, his grip still tight upon the hilt, staggered off balance, head bowing in the downward motion. Finlay tossed her cloak out of the way and brought her elbow down hard between his shoulder blades, forcing him to wheeze and fall to his knees.

His hand shot out and grabbed her cloak, pulling down. Finlay didn't fight the motion, pulling her arm back and sending her fist against his jaw when he pulled her close and her knees met the ground. His own punch to her stomach stole some of her breath, but hers did more damage, being so close up and packed with momentum. The Mage sprawled back on the rocky ground with a groan.

Finlay turned her head, catching the female Mage who'd made her fingers into talons in the corner of her eye. The woman was close to Jupiter's tail now. Jupiter was snapping and swiping at two Mages near his front. Finlay pressed her heels into the ground and sprinted toward Jupiter's tail, doing the only thing she could think to keep the woman from delivering the wound that would cut through Jupiter's scales and, most likely, cause him to rear in pain, giving the two at his front an opportunity to make a fatal blow. Though it pained her to let it leave her hand, Finlay adjusted the dagger in her grip and threw it forward.

The gold and silver of the weapon gleamed as it hurtled through the air between them, spotted with crimson. Finlay's aim wasn't perfect. Far from it. The blade didn't strike point first. It still did its job. The sharp edge scraped along the Mage's raised arm, the hilt colliding with her chest.

It distracted her enough to keep her hideous talons from meeting Jupiter's scales. Unfortunately, it also left Finlay without a weapon when she faced her, and Finlay's cloak wouldn't be much help again. If the woman's claws were as strong as a dragon's, the fabric would shred in an instant if Finlay tried to capture them the way she'd captured the short sword. Only shavings from dragon claws added to the fabric before it was sewn let it stand up to weapons as well as it did.

The woman threw Finlay's dagger aside and flexed her hands. Her fingers lengthened further, bleached bone nails sharp at their tips. "Are you actually a challenge?" she asked, a predatory gleam in her frost-blue eyes.

"You're losing," Finlay told her.

"You're dying," the woman countered, springing forward. She must have killed a sky dragon of some form, because her movements were lighter and more rapid than humanly possible—as if the air boosted her forward. Finlay dove to avoid her claws, wincing when they grazed her cheek and pulled several strands of hair from her head. The claws had barely touched her, yet Finlay felt warm blood bead on her cheek.

Finlay's dagger lay on the ground in front of her, several paces away. She scrabbled forward with a reaching grasp, her fingers touching the still warm metal of the grip—a strangled cry made her hand falter over pulling it closer. Sharpened bone nails perforated the cuirass that protected her torso, four points driven so deeply and forcefully into her back that the tough, magically enhanced armor couldn't completely block the blow. Not deep enough to kill her, but deep enough to make her flinch in pain, the tips digging into her skin.

The Mage stood over her, crouched low with a foot on Finlay's back, her taloned-hand still reaching into Finlay's skin. Finlay twisted to see her, and found the woman smiling at her insanely. When Finlay met her eyes, the woman jerked her hand. Lancets of pain speared through her as the talons widened the wounds in Finlay's back by almost half an inch, so they were no longer small points stabbing painfully but gouges, seething angrily. The woman's smile grew. Finlay gasped when the woman pulled her talons out, the motion further aggravating the area.

"Maybe you're not a challenge after all," the woman said, inspecting her reddened claws.

Adrenaline and fury overrode the pain and Finlay flipped onto her back in a sudden, forceful motion. The woman stumbled backward. Finlay jumped to her feet, dagger in hand.

"Finlay!"

Isla's voice. Finlay didn't take her eyes off the Mage; the woman lunged for her again immediately. Finlay parried one of her outstretched hands with her dagger and the other with her arm. Her bracer deflected the talons well enough. Thoughts racing, Finlay thrust her foot forward, planting it against the woman's stomach. Her armor dulled the blow, but it did send her a step backward. Finlay shoved her arms out and pressed closer, stabbing with her dagger. A torrent of air buffeted her back.

"There we go," the Mage said.

A sphere of water appeared over her head at the same moment, crashing down on her and surrounding her. Finlay looked up to see Isla and Muir circling just above. Muir flew lower, allowing Isla to jump off his back and land softly next to Finlay.

"You all right?" Isla asked, glancing at Finlay while keeping her attention on the Mage struggling in the dome of water.

"Okay. Thanks."

Isla raised her hand in a signal to Muir, and the water on top of the Mage lost its shape. The Mage sat up, coughing and spluttering. Finlay noticed her hands had retracted closer to their normal size and shape. Isla strode to the Mage and struck her hard, and the Mage collapsed, her hands returning to human form completely as she lost consciousness.

Jupiter charged over. *Finlay, come with me! Ghillie needs help!*

Alarm overwhelmed everything. In a moment Finlay was astride Jupiter's back, Isla back on Muir, both flying across the clearing, where five Mages had surrounded Ghillie and Chief

Stewart—who had lost his weapon. Cormac and Jasper were engaged with three in the middle of the clearing, two of whom were using abilities like the one Finlay had just been fighting, and appeared to be mostly immune to fire, from the flames they wielded themselves. Their most powerful form, Finlay realized, especially when they used a dragon's claws and magic together. Calum was trying to reach Ghillie and Chief Stewart, separated from Louis, but he was caught in a duel of blades.

A roar of pain from Ghillie cut through to Finlay's heart; one of the Mages around him had sent a concentrated, icy blast against his back leg. Finlay tensed, ready to spring from Jupiter's back and burn that Mage alive herself. A blast of lightning knocked Jupiter off course. Being a storm dragon, it didn't hurt him. Finlay's legs shook as some of the electricity reached her. Her eyes scoured the ground to find the dark-skinned female Mage from earlier directly below them, her gaze fixed on Chief Stewart.

"She's going to kill them!" Finlay cried.

The Mage drew her arm back, static springing into being on her chest and gathering, combining, forming an arc of leaping yellow energy that danced over her shoulder and hurtled along her arm when she threw it forward with the precision of throwing a spear. The lightning expanded when it hit the air, sizzling and popping. Finlay and Jupiter were flying again, but there was no way they would reach them in time.

A blur of blue and green shot in front of the bright yellow light just before it would have hit Ghillie and the chief. A long, serpentine blur of blue and green, illuminated horribly when the lightning struck it.

Finlay's scream shattered the night.

CHAPTER THIRTY-THREE

Time could stand still, Finlay found—in moments so horrible they seemed unreal, moments that stripped meaning from everything with how fundamentally wrong they were—time took its own despicable pace, as if flaunting its power and savoring the knowledge that, when the moment did finally end, nothing would ever be the same again.

That moment was when Isla and Muir took the bolt of lightning intended for Ghillie and Chief Stewart. When Muir's long body rippled and arched in response to the voltage racking his system. When Isla, sitting atop his back, convulsed, limbs thrown wide, mouth open in a silent scream of agony to match Muir's. When their bodies seemed lit like candles against the darkened sky, and then wilted and collapsed, falling limply, sparks still trailing in a sickening parody of falling stars.

Finlay didn't know how long she screamed. She didn't know where the scream came from, how she could give voice at all to the void of nothingness opening up inside her, but she did realize it came from her, from that long, drawn-out moment through to after Muir and Isla had crashed to the ground, utterly still and soundless.

The din of battle around them ceased, in the wake of that horrible moment, Knights and Mages alike turning to stare at the fallen dragon and human, and at Finlay. The sound tearing from her throat ceased as she took in just how wrong they looked, prone on the ground. Lifeless. Grief gave way to a rage the likes of which Finlay had never known, burning through her, overwriting her thoughts, her very identity, and demanding one thing: to burn through the one who had done it, to hollow them out the way they'd just hollowed her.

She dropped from Jupiter's back, barely noticing the shock that shot up from her feet after dropping from several feet up, and ran to the lightning Mage. The woman looked at Finlay as she approached, something like fear flitting in her expression. She held a hand up to ward Finlay off, sparks crackling feebly on her palm. She couldn't muster a formidable charge so soon after her last attack, and Finlay swatted her hand aside as if it were a feather, the charge an annoying tickle.

Finlay shoved the woman back, pinning her to the rough stone of the mountain's side, pressing her dagger against the woman's throat. There was definitely fear in the woman's eyes now. The flames inside Finlay relished in it, taking it in like oxygen and expanding into a devastating blaze.

The choker around the Mage's neck warped and melted. The woman's eyes widened, and a scream of fear and pain left her lips.

That was when Finlay consciously became aware of the fire surrounding her hands and rippling along her blade. Her blade, which had been pressed to the woman's choker, and was now against her bare skin, and still burning . . . Finlay drew it back. The Mage put a shaking hand near her throat, which was sizzling, badly burned. Finlay stared at her dagger, still coated in flames.

She'd never done that before. She could have killed the Mage. She still could. The fire was right here, at her beck and call. She still wanted to do it.

A glance at the Mage, cowering before her, fear and pain the only things written in her expression, made Finlay pause in this line of thought. The damage to her throat looked severe. She'd already been burned. She'd already paid. Not enough. Not nearly enough. But Finlay would let her live.

Bloodlust faded. So did the external flames, slowing and then disappearing entirely. She took in the fear in the woman's eyes once more, hoping she lived with it the rest of her life. Then she turned and ran back to Jupiter, climbing onto his back. As she did, she noticed a familiar figure in her periphery. Alistair. He stood on a boulder beyond what had been combat. She slowed for a second, facing him. He shook his head slightly, as if to say he didn't mean for this to happen. That he'd kept his word. Finlay couldn't remember if she'd seen him attack anyone. She also didn't care at the moment.

Muir was draped across Jasper's back, in front of Cormac, and Finlay could see them flying back in the direction of Aerouant Glèidh. A blue-green sparkle surrounded Muir—his body, dissolving as all dragons' bodies did, minutes after death. Chief Stewart and Ghillie were flying just behind them. Finlay recognized Isla's long black hair in front of the chief, and knew he had her.

"Finlay!" Calum called.

The remaining Mages let Finlay, Jupiter, Calum, and Louis leave. Maybe they were feeling generous. Maybe they knew if they tried to fight, they would die. Very little stopped a dragon's rage, and whatever they thought they knew of Calum and Louis, they all knew the rage in Finlay. She wasn't a dragon, but with the hatred coursing through her, she felt as powerful as one. If the lightning Mage had moved to retaliate, or any others, she would have surrendered to the bloodlust she could still feel under the surface, let the flames rule out all thoughts, and done something she would regret later. She would have tried to kill them all, and knowing Jupiter would have her back, she would have.

She wondered how many had seen her attack the lightning Mage. It was a fleeting wonder, as was the concern that Calum, Cormac, or the chief had seen. Finlay was too empty of anything but that simmering rage to feel something as trivial as that. She clung to the rage as they climbed into the air and pushed toward

Aerouant Glèidh, not letting herself sink back into that horrible realization that Isla was dead.

A pleasant doubt crept in, suggesting she might not be dead yet. She might still be saved, if they could get to her in time.

Finlay jolted so severely Jupiter turned his head to look at her. *What is it?*

"Phoenix fire," Finlay said. "Jupiter, get us home as fast as you can! We might be able to save her!"

Jupiter put on a burst of speed. Finlay's rage cooled, hope pushing through. Aithne had said they might have been able to save John, and Finlay hadn't known. She knew they could try to save Isla. A bit of her fire . . .

Almost all of the Knights stood in the compound when Jupiter landed. It was as full of people and dragons as Finlay had ever seen it, well-lit with torches, and she knew Chief Stewart must have run into the other Knights on their way to help and turned them around. Someone had already fetched Moira; Finlay could see her frizzy gray-brown hair where she crouched over Isla, though her body blocked Isla from view.

Evander appeared by her side as she slid off Jupiter. He brushed her hair from her face and inspected her closely, his eyes fixing on the blood on her cheek and raking over her to look for other injuries.

"I need to get to Isla," she heard herself say, and pushed past him.

She stopped when she reached Moira, now kneeling next to Isla with her head in her hands. Elsie stood next to Isla, rigid.

In shock. Finlay let her eyes fall to her adoptive older sister and see what she'd known she would see all along. Someone had closed her eyes, but there was no way to pretend she was just unconscious. The lightning damage was visible, and a light pallor had already come over her features. Isla was already gone.

Elsie looked at Finlay and blinked, as if just realizing she was there. She looked as hollow as Finlay felt. And Finlay felt hollow again. More than before. Before she'd had anger to war with the nothingness. Her anger was spent, the fire quenched.

She turned to walk away, surprised by how hard it was to lift her feet to walk, and how unsteady she was. It wasn't just her anger that was gone. The last traces of adrenaline from earlier abandoned her in a wave, leaving exhaustion and pain, dull and all-encompassing. Her thoughts slowed to a trickling pace. The air itself felt heavy on her shoulders and in her chest.

Something was wrong.

Nothing and everything was wrong.

Finlay made it two steps back toward Evander before the world took a darker hue, shifting before her eyes. Dizziness slammed in her temples.

The ground rushed up to meet her, but a pair of arms intercepted. Familiar, lean arms. They captured her as gravity drew her down, drawing her close, and the world darkened into nothingness before they hit the ground.

CHAPTER THIRTY-FOUR

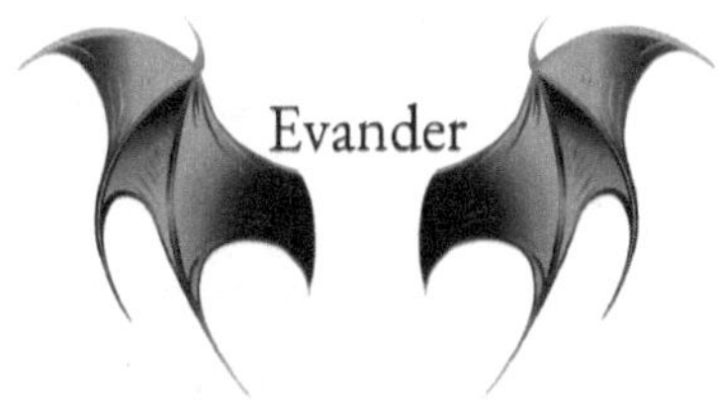

Evander

His conversation with Robin seemed to have taken place ages ago, yet it had only been hours.

Evander, Robin, and Forrest walked right to the sanctuary from the celebration, as Elsie reluctantly went home and Finlay went with Isla to change for the patrol. Elsie claimed Isla would just rub it in if Elsie followed them to the sanctuary, and said she'd hear enough about it from Isla later.

They didn't have long before the Knights going on the patrol would reach the sanctuary. Evander asked Forrest to fly to Jupiter and tell him it was time, and sent a mental message to Gaea asking him to find Muir and Louis. As the dragons did him that favor, Evander faced Robin in his cottage, and loosely crossed his arms over his chest.

"I thought we might take a minute to talk, if you want," Evander said. "No other ears. Say as much or as little as you want. I think you're looking for something. And from what you said earlier, I'm guessing you're looking for others like you. Am I right to think you're looking for your family?"

Robin stared at the ground and took several long seconds before he spoke. "I am. The trouble is, I don't know who that is. Or where. The first thing I can really remember is a face. A girl, leaning over me, telling me to go and be safe. She looked and sounded terrified. I can recall her voice perfectly, and everything about her face. I know she was a faerie, and she looked like me, except her eyes were ringed in yellow, not blue. I think she was my sister . . ." He trailed off, and then seemed to remember he had been talking to Evander and looked up with gently drawn eyebrows. "The next definitive thing I remember is wandering, a pack on my back, feeling like I needed to get somewhere but not knowing where. Totally alone, until an elven family took me in. Dim memories that aren't really memories, but feelings, have returned over time, so I've been traveling. I need to find her."

Evander studied him. "How old are you, Robin?"

"I don't know for sure, but somewhere around fourteen, I think."

He didn't just look young, then. He was young. "Have you told Finlay any of this?"

Robin shook his head. "She has enough to worry about. You do, too, but since you asked . . ."

"I'll do what I can to help you," Evander said, standing up straight. "We'll find your family. It just might take some time."

Robin ducked his head down and murmured, "Thank you," and Evander had a fleeting urge to hug him. Commotion outside drew the thought from his mind, and he nodded at Robin before leaving his cottage to greet Calum and wait for the others.

It had only been a handful of hours ago, but they were tense, agonizing hours, waiting for information after he found Elsie and several other Knights, and waiting even more agonizingly after they left, what had to be almost half an hour after the others.

When he saw Elsie and Kenna leading the large group Evander had asked to fly after Finlay and the others back, Evander's heart pumped faster than it had in all the time he'd been waiting. Elsie was flying in a rush.

"Get Moira!" Elsie yelled over her shoulder, and Evander saw Aileen's partner Tempest break off of the group. They landed, swiftly crowding the space that had been utterly empty apart from Evander, and Evander scoured their ranks for Finlay's bright hair.

Elsie dropped to the ground and ran to Ghillie. That was when Evander noticed Chief Stewart atop his back, a limp form with long, dark hair in his arms. "Oh no," he breathed.

Elsie took all of Isla's weight and moved several paces away before going to her knees and letting Isla rest against the ground. Evander hurried to her side, horror rooting inside him when he took in just how wrong Isla looked. How damaged. "Elsie, what happened?"

"I don't know," Elsie said in a toughened voice, feeling for a pulse on both Isla's throat and her wrist. "We met them in the air, on their way back. Muir's gone. They must have taken some kind of blast together."

"Let me see her," Moira said, running over with her limping gait. Evander stepped back. Elsie stood but didn't move away, staring at her sister with eyes that were both blazing and hollowed, while Moira knelt by Isla's head.

Evander moved closer to the crowd, intent on asking exactly what had happened, and where Finlay was. He didn't need to ask. He could see a pair of dragons and riders approaching, and ran to Finlay's side when she slid from Jupiter's back. Her eyes slid over him before returning when he said her name, and though he saw she recognized him, it was like she didn't take it in fully.

"Love," he said, brushing her hair back, trying to get her out of the daze she'd apparently slipped into. "Let me see if you're hurt."

"I need to get to Isla," she said in a dull sort of voice, and walked past him. Though walking may have been too orderly a term for the unsteadiness of her gait. He watched her closely as she stepped close enough to see Isla, and saw, when she turned to him once more, that whatever vestige of focus she'd had was gone.

Alarm shot through him when he saw how much paler she suddenly became, and her shoulders swayed. Evander scrambled forward, sliding to his knees to catch her as she fell. "Finlay?"

He adjusted his grip on her, pulling her head onto his lap. Was there a wound that was causing this, or was it the horror she'd just experienced? "Moira!" Evander said urgently. The woman was by his side in an instant, tear-stained face showing fresh terror at the sight of Finlay in his arms. "She's alive, but I'm not sure why she passed out, if she's wounded or not." He breathed in sharply and focused himself, and willed some of the healing magic Gaea had shared with him to the surface. He could sense any serious injuries, with a light application of his magic.

He didn't feel any life-threatening injuries, and sighed. "I think it's mostly shock, though she does have a few wounds."

"She's to be taken to the war room," Chief Stewart said. "She needs to be questioned when she regains consciousness."

"She needs to be taken where she's comfortable," Evander insisted, "so she can start to heal." The chief's words finally sank in. "Why do you want to question her?"

"We learned a dark truth about Finlay tonight, Evander," Chief Stewart said.

Evander could see it in the man's eyes: his hatred, and also, his triumph. He thought Finlay was a Mage. She must have used her fire at some point. "I'm bringing her back to the sanctuary," Evander said firmly. He scooped Finlay into his arms and stood. "I'll bring her to you when she's recovered."

"Evander," Chief Stewart started, but Moira held up a hand.

"She needs medical attention, Stewart. Surely you don't think Evander would try to sneak her away?"

Chief Stewart looked at her levelly. "He might not, but he might let her try it herself, once she wakes. So I'll take this as a reassurance." He reached over and pulled Finlay's prized dagger from her belt.

A protest rose in Evander's mouth, but Moira shook her head at him, and he kept silent. He didn't say anything else to the despicable man, but brought Finlay to Jupiter's back and asked the dragon to fly them home.

"I won't let him hurt you," Evander said to Finlay, despite knowing she couldn't hear him. "I won't let him take you away from me."

Chapter Thirty-Five

Finlay

Her nightmare was the same. It was also more.

The last night with her family, and finding their charred remains, never knowing who was responsible. The grief and terror when she'd first met Aithne, and thought she'd killed her. Chief Stewart laughing as he kicked Ghillie while she watched, restrained and unable to stop him. Isla and Muir, illuminated by a deadly shock, and Finlay's scream as they fell. The fear on the lightning Mage's face. The blankness of Elsie's expression.

Tears clung to her eyelashes as she blinked away sleep. She wasn't in her bed, though her surroundings were immediately familiar. She was in Evander's cottage, in his bed. Forrest lay beside her, curled into a ball with his snout tucked beneath his tail, breathing deeply. Bright light filtered in through the open door and window, and warm, humid air pressed close, so strands of hair clung to Finlay's neck and her clothes slicked to her skin with sweat.

Moving her head, she saw a clean pair of pants and a shirt folded on Evander's table, which she recognized as her own. More importantly, once she realized how achingly dry her throat was, she saw the glass of water next to the clothes. The action of getting up roused Forrest, and before she'd done more than swing her legs around him (she'd had some practice getting up around the sleeping dragon) and sit up on the edge of the bed, he had jumped upright and run onto her lap.

Don't stand up yet, Forrest said. He reached up, balanced his paws on her shoulders, and nuzzled her face. *I'm really glad you're awake. Just let me get Evander.*

He zoomed away, raising his voice and calling for Evander in an excited tone. Finlay waited on the bed's edge, as Forrest requested. Her back didn't hurt anymore. Moira must have used a salve on the wounds after Finlay had passed out. Or perhaps Evander had used some of Gaea's healing magic.

Forrest was back within a minute. Evander ran in behind him, tightness in the skin around his eyes. When he saw Finlay that tightness vanished and an open-mouthed grin graced his face. "Finlay." He ran over and went to one knee in front of her, looking at her searchingly. "How are you feeling?"

"Like I need a drink," Finlay croaked.

Evander retrieved the glass and handed it to her. The water was warm but soothed the dryness in Finlay's throat, and she felt just a bit more herself after drinking it.

Evander took the empty glass back, set it down next to him, and then took Finlay's hand. "Gaea used his healing breath on you, so I expected you to sleep for several hours, but you were unconscious for more than a day, Finlay. I was so worried."

Finlay looked to the window again. The light filtering through spoke more of afternoon sun than morning, more muted in shades of gold. More muted than usual, actually, like darker gray clouds than normal were blocking the sun. "More than a day?" A horrible thought that twisted her empty stomach occurred to her. "Isla's ceremony of life."

Evander moved to sit beside her on the bed in a slow, gentle motion. "They did it last night. Elsie asked them to wait, but it's custom to do it within a day, and Chief Stewart insisted."

He wouldn't have let you go anyway, Forrest said.

Forrest's comment pulled Finlay from her contradictory emotions: undeniable relief that, after everything, she didn't have to face another blazing flame, and bitter regret that she missed her last chance to say goodbye to her sister. She blinked at the dragon. "What?"

Evander cast Forrest a harried look. "We can explain later, after you've had a bit more time—"

"Evander, what is it?"

Evander was still looking at Forrest, who nodded, and with a sigh, Evander turned back to Finlay. "You're under a sort of house arrest. Chief Stewart wanted to keep you in the detention ward, under watch. Elsie, Moira, and I convinced him to let me take you here."

"Why am I under house arrest?" She reached for her dagger and felt only empty air. She wore simple pants and a loose shirt. No belt or string to attach her dagger to. No dagger, sheathed near her. "Where's my dagger?"

A muscle in Evander's jaw tensed. "The chief has your dagger. Insurance, he said, that you wouldn't try to escape on a dragon. He knows you would never leave it behind. They saw you use Aithne's magic, and there's going to be a meeting. I think they've already had one, but they have to include you in one as well, before they can make a decision."

Finlay stared ahead without seeing. "They think I'm a Mage."

Evander took her hand firmly between his and demanded her gaze. "We'll tell them the truth of your situation and they'll see you're not. I'll be at the meeting too, and Elsie. Robin too, if they let him. I know Elsie's already been telling anyone who'll listen that you're innocent."

Elsie. A pang went through Finlay's heart. "I'm not innocent of everything. It's my fault Isla died."

Evander stood and refilled the glass with water. "I think Cormac holds more blame for that than you do. And the Mage that actually killed her."

The chief is only stirring people up about this because he hates you, Forrest said.

Finlay knew that much. Chief Stewart had been waiting for an opportunity to ruin Finlay's life. "What happened with Ghillie?"

Forrest snorted smoke. *He's in his usual spot. Robin wants to stay to see how he can help you before he gets Ghillie out.*

Finlay stood and swayed immediately. Evander braced her and eased her back onto the bed. "You need to drink some more and eat something before you try to get up, all right? Your wounds are all healed, but your body is very low on energy."

Finlay swallowed and moved back on the bed to lean against the wall. "All right."

"I finally get to make you eggs," Evander said in a lighter tone, a teasing tilt to his lips. "You need the protein. They'll be ready in a few minutes."

Forrest sat down next to Finlay again while Evander made a hearty plate of eggs for her. As the eggs cooked she drank another cup of water, this one slightly bitter due to the energy-boosting powder Evander added. "Help me eat all this," Finlay protested when he handed the full plate to her with a fork.

"Not a chance. You need to finish it."

Finlay wanted to protest again, as she took a bite. That desire vanished after swallowing that bite, and tasting the cheesy eggs. Her appetite roared to life, her empty stomach demanding sustenance, and in a very short time she had the plate cleared.

Not even a scrap for me, Forrest grumbled.

Finlay was tempted to smile. "Sorry, Forrest. I didn't realize I was so hungry."

You feel better now, right?

The slight shakiness that had lingered after she tried to stand was gone. "Much." Finlay blushed so fiercely she felt the tips of her ears warm. "Thank you for the eggs, Evander."

He rubbed a hand along the back of his neck. "My pleasure."

Forrest looked between them. *You two are so weird sometimes.*

Finlay scratched under his chin. "You would know. You're the weirdest one of the three of us."

I think you mean most amazing.

A breath of a laugh broke through the swirl of grief and anxiety inside. Only Forrest. "Maybe."

"Ready to get up?" Evander asked.

Finlay stood in answer. Between the eggs and the energy-boosting powder, she felt in peak physical condition. It was just mental and emotional strain that remained, and those wouldn't be lifted as easily. "Can I wash up?"

"I'll fill the basin."

With the humidity so high, it didn't make sense to take a full bath, though Finlay did want to. She would want another later. She settled for taking the lukewarm water and rinsing off. Twenty minutes later she'd finished that, brushed out her hair and put it into a loose knot on the back of her head to keep it from sticking to her again, and changed into the clean outfit Evander had gotten for her, and felt about as good as she could, knowing everything about her day would get harder as soon as she walked out the door. She looped string around her waist too, fashioning the knot she used to hold her dagger in part of it—she would be taking it back, whatever happened.

Evander waited outside, leaning against the wall of his cottage.

"Where are you supposed to take me?" Finlay asked.

"Straight to Chief Stewart. He wants to talk to you before he calls the meeting." They set off toward the sanctuary's border closest to the compound, walking in silence for several minutes. "Walk a little slower," Evander said as they neared the sanctuary's edge. The crystal blooms were in view now.

Finlay started to ask why, but the question faded from her tongue when she saw Forrest flying in her direction, coming from past the border mark. A few seconds later Elsie came into view as well, jogging behind Forrest. Robin, who could have outrun her, stayed several paces behind, as though holding himself back. "You sent Forrest to get Elsie and Robin?"

"The chief doesn't need to know you've been awake for a bit. Robin was here until a few hours ago, waiting for you to wake up. Then he went to check on Elsie. They've been wanting to see you, and I know you need to see them."

Finlay was embarrassed by the tears that pricked at her eyes as Elsie approached. Her adoptive sister didn't say anything about them, though. She just charged in and trapped Finlay in the biggest bear hug she'd ever given. Finlay felt the shudder that ran through Elsie's frame and held her back just as fiercely, for a long moment. When they let go, Elsie's eyes weren't quite dry either, though her tears hadn't spilled free like Finlay's.

"I'm so sorry," Finlay said in a choked sort of voice, when Robin took Elsie's place embracing her. "I wanted to try to heal her with Aithne's magic, but I was too late."

Elsie took a deep breath. "It's not your fault. Moira said—Moira said she probably died immediately after the shock. There was nothing you could have done. Me either, even if I'd been there. I just . . . I can't believe my sister is gone."

"My sister too," Finlay whispered. Maybe it was stubbornness to say this to Elsie now, maybe it was stupid and might make her mad, but Finlay felt the need to say it all the same. To lay some legitimacy to the grief still threatening to swallow her, and hear it validated from another. "She was my sister too, in all but blood. Same as you."

Elsie swore and tackled Finlay in a hug again. "Damn it, Fin, you know I feel the same," she said over Finlay's shoulder. She stepped back and rubbed a hand hard across her face. "Which is why I've been telling them it's ridiculous to think you could have killed a dragon to take its power. I know you, and I know the truth. Let's go clear the air."

Robin ducked his head slightly. "I'm sorry I didn't follow through on my promise to free Ghillie yesterday. I know as soon as I do, I can't risk coming back, and I wanted to make sure you . . ." Finlay touched his arm in understanding, and he trailed off. "I'll glamour everyone if I have to. I need to make sure you're safe before I get Ghillie."

So much like her brother. "It'll be all right."

Forrest nestled in Finlay's arms. Elsie, Robin, and Evander walked on either side of her. In minutes they reached the compound, passed Graham at the gated entrance, and found their progress blocked by several Knights.

"We'll take her from here," Cormac said.

"She doesn't need to be *taken* anywhere," Evander said, bristling.

"Chief Stewart says differently," Cormac said around a sneer. He pulled out a rope and stepped toward Finlay. "No more special treatment."

"No punishment before it's been proven she did anything wrong!" Elsie said, stepping in front of Finlay.

"Hey!" Calum said, approaching swiftly from across the courtyard. He assessed the situation in a heartbeat. "Cormac, I hardly think rope is necessary. Finlay is perfectly willing to cooperate, right?"

Finlay dipped her head.

"It's not to be mean," Cormac said. "It's to keep the chief safe while she talks to him. No saying who else she'll try to burn. No fire magic with this about her wrists."

Finlay narrowed her eyes at Cormac but didn't dignify his words with a response. She'd never had a problem with him before, but losing John, something inside him had broken, and the jagged pieces were being aimed at her. She'd been with John when he died. She'd helped bring about that situation. Seeing her use Aithne's fire, she understood Cormac's concern. She understood the leap he had made, thinking perhaps she was working against them. It was ridiculous, but putting herself in his perspective, knowing how frenzied his mind must be, Finlay understood.

She hated him a little for it, all the same.

"I'll take it," Calum insisted, holding out his hand for the rope.

Cormac's jaw twitched, but he handed it over.

"Everyone, back to what you were doing," Calum ordered. He looked at Finlay. "I'll bring you to the chief. He wants to meet in the war room."

He led her there silently, past the storage sections of the armory. Finlay purposely avoided looking at Isla's section, fearing it would already be emptied. Calum opened the door to the war room and stood back to let Finlay inside. "We'll get this sorted out," he said under his breath as she walked past. That was when she realized he had the rope from Cormac still tucked in his pocket, and didn't make a move to retrieve it. Her pulse leveled for a moment, appreciation for her mentor calming her.

The door closed behind her, and Finlay faced Chief Stewart. The paunchy man stood at the far head of a long table that dominated the space of the room. Nothing ornamented the space; it was simply a long table surrounded by chairs, in a very plain room. Still, it was slightly intimidating. Maybe it was the name, calling it the war room. Finlay had never been in here before. Emergency meetings occurred outside when the weather permitted, and she hadn't been a Knight long enough to see bad weather that would warrant this room's use. Finlay wondered if this room was used very much at all, other than for

Chief Stewart to meet with Calum, and occasionally Moira and perhaps Evander.

The chief stood with his hands clasped behind his back, gloating triumph written in the set of his shoulders and swell of his chest. "To think I've spent all this time trying to figure out how to get rid of you, and you've damned yourself. You're a dragon killer."

"I've never killed anyone."

"It's possible you couldn't help it, given the filth running through your veins."

Finlay pressed her lips together for a long moment. She'd never noticed before she discovered Ghillie's situation, but since learning how effectively the chief could hide his disdain for her . . . paired with this comment about what runs through her veins . . . "What don't I know about why you hate me? Why you've always hated me?"

Chief Stewart produced Finlay's dagger from behind his back. "One look at this dagger was all I needed to know who you were, that day you stumbled into our midst. The daughter of a murderer." He looked at her with narrowed eyes. "I knew you'd grow up to be just as despicable a creature."

CHAPTER THIRTY-SIX

Finlay had to force herself to stay in the same spot when he insulted her father—the urge to rush forward, grip him by the collar, and demand to know what the man knew of her family was hard to tamp down. She knew the chief, though. He would tell Finlay, anyway, wanting to lord it over her.

"You really never knew your father was a Mage, you ignorant girl?"

"There's no proof he killed a dragon."

"The proof is in the conversation I had with him, the day he came here!" the chief said in a louder voice. Finlay sucked in a breath. Chief Stewart looked at the door and said something in the elven language. "There. Now we have a bit more privacy."

Part of Finlay wanted to ask what he'd done. She needed a different answer more. "My family was here?"

A wicked little smile curved on his lips. "I think it's time I told you this story. Yes, Finlay, your mother, your father, and your brother came here. They wanted to live here. They even met with me, to see if anyone could train to defend dragon-kind when they came of age. It was clear they wanted the boy to become a Knight. I saw no problem with it, until I saw the pommel of this dagger on your father's waist.

"It's a finely crafted weapon. It didn't match their worn clothing. Your father noticed me eyeing it and made a joke, saying it was just for protection before moving to conceal it. I asked to see it more closely and suggested Meric show your mother and brother the courtyard. We were more relaxed with admittance, then. They left and your father drew this blade with a palpable reluctance, turned it over in his hand, and held it out to me by the hilt."

Chief Stewart held the dagger loosely in his hand, his eyes trained on it as if reliving the memory. "I told your father I'd seen daggers like this before. That I'd grown up seeing men and women wielding them, after they'd harnessed the powers of dragons they'd slayed. And that only those who have killed dragons and been named royal Mages have them awarded. Those in the inner circle of the queen. He didn't deny it.

"He lowered his head, faking grief or something similar, and said he used to be a Mage, but that he couldn't continue. He said he couldn't condone killing anymore, and ran off shortly after he earned the dagger, marrying your mother and starting your little family. He'd heard rumors of our settlement, but thanks to Ghillie's magic, he could never find it. It took them years to track us down, and your mother had to lead your father in by the hand for him to see it. Apparently the magic didn't think she consorted with a dragon killer, since he'd left the Mages' ranks before they met. I say she was garbage for being with him at all."

Finlay's rage sparked and kindled with the chief's words.

"I gave him the dagger back, and he asked if it would be a problem. It wasn't like I could tell him the truth. Meric and several of the others had met with them as well. Their permission to live here had already been all but granted." His grip on Finlay's dagger tightened, his stubby fingers whitening over it. Finlay's fingers twitched at her sides. She wanted his fat hands off her father's weapon. "They stayed a short while before leaving, saying they would pack their things and return in the coming days."

Chief Stewart threw the dagger onto the table. The clatter made Finlay flinch. "Your father was a cowardly murderer. He didn't recognize me from the kingdom, though I could vaguely remember him. He didn't have the courage to leave that life behind, to form a settlement dedicated to fighting back!"

"He had the courage to leave and start a family!" Finlay said. "He was kind!"

The chief slammed his hands down on the table. "He was tainted, the second he killed a dragon!" He drew in a large breath. "And that kind of darkness isn't contained to one person. It leeches into their loved ones, infecting them, propagating so it can spread. It tainted your mother by association. You and your brother never had a chance to avoid it. So I did what had to be done: I destroyed it."

He walked around the edge of the table, taking slow, measured steps closer to Finlay. "I went out with Ghillie the next night, Finlay. He was so opposed to my intentions that I had to drug him to get him to obey me and fly; it was the first time I ever had to do that, and the reason I've had to do it every day since. When I saw your mother and brother in that clearing, and ordered Ghillie to use his fire, I felt our bond break. I felt him rebel against me, only submitting because of what I'd given him and the force of my will, in that last moment we were connected. I burned the house for good measure. Didn't occur to me that they had another child. That anyone else could survive, if there was anyone else. I wanted all traces of that darkness gone."

Finlay's body shook violently. Dimly, she heard the chief say something else in that elven language. Her vision tunneled, the rage that had kindled inside exploding to the same level as the night Isla died; a blaze that threatened her very identity, it wanted so badly to destroy the one who had caused her wounds—wounds which felt as new and deep as the night they'd been inflicted, learning their true origin. Her voice came out in a forceful whisper. "You killed them."

He stopped just beyond arm's reach from her. "I thought you'd like to know. And I'm sorry I didn't check for survivors that night. We could have avoided all of this if I'd killed you then, with your family. It wasn't like I could kill you when you came here. There's another in your situation, born with that darkness in his veins, but as we live now, my hands are tied with him as well. I'll just have to keep hoping he meets the same fate as Isla, with a tragic accident . . ."

His casual tone was the final straw thrown onto the inferno inside her. The rational part of her screamed for her not to do it, knowing it was what he wanted, and why he'd so theatrically told her everything. The fire overrode it, propelling her forward. *Burn,* it urged her, filling her sight with red. *Burn!* Flames licked along her shaking limbs, vibrating so strongly she felt she could burst. "You took them from me!"

She saw the gleam in his eyes, the satisfaction in his face. Her own sort of satisfaction filled her when her nails scratched his cheek. Blood beaded and trickled down the linear grooves, scorched pink and blistered by the heat in Finlay's fingertips, and he smiled through the pain as she gripped his collar and pulled her fist back to strike again. "Just what I needed to be rid of you for good."

Finlay backed up, rage cooling as horror replaced it.

"Help!" Chief Stewart cried. "She's insane!"

The door behind Finlay burst open with Cormac gripping the handle, Calum behind him—and Lachlan, Bryson, and Elsie beyond him.

"I told you it was necessary!" Cormac said, pointing at Chief Stewart's cheek as Bryson and Lachlan rushed in and blocked

Finlay from the chief. They seemed to want to grab her, but were too wary to touch her.

"Shut up," Elsie said, looking like she wanted to punch him.

Cormac held his hand out to Calum. "Give me the rope!"

"I'm not trying to kill him," Finlay spat.

Calum had half-pulled the rope from his pocket, looking from Finlay to Chief Stewart with the most closed-off expression Finlay had ever seen him wear. Cormac snatched the rope and went over to tie Finlay's wrists together in front of her. It cinched tightly, and Finlay slumped, every bit of magical fire inside her muffled. How had they made a rope like this?

Elsie marched over and jerked Cormac's hand away from Finlay's wrists. "Leave her alone!"

"She attacked the chief," Lachlan said.

"He killed my family," Finlay seethed, glowering at the chief. Lachlan and Bryson gripped Finlay's arms and pulled her toward the door.

"We'll hold the meeting immediately," Chief Stewart said, as if she hadn't spoken. "I don't want to drag this out any further."

"Did you hear her?" Elsie asked Lachlan and Bryson. "She just said he killed her family. How can you take that without pause?"

They ignored her and shoved Finlay through the door.

Finlay craned her neck to look behind her. Calum still stood in the doorway, his guarded expression locked on the chief.

"Call the Knights," Chief Stewart told him.

Calum turned on his heel to walk after Finlay and the others, and Finlay observed a hardness to his jaw that betrayed his emotion. Anger.

She didn't resist as Bryson and Lachlan escorted her to the courtyard, Elsie and Cormac having a heated exchange behind her. Calum followed close behind them, a storm rumbling beneath his seemingly-placid brow.

It wasn't the only storm Finlay sensed. The heavy, humid air weighed down on her like a choking blanket, stirred feebly by a hot breeze. The clouds, which normally looked more gray than white, hung uniformly in the skyline above, several shades darker than usual. Darker than they'd been when she first woke up, even.

She remained silent as everyone gathered, surprisingly numb to the situation. Chief Stewart would have his way. Robin walked to the front of the crowd, a question clear in his eyes. *Do you want me to glamour them, and get you out of here?*

Finlay shook her head in a tiny motion. She couldn't put Robin in danger like that. They would absolutely pursue him as an enemy if they found out he was a faerie and hadn't told them. Besides. She was sick of pretending everything was all right, and keeping secrets.

"I'd like to start by explaining my situation," she said, before Chief Stewart could say anything. She didn't look at the man to receive permission. She raised her voice to speak over him, and kept going after he reluctantly stopped trying to take control, telling everyone the truth of her bond with Aithne, her discovery of Ghillie's mistreatment, and her plan to expose the chief with the Mages' help. She told them how the chief had confessed to killing her family, just now. Several times, she noticed disbelieving sounds coming from the crowd, and heads shaking in refusal to accept it. Sometimes it seemed they overrode her own voice, but she pushed through until she'd said everything she wanted to.

And then the onslaught began.

"What a story," Cormac sneered.

"Only telling something so horrible about Ghillie after the chief wants to question her, and after she's attacked him? More than a little suspicious!" Lachlan said loudly.

"Why wouldn't she tell us about the phoenix dragon before?" Bryson challenged in the same breath, addressing everyone. "Why hide it, if it really happened like she said?"

"Because you lot jump to conclusions!" Elsie interjected, her face reddening.

"What she's telling you isn't possible!" Cormac raged.

"It is, because it happened!"

"You expect us to believe the chief, who hates Mages and all they stand for, would abuse his dragon partner?" Aileen asked.

"Everyone, calm down," Calum ordered.

Elsie seemed ready to retrieve her war hammer and fight Cormac. Finlay found Robin's eyes and gestured to Elsie, in a silent plea. He seemed to understand. Elsie paused after taking a great breath, noticing Finlay's gaze shift from her and over to Robin. Robin's eyes swirled slightly when Elsie met them, and the heavy breath Elsie had taken rushed out in a reluctant sigh. *Thank you,* Finlay thought to Robin. He'd understood. Elsie was still angry. She was still perfectly herself. But if Robin hadn't taken the edge off of her rage, she would have done something she would regret. Elsie would forgive them later.

"Finlay's said her piece," Chief Stewart said. "I think we need to make it clear why we're meeting here. Finlay has been accused of being a Mage. She just admitted to colluding with Mages. I, along with Cormac and Calum, witnessed her use fire magic reminiscent of a Mage. She was there when John died. Who's to say she didn't have a role in that death, as well as Isla's? As for the accusation that I abuse Ghillie, have any of you seen signs of that? Because I wouldn't call it abuse to give him the support and care and privacy he needs, in his frail condition."

"Did anyone ever verify that he still has a condition?" Elsie demanded loudly. "Evander, or Moira? I don't think so!"

"She's trying to shift the focus away from herself, that's all," Bryson said.

"Let's ask Ghillie," Moira said. "I trust Finlay."

"You also apprenticed her," Lachlan said.

"I trust her as well," Meric said.

"Okay, surrogate father," Lachlan stage-whispered.

"So the words of those closest to her, who know her best, aren't trustworthy?" Elsie asked. "Who's shifting focus now? Let's ask Ghillie!"

"Let's focus on Finlay," Cormac said. "Then we can investigate the claims about Ghillie."

Finlay stared hard at the ground as the bickering continued. Moira's support, and Meric's, meant a lot. They also weren't enough. Not if most of the Knights felt as Lachlan and Bryson did. Especially not if they felt as strongly as Cormac did. Anything else she said would seem like trying to make excuses. If they didn't believe her, Finlay saw quite clearly that she wouldn't be the one to convince them otherwise. Someone else had to do that, and Finlay saw someone step forward as she thought this. Evander. Finlay's gaze lifted to him, and to Forrest, who clung over one of his shoulders.

"Look at her eyes," Evander demanded, after a long, tense moment, in which everyone whispered amongst themselves. "Those eyes don't lie. You all know Finlay, and how much she loves dragons." He looked around, chest rising and falling rapidly. Few looked at Evander or Finlay. A spasm of indignation rippled across Evander's face. "SHE'S DONE NOTHING WRONG!" he bellowed.

"Well defended, young Evander," Chief Stewart said. "But your relationship with her prevents you from seeing this clearly. Whether or not you believe she killed a dragon, she consorted with a Mage, and set up the fight that led to the deaths of Isla and Muir."

"Cormac was the idiot that started that fight," Elsie spat. "It wouldn't have happened without him."

"It wouldn't have happened at all without Finlay's collusion with a Mage," Chief Stewart insisted. "This is the latest in an alarming pattern of behavior on her part, which can regrettably be traced back to her family." He produced Finlay's dagger. "Few here would recognize this as the symbol of a full-fledged Mage, but I'm not the only one to know it. I turned a blind eye when she wandered into our midst, hoping she didn't understand its significance. I now realize she's known all along, and embraced that path, as her family did before."

He brandished the dagger. "Those recognized as Mages aren't recognizable only by the rings they wear, and for those in the inner circle, daggers like this. They also suffer from nightmares on a regular basis. Finlay is known to have frequent nightmares. She treasures this dagger over all else. The magic she displayed when she 'fought' that Mage, and when she attacked me just now, is unlike anything we've seen someone who has not fully claimed the power of a dragon possess. All of this paints a very unflattering picture, one even Evander can't ignore. Verified Mage or not, as a willing conspirator in the most recent battle that led to the death of one of our own, and paired with this other alarming evidence, it's clear Finlay has no place among the Knights. Her actions were severe, which merits severe consequences.

"I call for Finlay's total banishment from our community."

"That's insanity," Evander said, pressing forward. "You're twisting words. She's always had nightmares, because she experienced real trauma as a child. She favors her dagger because it's the only thing she has to remember her family." He shook his head, his lip curling in disgust. "You'll stop at nothing to be rid of her, because she knows what an absolute monster you truly are."

Hatred flickered in the chief's expression. "You're lashing out because you're upset, of course."

Evander looked like he wanted to walk away, but he looked to Finlay and dug his heels into the ground. Forrest had his eyes shut tight.

"That's too extreme," Moira said.

"She doesn't deserve to be punished," Elsie growled.

Calum, who had stood nearby, staring at the ground with an impenetrable expression all along, moved to face the chief, something broken, angry, and pained in his expression. "I—"

"Finlay wouldn't make an unfounded accusation about a dragon's safety. Show us Ghillie," Meric demanded.

Calum stopped and looked between them, waiting for the chief's response.

Chief Stewart looked to Meric, feigning betrayal. Robin moved in an instant to stand behind Meric and capture the chief's eyes. A cry rose to Finlay's lips, though she kept it in. Why would he risk his safety, when the chief's mind was made up?

"All right," Chief Stewart said, somewhat dreamily.

"What did you just do?" Lachlan asked, looking at Robin.

Finlay saw Robin's eyes swirl again, and heard Lachlan say, "Never mind," but the damage was done. All eyes were now on Robin, ranging from confused to curious to suspicious and hostile.

"Magic," a Knight called Lionel said. "He used magic." He gasped. "He's a faerie!"

"Robin, go!" Finlay yelled, rushing forward as chaos overwhelmed the scene. Hands appeared and held her back. Evander and Elsie surged toward her, trying to help. Calum was pushed back, confusion in his brow—*don't let this keep you from believing me,* Finlay pleaded. She was sure he'd been about to say he believed her. His voice would be enough to stay the Knights. He seemed stunned into a temporary paralysis, though, his thoughts spinning in his eyes. Forrest flew off Evander's shoulder to ram toward Lionel and Iris as they tried to grab Robin. They startled back, and Robin ran toward the dormitory, Forrest flying at his side. Meric drew his staff and ran after them. Three Knights chased after *him.*

"Oh no, you don't," Elsie said, tearing after them.

"Mutiny!" Chief Stewart yelled as all of this happened. "See what Finlay has brought us! Division, secrecy, and lies! She vouched for the faerie boy! She must have gotten him to sway several of our Knights to her side, as he just tried to sway me! I call for her banishment, and I call for it now!"

Calum startled out of his paralyzed state. A glance told Finlay she'd guessed correctly earlier, and a rush of adrenaline went through her when Calum stepped in front of her, pulling his sword and leveling it at Chief Stewart's chest. "I call for your silence." He raised his voice. "Knights, stand down!"

"Finally, someone with sense," Moira said loudly.

"The faerie's gotten to you," Cormac said, his own sword drawn.

"The chief has gotten to us all," Calum protested.

Chief Stewart said something loud and low in that elven language, and a tremor went through Finlay. Abruptly, she found herself unable to move, utterly stuck in place.

The chief moved to stand directly in front of her frozen eyes, a grim smile upon his suddenly sweat-slicked face. "I'll have some explaining to do where Ghillie's concerned," he said quietly. "They may take my leadership from me. But there's a chance to spin my innocence in your death, this way. Regardless, I'll see what I started over a decade ago finished, and wipe out the darkness in your veins. I'll get the other one in time." He grabbed her, hoisting her over his shoulder. Finlay couldn't react externally because of his damn spell. Inside, she raged. She tried calling fire to her hands, to burn away the rope. That didn't require movement, just thought and feeling. Whatever had been done to the rope still kept her from accessing the flames.

He carried her to the sanctuary, huffing at his clipped pace within seconds. "I should have a good five minutes before anyone in the vicinity can move," he said between panting, as if to himself. "That spell is costly, but beneficial. More than enough time to get you out of reach." He dropped her to the ground after they passed the crystal blooms at the border. "Help!" he called. "I need a dragon's help!"

Finlay couldn't see which dragon approached, the chief's boots filling her field of vision. She heard the sound of wings cutting through the air, though, and a sturdy but gentle footfall. *What's happened to her?* a deep voice rumbled.

Gaea.

"We need to act quickly," Chief Stewart said, feigned but convincing panic in his voice. "Poison. Only one cure I know of. There's an herb that grows higher up on the mountain, by the far side of the lake. If you can take us there, I can help her."

Let me use my—

"Dragon magic won't work! I've seen this before!"

Then let's go.

Finlay's heart sped. *No, Gaea!*

He didn't hear her plea, and in seconds Chief Stewart had lifted Finlay and draped her over Gaea's back, and seated himself behind her. A tingling sensation started in Finlay's fingertips as they ascended. Concentrating, she made her pinky twitch.

The air moved restlessly higher up, whipping itself to make a storm, droplets of moisture clinging to each angry gust. Finlay focused on the muscles in her jaw, fighting to make them obey her and open. If she could just speak to Gaea . . . her mouth opened, and she forced sound through her constricted throat. A feeble gurgle, quickly stifled by the chief's heavy hand.

Are we close to where you need to be? Gaea asked a minute later. Finlay, who could now move her face and all of her fingers, but not the entirety of her body, glared at Chief Stewart as the man urged Gaea to move a bit further out. Rain began falling in earnest.

"This will comfort you," the chief said, pulling Finlay onto his lap and securing Finlay's dagger in the string she'd set up for it. She could move her head and her limbs, and went to strike him with her hands, despite them still being bound. He still had one hand on her mouth, and with the other he pulled her too close for her still-clumsy movements to do anything. He leaned in close, his voice the faintest whisper in her ear. "You claimed a fire dragon's power, Finlay. Have fun in the water."

He thrust his torso to the side, arms extending. Finlay felt open air all around her, weightless for a singular moment—and then she was falling. Hundreds of feet separated her from the lake's surface, a distance she knew would be breached in seconds. She reached for her dagger, turning the blade up and sawing at the rope around her wrists with furious desperation. She kept the blade polished and sharpened, which was good. She cut through the rope, nicking herself a few times in the process, in what she guessed was about half of the time she had to fall. The frayed edges fell away.

Gaea roared above her. Finlay twisted in the air and saw him angle his body down, diving to save her. She looked down and knew in an instant he wouldn't make it in time. She would collide in a handful of seconds, and from that height, at this speed . . . it wouldn't feel like water at all. There was no coming back from this fall. Terror stole the scream she felt inside, or maybe the wind rushing by her ears simply kept her from hearing it. She curled in on herself, hugging her dagger to her chest and closing her eyes just before she hit. Evander. Elsie. Forrest. Robin.

I'm sorry.

She didn't feel the warmth until the instant before she hit, or see the flames licking along her body until the split second before she shut her eyes, and any thoughts as to what it meant stopped with the collision. All thoughts stopped, only sensations remaining. It wasn't like water. It was harder than stone, and it was with a heavy slapping sound that she collided with it and barreled through it, stone giving way to liquid. She felt the bones on the right side of her body, which hit first, shatter, and her eyes shot open, a scream of agony tearing from her throat. It came out in a torrent of bubbles, her broken body sinking beneath the surface. How was she alive? Was she alive?

Bright light played at the edges of her vision. Red and orange light . . . warm . . .

Agony speared her, more intense than before, when she inhaled and water burned her lungs. It wasn't just her lungs that were burning. Focusing was hard, but certain things demanded recognition: water all around, and fire, cool and hot, both somehow burning; pain inside and out, levels she'd never imagined possible all exceeded; light and dark warring in her eyes, vision popping in and out . . . all of these, everywhere . . . it was hard to think. What was happening? Where was she?

There was a warm, liquid feeling inside her—a very wrong liquid feeling, almost pooling. Blood? A sharp pain near her shoulder. Her dagger? A particularly hot spike in Finlay's chest pulled her into Aithne's mindscape, and a stab of clarity pierced Finlay's broken, muddy thoughts.

You need to fight! Aithne told her. The phoenix dragon was surrounded by fire, trembling with effort. **I can heal your body with time, but you have to keep yourself from drowning! Get to the surface, now!**

The surface . . . the lake. She was in the lake. She'd been thrown into the lake. That was the water all around, which meant the fire was all from Aithne. Burning from the inside out, healing as it did.

Get to the surface, Finlay told herself, bracing for the pain and disorientation to return full force when she left the mindscape. *Get to the surface, get to the surface.*

The words were an anchor, and though they lost individual meaning, Finlay kicked her legs when she found herself sinking in the lake again, stretching her broken body. The shattered and splintered bones resisted movement, limbs moving grotesquely, but she forced herself to move through the agony. Healing fire raced along the bones, knitting them together, rebuilding muscle, so her next kicks were stronger. With the power of the storm-fueled water, she needed all the force she could muster to stay oriented.

Keeping her eyes open, Finlay fixed her attention on the light coming from above, gray as it was. *Get to the surface.*

She was soaked but still burning when her head broke the surface. The breath she took in was a relief and a worse pain than being without it. Rain splattered down, as if trying to force her back beneath the water, or convince her she could never escape it. *Land,* she thought dimly, after several seconds. She saw the shore and feebly kicked toward it, paddling with one hand, bracing her dagger—the point still embedded in her shoulder, because she didn't trust herself not to drop it simply holding it in her shaking palm—with the other.

In what she knew to be the most difficult thing she'd ever done, slowly, painfully, Finlay paddled her way to the shore. Her clothes, soaked with water, weighed her down. Her mending bones, still broken and still covered in healing fire, throbbed. Every bit of energy abandoned her after she pulled her dagger out and set it next to her, gripping it as tightly as she could, and Finlay couldn't fight it any longer. She had no more attention to spare, woolly thoughts slow and water-logged: her cheek fell heavily against the pebbled shore, her eyes slammed shut, and only halfway out of the lake, Finlay drifted in and out of consciousness.

Pebbles scraped her cheek; a light splashing sound entered her hearing. Something was pulling her. Her legs hit the rocky shore, dragging uselessly. The pulling stopped.

The next thing she was aware of was a feeling of being carried, arms holding her. "N-No," she managed, trying to get away. Chief Stewart wanted to drop her from Gaea's back.

"Shh," a warm voice said. "It's all right, love, I've got you."

Finlay wanted to open her eyes to make sure it was really him. A light feeling started spreading through her, bright and nurturing. Gaea's healing magic? It had to be Evander . . . everything faded before she could make sure.

Aithne, she thought, some unknown amount of time later. She went into the mindscape and found the phoenix dragon in the grassy clearing, no trace of flames on her body. "Aithne?"

Aithne lifted her head slightly. **Finlay.**

"Are you all right?"

I used a lot of my magic to keep you alive. I'll be fine in time. I promise, I'm not dying. I didn't use every drop of magic I have left. But I am utterly spent. As you are. Rest now.

Relief washed over Finlay, with the lingering exhaustion and pain, and she was happy to comply.

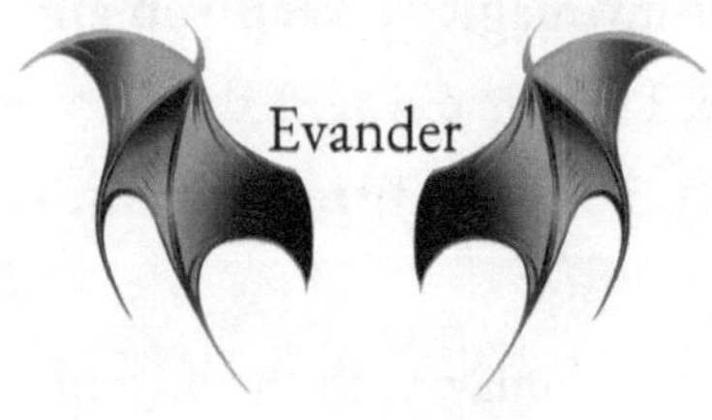

CHAPTER THIRTY-SEVEN

Evander froze after the chief said something in a loud voice. Every muscle seized and even his eyes locked in the direction they'd been when whatever the chief said was uttered. Everyone seemed frozen around him. It meant he had a clear view of Chief Stewart walking close to Finlay, saying something too low for him to hear, and picking her up, and that he was entirely helpless to do anything to stop him.

Chief Stewart slung Finlay over his shoulder, glanced around swiftly, and stepped into a jog that carried both of them from view. Terror doused Evander like a cold bucket of water. The chief wanted Finlay dead. Robin had said that, recently. Evander had seen that, in the chief's insane attempts to turn the people against her. Where was he taking her?

Evander strained his frozen limbs as a protective kind of fury roared inside him. He'd promised to keep her safe. All too slowly his fingers were able to twitch. His eyes could shift. His hands, feet, head, could move.

He was in the process of beating his hands against his still frozen legs, trying to force them to thaw faster, when a loud roar nearly deafened him, followed by a massive crashing sound. Evander turned his head in the direction of the noise, looking over his shoulder, and his breath caught.

A column of fire lit on the back side of the dormitory, and with another loud crashing sound, Ghillie appeared. The towering flame faded once Evander saw Ghillie's head, as Ghillie let out a second roar. He rose higher into the air, wings spread wide, bits of broken stone and wood showering down around him.

Several figures were visible on his back. Evander saw Meric standing on Ghillie's shoulder, one hand holding onto one of the spines along Ghillie's neck, the other brandishing his staff toward any potential attackers. Forrest held on to Ghillie's other shoulder with both front paws, a green speck on Ghillie's mountain-hued scales. Robin sat astride Ghillie, behind them, and Elsie sat closer to Ghillie's tail, facing away, a heavy rock in her fist.

Broken chains dangled from Ghillie's legs. They clanked against each other when Ghillie pushed his feet and wings back, and Ghillie shot forward and upward, into the now rain-filled sky, away from the compound. Away from Aerouant Glèidh, and the Mage-ruled Alocasia, in a direction over the lake toward the southern part of the mountains.

Trapped as he felt, furious and terrified as he was, a giddy joy swooped low through Evander at the sight of Ghillie finally finding his freedom. He was sure they would be back, but knew they may take their time.

Evander's legs and torso thawed and he raced in the direction Chief Stewart had taken Finlay. He had a guess they'd gone to the sanctuary. *Gaea!* he called as he ran. *Gaea, I need you!*

Gaea had told him the range of their mental connection wasn't overly far. Up to a mile, if both were strong and well-rested. When Evander didn't receive a reply at the border of the sanctuary, he did something he knew Gaea could feel from further than a mile. He summoned a burst of healing magic and slammed his hand down into the ground. The magic made the coarse grass shoot up in bright green tufts and made the nearest crystal blooms increase in size.

Evander stood, panting slightly. A surge of the power they shared would surely be felt by the great dragon. "Gaea!" he yelled anyway.

I'm coming, his deep voice replied. Evander staggered at the pain in his tone. Something was very wrong.

He reached Evander and crouched, and lifted off the ground before Evander had fully seated himself on his back. "You know where Chief Stewart took Finlay?"

I know where I took them, Gaea said miserably. He flew faster than Evander had ever seen him fly, so rain drops slapped against

Evander's face. He listened as Gaea told him how the chief had tricked him, and thrown Finlay from his back.

I threw the man down the instant after he pushed Finlay, Gaea said with a trace of pleasure.

Evander only dimly took in that fact. "Finlay was burning when she fell?"

Gaea stopped and looked down at the water. Evander searched the murky surface as well as he could through the darkness of the storm and the force of the rain. *I think Aithne used her magic to brace her fall. It was the only way she could have survived. But I stayed for a moment and didn't see her come up.*

They spotted it at the same time: a tiny patch of brightness in the heavy rain, on one part of the lake's edge. Evander had barely spoken a command for Gaea to go before Gaea dove. Evander got off his back so quickly he fell to the ground, but he scrambled upright and reached Finlay's side in the next instant.

If not for the fire flickering over her body, he would have thought she was dead, she was so pale and still. She was mostly out of the lake, part of one leg still in the water as if she'd collapsed before she could pull herself up all of the way, and though she was completely soaked, red and orange flames burned everywhere. They caught the copper color of her hair and brightened it. They made her skin seem paler than ever, alarmingly so. The hand that bore the dragon paw tattoo curled around her dagger, flat on the ground beside her.

"Finlay," he said, despite himself. He reached for her arms to pull her out of the lake, and recoiled when the heat of those seemingly small flames burned his palms. He took a deep breath, shook his hands out as if to brace them, and reached for her again, pulling her fully from the water. His palms ached even after he took them away, but the healing energy he called to them rushed past them and went straight into Finlay.

"We'll need to bring her back to Moira," Evander told Gaea, not taking his eyes off Finlay. Her chest rose and fell shallowly.

We won't be going anywhere, Gaea said. *You may not have noticed, but the winds are too strong, and with the rain getting heavier by the minute, I might lose you both trying to fly through it. I could do it alone just fine, but I won't risk either of you. I'll make you a shelter.*

Evander realized he was as soaked as Finlay. Wind tore at his hair. His focus had been so singularly on Finlay he hadn't noticed how severe the weather had become. How long would it take for Aithne's magic to heal her? Would Gaea's healing breath, more powerful than what Evander could do, help her efforts, or hinder them, as Jupiter and Aithne's magic had combatted each other at the recognition ceremony? With this much damage he wasn't sure it would be safe, as it had been last time. Last time, she hadn't been burning with Aithne's magic when Gaea used his.

Evander wouldn't risk hurting her further. Maybe his smaller scale healing magic would help, without posing a threat to Aithne's fire. Evander continued his supply of magic, willing it to go to the places he could sense broken bones. So much had been broken, and if the flames were any indication, much had already healed from the worst of it . . . his stomach rolled at the pain she must have been in.

It's ready, Gaea said.

Evander braced himself once more and pulled Finlay half onto his lap, then scooped her into his arms and moved her dagger to rest flat between them. He staggered slightly upon standing, and bit down hard on his cheek. His hands, arms, and chest seared where Finlay touched him. She stirred slightly, her head moving to one side, brow pinching. "N-No," she said loosely.

He made a shushing noise. "It's all right, love, I've got you." He wasn't sure if she heard, or if she just lost the thread of consciousness she'd found. She burned brightly in his arms as he carried her into the structure Gaea had made to shelter them from the storm. He heard her mutter several times as he attempted to light a small fire, and as he drew off her soaked cloak. Something about Aithne, he thought.

Once he managed to light a fire near her he sat down by her head and resumed what healing he could. The fire rippling around her began to fade after some time. Not long after that he felt his magic energy wane considerably, and couldn't risk using more and passing out. Finlay needed him to be alert right now. When the flames covering her body seemed to fade away completely, she sighed in her sleep, and Evander leaned against the rocky wall, almost lightheaded in relief.

Gaea, he thought, a trace of a smile on his lips, *I think she's all right now.*

Chapter Thirty-Eight

Waking was like drawing aside the curtain and opening the window on a bright spring morning: refreshing, and at the same time, too fierce for several long seconds.

Heavy winds ripped across Finlay's hearing, and it wasn't brightness that was too fierce, but the force of the downpouring rain she could hear all around, and see in large cracks between stone as she opened her eyes: droplets raining down so fast they were large streaks of silver against a gray sky, curiously rimmed in soft light . . . a small fire behind her, its cozy crackling muted by the tempest.

She lay on something soft but thin, on a hard stone floor. Where . . . ?

A bass rumble Finlay felt in her bones drowned out the wind and rain for several long seconds. She breathed in sharply. *Bones.*

Finlay raised her arms, turning them over in a kind of wonder. They didn't hurt anymore. Her bones felt as they always had, solid and, unless she focused on them, simply a part of her, rather than the splintered, stabbing fragments they'd been before.

"Finlay?"

She pressed her hands to the floor to push herself upright and swivel to face Evander, who had apparently been leaning against the wall just behind her. He scooted closer, warm eyes searching her. She had to finish her inspection, reaching down to feel along her ribs and legs. Everything seemed mended. No pain. Just a lingering tiredness.

"Love, are you all right?" Evander asked, a little more insistently.

"Wh"—her voice came out a raw croak, and she swallowed hard and tried again. "Where are we?"

The firelight cast a flickering glow over the structure in which they sheltered. The walls were too strange to be natural, large, uneven slabs of stone pressed together to create a room of sorts. "The storm picked up too quickly. Gaea is one of the sturdiest dragons I know, but he didn't want to risk flying through it with us. He knocked down slabs of stone from the mountain and made this hideout for us, to keep the worst of the storm away." Evander looked up at the cracks between the stone slabs, where water ran in. "It's not perfect, but it won't fall. He's just outside.

Apparently he loves the storm, though he won't fly through it. Says he'll make himself shelter if he needs it."

A flash of brilliant white lit the visible sky. Finlay's heart rate sped. That horrible, time-defying moment of Isla and Muir's deaths flashed across her mind along with the lightning visible through the cracks in their shelter, and though there was no physical impact, it struck Finlay all the same.

Evander had closed the distance between them in a second, enveloping her in his arms. "It's just lightning, love, it's all right."

Finlay pressed her lips together to stop their wobbling and leaned against Evander, holding him tightly. She pressed her nose closer to his collar and inhaled his rain-washed scent as the sound of the lightning reached them in a booming rumble of thunder. "You pulled me out of the water."

"You were mostly there yourself. I just carried you the rest of the way."

The firelight playing across Evander's face was much more interesting than the light warring with the storm. It gave his deep brown eyes a golden sheen, as if the sunlight he exuded was visibly emanating from him. Angles made shadows, which were more noticeable on the reddened patch of skin on his neck compared to his usual sandy tone . . .

Finlay pushed back and looked at him more closely. That had never been there before. Her eyes traveled down his frame, taking in how ravaged his clothing was, following the heavily pinked skin down his chest and all the way down his arms. She turned over one of his hands to reveal a red and blistered palm. "You're burned." Her attention went back to his face. "When you carried me, I burned you."

His throat bobbed when he swallowed. "I'm fine."

"Why didn't you heal yourself with Gaea's magic? You might still be able to, to keep it from scarring—"

"I was more worried about you," Evander interrupted. "I used most of my magic to stimulate your own healing. I might have a bit restored, since it's been about an hour, but it doesn't matter."

Finlay leaned down and brushed her lips against his palm, watching carefully. He didn't wince. Still, it had to hurt. Guilt snipped at her spine. "Please try," she said against his wrist.

He breathed in deeply and a brown light rippled above his damaged flesh. The blisters faded into smooth skin. The angry red most prominent on his palms and chest faded to a pink color. "That's the best I can manage. I don't mind having scars, Finlay. I'd rather have scars and you than have risked losing you."

Moisture dewed in his eyes, and his throat bobbed again, as he tried to swallow back what Finlay now realized was lingering grief. "I really thought I'd lost you. When Gaea came to get me and brought me here . . . and then I saw you on the edge of the lake . . ." He blinked hard, and droplets collected on his eyelashes. His voice came out strained. "I knew you were all right when I saw the flames, but I was still so scared, Finlay."

She swept the tears away with a feather-soft movement, slow and purposeful. "So was I."

They sat like that for several moments, Finlay stroking the side of his face and sweeping back his hair, brushing away any tears that spilled over—always keeping her hand on him, in soft, intimate motions to reassure him she was here, and safe.

"What happened to the chief?" Finlay asked, once she judged both of their heart rates to have slowed to a normal pace.

Evander's face darkened. "Gaea threw him off his back just after you fell in. He's dead. He can't hurt anyone ever again."

Finlay closed her eyes as a wave of relief swept over her. "So everyone will know the truth, now."

"And Ghillie is free." The darkness in his expression faded, his usual optimism breaking through. "I wish you'd gotten to see it. It's over."

Thunder and lightning cracked overhead again before Finlay responded, throat tight. "It isn't over, though. There's something else I have to do. Something you're not going to like." *Something I don't like.*

"Look at how easily everyone turned on me," she continued. "How divided we really are, so desperate to take a stand against the Mages that we're putting ourselves and others at risk. I think Calum is right when he says the final fight is drawing near. I can make it happen sooner, if I go into the kingdom myself."

"Don't be rash," Evander urged. "You've just been through a lot."

"That's why I know I need to do this." She watched his face carefully as she explained her plan. "While Aithne was healing me, we had a conversation."

The joy of discovering her mended body upon waking, and finding Evander so close, had hidden the grief that conversation had instilled. It returned now, her heart thumping heavily, as if trying to extend the time it could feel as it should. "Some of Aithne's healing fire is still burning in my veins right now. Phoenix fire doesn't only heal, but transforms. She can give me the strength I need to infiltrate Alocasia. She can do it before that fire goes out, without using a significant amount of magic. If I wait and ask her to do it later, I don't know how much magic she'll be left with.

"When I say she can give me strength, I don't mean physically. Aithne can dampen my emotions, make me more ruthless; transform me into a harsher version of myself. It's the only way I can be sure I'll do what needs to be done to get in a position to make a difference."

She would need to be unfeeling. That idea she'd had the night she met Alistair, of how she could use Alistair to help all dragons? No more time imagining it. It was time to make it happen. Time to do what she'd known she would end up being the one to do when she saw the visions the Seer Sisters showed her on her first day of training, and infiltrate the Mages' ranks. The first step was helping Alistair become a Mage—standing by his side when he killed a dragon, feigning devotion and affection that, with any luck, he would return—and securing a place within the circle of Mages closest to the queen. Close enough to take any other steps necessary to clear a path for the Knights.

Evander's horror kept him from noticing her hesitation to speak further. His shoulders tensed. "Dampen your emotions? In a permanent way?"

Finlay's voice trembled. "I really hope not."

He crossed his arms and leaned against the stone wall, gesturing for her to finish explaining.

She told him only the essential information. "I'll tell the Mages the Knights betrayed me, and with my abilities, convince them I killed a dragon and want to join them. It'll get me into their ranks, and I can see about rallying support within the kingdom. Then I can send word somehow, and we can take Alocasia back for good."

He looked at her with solemn eyes. "Why do you feel you need to do this alone?"

Her control over her voice was failing her. "So I know everyone I care about is safe."

"But it isn't safe for *you*!"

Her control broke. "It has to be unsafe for someone, and I can't bear it to be anyone else!"

It wasn't fair to do this to him. She'd told Aithne she could be strong, in telling Evander her plan and in following through with it, yet here she was, balking at the first task. The easiest one. The thought of how she'd be after . . . how she wouldn't be able to feel . . .

Evander was quiet for a long moment. Finlay feared she would drown in the sorrow and worry in his gaze, and cupped his jaw and ran her thumb across his cheek. Her touch softened his forlorn expression, if only slightly. "Please tell me you understand."

He pressed his hand over hers, though he wouldn't meet her eyes. "I know you. Of course I understand. I just wish there was a way to change your mind."

She scooted closer, and saw his jaw tense. "Evander . . ."

A million things shone in his eyes when they acquiesced and slid to meet hers, but one dominated: determination. Next thing Finlay knew Evander had pulled her onto his lap and started kissing her. "Don't," he said between kisses, his voice low and husky. "Let me help you. Don't do this alone."

"I'm not doing it alone," Finlay said, forcing herself to keep her head and defend herself. It was incredibly difficult, when everywhere his lips touched, a well of pleasure formed and spread. She wanted to sink into him, to promise she would never leave his side again. No doubt that was his intention. He'd never used his affection like this before, sneakily lowering her guard. She'd also never given him a reason to use every weapon in his arsenal to sway her opinion. She clung to her resolution, knowing she would return to his side after it was done, and never have to part from him past that point.

"You'll be with me the entire time." She drew back, staring him full on, and took in the desire darkening those earth-toned eyes, the surprising anger in his jaw; the pain in his lightly arched brows. "You're the only reason I can do this. Someone needs to go inside. I'm counting on you to help me get out, when it's done. To bring me home."

The anger that didn't belong on his face lessened, a trace of guilt discernable in the rush of blood to his cheeks. "Finlay—"

She pressed a finger to his dry lips, still warm from the heat of their last kiss. "It's all right. I would do the same thing if our situations were reversed."

"It was foolish to think kissing you might change your mind," he said anyway.

"It won't change my mind, but it does tell me how much you care for me."

A smile fizzed on his lips. "Those paltry kisses? They couldn't convey a dragon's scale of how much I love you."

She touched his sculpted chest, now marked by a burn but still completely perfect. If anything conveyed how much he loved her, it was this. She felt his heart pounding beneath her touch, and knew before she threaded her gaze to his that he'd accepted, however reluctantly, that she wouldn't change her mind, and maybe realized how limited their time was. Who knew how long the storm would last, after all? Aithne could keep the embers of the restorative fire going for several more hours, but had to act to change Finlay before they went out. Finlay wanted to enjoy every moment she had with Evander before that point.

Desire was clear in his heat-washed cheeks and blown pupils, and Finlay worked to remove the tattered remains of Evander's shirt while he placed kisses along her jaw and trailed them down her neck. She lifted the shirt over his head, want burning low in her gut. He pulled aside the sleeve of her tunic to kiss the scar from her dagger, inflicted as a grieving child all those years ago, and that burn, that need, doubled and spread through her entire body. Grief was the last thing on her mind right now.

Finlay's hands roamed over his bare chest and to his waistline. His hands stilled against her back, where he'd been holding her close. "Are you sure?"

Rain continued to fall around them, torrential in its force as it collided with the stone of their little shelter. Lightning flashed. "As sure as I've been about anything," she whispered against his ear, to be sure he heard through the clap of thunder.

He captured her mouth with his, and Finlay surrendered all thought, sighing against his lips. She couldn't tell where she ended and he began, they were so closely entwined. Slowly, the last pieces of fabric between them vanished, and Evander pulled Finlay tighter in his arms as they lay back on the warmed stone floor.

The crashing roars and intermittent flashes of the storm, the force of the wind grating on the stone structure in which they stayed—all of it faded around them. Unnoticed. So separate that Finlay only dimly recognized the storm's abatement in snatches of awareness of the world outside.

What need did she have of the world outside? Her home was here, with Evander. It had always been with Evander, the gentle, dragon-loving boy who'd been there for her since the moment they met. The young man who'd completely claimed her soul with his constant compassion and warmth.

They existed in a sphere all their own, the storm, the Knights and Mages, every outside force banished from this extended moment that made Finlay realize perhaps, sometimes, time *could* be as kind as it was cruel.

Finlay lay tucked against Evander's side when the brunt of the storm had long since faded, her head on his chest, listening to the steady beating of his heart and the slowing rain; feeling more whole than she ever had before—more wonderful, more peaceful. More loved. Stars above, so loved.

She willed the rain to drag on forever, knowing when it ended, she would have to cleave her heart in two. No, she amended, closing her eyes as Evander toyed with a lock of her hair. She wouldn't fracture her heart.

She would lose it altogether.

Finlay

"Let me go with you."

Evander's soft whisper roused Finlay from the edge of waking and sleep, from a stupor of sorts where thoughts floated weightless and warm, drowsy contentment muted everything. His words brought reality back to light, and Finlay sighed and opened her eyes.

The storm had raged for several hours, the rain continuing gently for some time after that. Now, the rain had stopped. She could no longer hear the steady pattering of raindrops against their shelter, as she had been able to when she and Evander lay against each other, simply being, and she entered that pleasant daze. Their little fire had faded to embers, letting her see very little around her. Cozy as she was, nestled tightly against Evander, his body heating hers, she felt the change when she shifted upright. Cool night air touched her face, made worse by the warmth she'd just left behind and the break in the humidity after the storm. She summoned a spark and gave the embers another chance to roar, the glow faintly illuminating the shelter. That done, she reached for her damaged clothes and looked at Evander as he sat upright as well, leaning on his hands behind his back.

"I can help you," he said, in that same soft voice. His warm brown eyes pleaded with her, gentle. Fragile.

"You're needed here. Calum should take over. You and Elsie can help him get everything ready, knowing I'll be doing the same on my side."

His eyes cast down, and he said nothing.

Finlay needed him to understand. "You undo me, Evander. You always have, in the best way. And if there's any chance to undo the transformation I'll have to go through . . ."

His eyes lifted, surprise and love shining in them. "You need me."

More than you know. Desperately, with every beat of my heart. She met his eyes. "Always."

"I'll find you," Evander promised. "The second I can, I'll find you."

Her throat tightened. "I have no doubt of that. I just wonder what you'll find when we see each other again." *When, when,* because she couldn't stand the thought of it being an *if*.

He swept an errant strand of hair behind her ear with a lingering touch, his knuckles grazing her cheekbone. She breathed in deeply as that feather-light touch swept over her. His voice was low and sweet when he said, "I'll find the brave, selfless, caring young woman I'm looking at right now."

A concentrated heat in her breastbone told her it was time for Aithne's flames to do their work. "Tell Elsie, Robin, and Forrest I'm sorry I didn't say goodbye," she said, standing. "But there's no way Elsie would let me do this. Give me a head start, so she can't follow me." Evander, now clothed in his own tattered garments, stepped forward and wrapped her in a tight embrace, his pressed-together lips indicating he couldn't say goodbye. "I do love you, Evander," she whispered.

His hands tightened on her back. "I love you too," he managed in a choked, forceful murmur.

He called to Gaea, who removed the roof of their structure with his massive jaws, and then flattened what had been the walls. The great brown dragon looked at Finlay with palpable guilt, and Finlay hurried to reassure him he held no blame for what had happened.

Evander delayed going over to him only to do one thing: he picked up Finlay's dagger and placed it in her hands. Finlay took it with more than a trace of shock—she hadn't felt incomplete without it by her side, or truly realized she didn't have it. She slipped it into its spot on her makeshift belt. Then Evander hopped on Gaea's back and asked him to take off. Though Gaea looked at Finlay questioningly, they left without another word.

Only once they had faded from sight did Finlay focus on that tingling heat behind her breastbone, and enter the mindscape.

Aithne appeared in her grassy meadow, looking significantly better than she had during their last conversation, before Finlay had woken in the shelter with Evander. **I would ask if you're sure you want me to do this, but I know you wouldn't put Evander through that if you weren't.**

Finlay thought again of the visions the Seer Sisters had shown her, that first day of training. So much of what she'd seen had already come to pass. The image of herself, standing in a room high in a tower, stood out as something she still had to do. She knew that room was in the castle in the capital. She knew she had to go there. *Flames will change the kingdom whole,* they'd said, *sparked by the girl with the dragon's soul.* Finlay had fire, and Aithne was as tightly bound to her as any dragon could be.

It was her fate to do this.

Knowing that didn't make it any easier.

"I'm ready," she lied, meeting Aithne's kind orange eyes. Her heart pounded furiously, telling the truth while it still could. She lifted her chin and took a deep breath. "Stop up the access and passage to remorse. Compassion." She took an unsteady breath. "Love."

You won't remember him.

Finlay swallowed hard. The fear of losing her emotions was great. The fear of losing her memories . . . that instilled a deeper kind of terror. What if she lost herself, became a monster with no feelings and no memories? Aithne said her goal would remain clear, even if she didn't understand why she felt she had to follow it through. Finlay had to believe it. "I know."

She closed her eyes to keep sudden tears from spilling. Her memories of Evander, and of Elsie, and everyone else she'd made a meaningful connection with, would be buried by Aithne's transformation. To lose access to love, she couldn't remember those she loved most—those who personified it, gave it meaning. It was the only way to truly steel herself for what she had to do. She imagined Elsie giving her a bear hug, and Evander's dimpled smile, one last time. Her heart wrenched.

"He'll find me, and bring me back."

Tears leaked from the corners of her eyes, and her lips framed his name once more, savoring its sound.

"Evander."

End of Part One

A Glimpse at Part Two

Read the first chapter of *Lady of Dragons (Part Two)*!

Evander's name whispered on Finlay's lips. There wasn't time
for it to soothe her.

Despite keeping her eyes closed, Finlay heard the crackle of fire
transition to a roar, and knew if she looked, the flames would be
cresting beyond Aithne's feathery, sunset-hued wings. Reaching
for her. For a moment, she felt them, standing in the mindscape.
Soft wings enveloped her, flames leaping over her body.

The mindscape rushed away from her, pulling deep inside, as
flames overwhelmed everything. The tears on her cheeks dried
in a burst of steam. Every pore opened. Her eyes shot wide, sight
filled with rivulets of crimson and gold.

The warmth of the vestiges of healing fire inside her increased,
the sparks igniting and growing into a bonfire. The fire liquefied,
molten energy so hot it didn't seem to burn at all—it froze.
Ice-fire rushed through her veins, wilder than river rapids, and
Finlay felt she was in the lake again: submerged, stifled, com-

pressed. Especially when the ice-fire reached her head. It rammed into her thoughts, scattering them every which way, waterlogging many and dragging others into its depths, out of reach.

The name that had been on her lips . . . what had it been? Had there been a name at all? Had there been pain? She couldn't recall. She didn't care. Her anxiety faded. Everything faded. The ice-fire eddied and sluiced back within its bank, pulling something with it. Ice filmed over the fire dominating her sight and burst apart, dazzling, disorienting, and everything settled.

Finlay took a deep breath and stared at the lake before her, her mind curiously empty for a moment. What had she been doing?

Hand resting on her dagger's hilt, she remembered. She'd been steeling herself to leave everything she knew behind. She tightened her grip on the dagger. If this was the sign of a royal Mage, it would serve her well now. It was the only thing she could bring with her.

She had to find Alistair. She needed to get moving, to be past the borders of Aerouant Glèidhby dawn, so she couldn't be pursued as easily. It would take much longer to reach Alistair's cavern on foot than it had on a dragon's back, but it had to be done. Others would delay her, or keep her from going, if she went to find a dragon to take her.

Finlay walked for almost an hour, leaving the lake behind and entering the sparse woodland that bordered the mountains on the side she needed to reach. The only sounds for a long time were her footsteps when she stumbled over unseen rocks or twigs and the occasional hoots of owls. Large wings buffeted the air above her. Night still served as a decent cloak. Finlay stopped and pressed herself to a tree's bark, watching and listening.

A dragon approached and landed several paces away. No rider.

Finlay?

Finlay kept silent.

I have supplies for you, the dragon said, looking around. *I know you're near. Evander sent me to help you. No one knows I'm here.*

The name sent a confusing tingle through Finlay's temples. Should she know who that was? She stepped out, recognizing the dragon's voice, at any rate. Hugh. The Knight Meric's dragon, known for his tracking abilities. "Why would someone send you with supplies?"

Hugh cocked his head to the side. *He's worried about you. He said I should bring you to where you need to go, if you'll let me.*

Finlay looked at the sky. She might be able to reach Alistair by dawn, flying on a dragon. "I *will* let you. You can bring me near where I need to go. Avoid the settlement."

Can do.

Finlay went through the pack of supplies on Hugh's back while they flew. She found two canteens, one of water, one of ale. A jar of a healing salve. Two strips of bandages. A sizable meat pie wrapped in cloth. Several apples. Beneath all of this was a folded blue cloak and spare set of clothes. She ate part of the meat pie and an apple while Hugh carried her toward the appropriate section of caverns, and washed it down with some of the water.

"This is close enough," Finlay told Hugh. The sky had lightened considerably, now gray with a pre-dawn glow. She could see

Alistair's cavern in the horizon. Hugh landed and let her slide off his back, and Finlay shouldered the pack. "Thank you," she said without looking back. Hugh's wings flapped, the breeze they generated as he flew away stirring her coppery hair in front of her shoulders. Why had someone sent him to help her? How had they known she was leaving?

She paused near the cavern entrance, more so because of the absence of concern than the concerning questions. Something wasn't right . . . vaguely like the fog too much alcohol imbued, her emotions seemed shrouded, out of reach.

Another heartbeat's reflection showed her it didn't matter. She should be glad of this foggy emotional state. Emotions made things messy. She needed to be clear-headed in every moment, from this point on. The future was what mattered: taking power from those too corrupted to wield it, and saving the current and coming generations of dragons.

"Alistair?" she called. "Alistair!"

She strode into the cavern, bringing a flame to her palm to see the inside more clearly. The man staggered to his feet and looked at her with bleary, pale green eyes. He raked a hand across his face. "Finlay? What are you doing here?" He stared at the fire in her hand. "I heard rumors you had fire powers during that unfortunate skirmish. You killed a dragon?"

"You said you would sway me to your side, didn't you?"

He let his arms fall from the stretch he'd been doing, and narrowed his eyes. "What?"

"I can't fight for the Knights any longer. Not after what they've done." She met his eyes, chin lifted. "I've come to my senses. I'm changing sides."

A slow smile spread across his unshaved face. "Please," he said with an inviting gesture, sliding down the wall to sit again, "enlighten me."

It wasn't hard to spin the story of discovering the chief's cruelty, and learning how he'd killed her family, into a reason to hate the Knights and all they stood for.

"I'd wondered what motivated you to plan the ambush." Alistair's neck tightened so she could see his pulse pounding in his throat. He tensed, ready to stand. "That murderous bastard. I don't know if I'd like to hear that he's dead, to toast it, or that he's alive, so we can kill him together."

Finlay sat down across from him. "He's dead. Fell from the back of the dragon he used to try to kill me."

"He tried to"—Alistair compressed his lips, breathed out through his nose in a huff, and sank back against the wall, motioning for her to continue.

She told him how she'd accidentally killed a dragon, and most everyone turned on her when they found out. She explained how Chief Stewart had thrown her from a dragon's back, and a dragon's healing magic had allowed her to survive. His hands twitched at his sides, then curled into fists, but though he opened his mouth a few times, he remained silent until she'd finished, pale eyes blazing fiercer with each sentence.

"I couldn't face the Knights again, and hoped to catch you here," she said, scrunching the fabric of her cloak. "I can't go back to them."

He stood and walked to her side, sliding onto the floor beside her. "To those traitors? Of course you can't. I'm sorry for the pain they put you through, but glad you sought me out. I'd feared you'd never forgive me because of the Knight that died in the fight. From your reaction, she seemed like someone close to you."

Finlay blinked. Had she been close to her? She couldn't even recall her name. "I saw that you weren't fighting more than you had to. You kept your word."

A roguish smile flitted across his lips. "I swore I would, my beautiful, dangerous lady." His smile grew when she didn't correct him about not being his lady, as she had last time. "You'll join me?"

"I'd like nothing more."

The blaze in his expression cooled. "They really did a number on you, didn't they? You're very different than the first time I met you."

"Change is the nature of life," Finlay said. "I can't afford to be as sentimental as I was. The only thing it brings is pain."

He took the hand she was scrunching her cloak in and traced the dragon paw tattoo on its back. "You know I intend to kill a dragon. You've understandably turned on the Knights. What about the dragons you held so dear?"

A dull anger snaked in her chest like a vine, thorns of guilt along it—faint, as noticeable as a fly, and therefore easily ignored. "I was thrown from the back of one, and learned a dragon killed my family. I've said I've given up on sentimentality. Maybe you didn't fully understand my meaning." Finlay freed her hand from Alistair's loose grip and trailed it up his arm, lowering her voice. "I think I'd rather have power."

His posture inflated almost as much as his ego, chest puffing out, shoulders going back. Gods, this was easier than she'd anticipated. "I can help with that."

The smile she gave him wasn't forced. *Yes*, she thought. *You can.*

"Come with me to Inverness. I was planning to return soon anyway, to replenish my supplies. After the ordeal you've been through, I can give you a steaming bath, fine clothes, and a feast of anything you'd like."

As much as she wanted to urge him to find a dragon first, Finlay knew she had to play this right, to earn his trust and secure his affection. "That sounds wonderful."

Acknowledgments

A huge thank you to Kate Macdonald and E.P. Stavs, for being my fabulous beta readers and authors extraordinaire! Your insight into this novel made it so much stronger!

To Cat, thank you for helping me name this series of Shakespearean-inspired fantasy romance novels! All the World's a Story is a perfect title for the series! And Alocasia as the country in this one is spot on!

And you, my readers. Thank you for taking a chance on my work. I sincerely hope you enjoyed it. Please consider leaving a review, to share your thoughts and help the book gain visibility for other readers!

Also By Shelby Elizabeth

Young Adult Fantasy Titles:
The Celestials Trilogy
Stars Begin to Burn
Stars, Hide Your Fires
Stars In Different Skies

Young Adult Contemporary Romance Titles:
Falling at Fredricks High
Don't Hate the Player

Young Adult Fantasy Romance Titles:
All the World's a Story
Lady of Dragons (Part One)
Lady of Dragons (Part Two)

ABOUT SHELBY ELIZABETH

Shelby Elizabeth is an English teacher in Upstate New York. She is also a major geek who enjoys writing both fantasy and contemporary romance. When she is not writing in her free time, she can be found playing with her nephews, reading, or watching just a bit too much television with her cats on her lap.